FINDING KAI

DAVID A. WILLSON

SEEKER
PRESS

Cover art and illustrations by Diana Buidoso
Map by Jackson Cunningham

For more information visit: www.davidawillson.com

THE GREAT LAND

PART ONE

He began his work, speaking the name of the earth, bringing mountains. He spoke the name of water, and the oceans rose. They formed out of nothingness, standing in defiance of the chaos. Then He spoke the name of light and it came alive, so all would see the beauty of His work. Then He smiled, for it was good.

— Creation Account, First Light 1:4

1

ENNIS

The man shuffled down the twists and turns of the dim corridor toward a room with a single cell in an isolated area of the dungeon—a special area, for a special project. He shivered; the thin cloth soles of his shoes provided little protection from the cold stone. He should have worn boots today.

As he got closer, he heard sounds of snarling and straining, pushing him to quicken his pace. He entered the well-lit chamber and the source of the sounds became apparent. The prisoner was flattened against the bars of his cage, arms reaching out to claw the air near a second figure that was just inches out of reach.

Dressed in leather trousers and a padded cloth coat, she looked simple today. Unassuming. Far from the fancy gowns and the pomp and circumstance that occupied the days of a monarch.

"Hello, Ennis."

She didn't look at him as she spoke. It was hard to read any emotion in her words, but that was always the case with her. He wondered if she felt anything at all. No notice. No courtesy. Yet another surprise visit, and he now became self-conscious about his appearance. His blemished, pale skin, balding head, and raspy voice gave him much in common with the broken people he worked on. These souls he tortured and sometimes killed. Losers at the game of life, trying to make the most of a poor hand.

The clawing, snarling creature in front of her was unceasing in its efforts, anger and hatred streaked on its face as it struggled in futility to reach its enemy. A young man of thirteen, it had pursued a normal life before its capture. Now it was huge, a misshapen monstrosity over seven feet tall, with odd bumps and torn skin where it had been hurting itself. Fitting that it would have its home in the cold dungeon, destroyed as it was, the scars of many burns over its body where tattoos once decorated its skin. The grand project. The grand failure.

"Good morning, Your Majesty," he said. "So sorry I wasn't here to welcome you. How long have you been waiting, might I ask?"

"Not more than an hour, I suppose."

An hour of watching him snarl and claw at her?

"I wanted to take a final look," she said. "We will move on from this one. Try again."

"So sorry, Majesty. This was the best one we've made. Even so, I hoped we might still learn something from him."

She continued to stare at the creature, and there was a profound contrast between the two figures. Beauty standing before ugliness. Order in the presence of chaos. Peace staring at pain.

"No. We move on."

She lifted a hand, and the immense creature flew backward against the stone wall, its head impacting with a sick, cracking sound. A moment later, the corpse fell to the floor. She took a step forward and reached a hand out, closing her eyes. The creature's body stiffened at first. Cracks started to form on its skin, and it shriveled, blackened, as if being scorched by fire. Within seconds, it was an empty husk, scarcely resembling the living being it had been a moment before.

Frightening as it was to watch, it was good that she now destroyed them. Too many of the early projects had escaped and were causing chaos about the Great Land.

She turned toward Ennis, a reddish-orange glow now fading

from her eyes as she stepped, coming close. His heart pounded in his chest as she reached out to place her hand on his shoulder. He worried that she would take his life in payment for the failure, but was surprised when he found her touch to be warm. A peaceful, even comforting feeling.

"Too many runes at once," she said. "He couldn't handle them all, and it broke his mind. It's not your fault. Not at all. Mine alone."

"Yes, Majesty. Um . . . I have been working on another method. Much more careful, I think. A mix of the old and the new."

An awkward silence intruded as her hand remained on his shoulder. She looked away, as if thinking of something, staring off into a corner of the room. "Why do they grow so much?" she asked.

"I don't know. When you stretch the container, it's as if the body resets. A child again, in some ways. Memory loss. And it grows like a new babe, but much faster."

"I never expected that."

He nodded. It was indeed fascinating. But she hadn't refused his suggestion. Nor had she consumed his spirit as a punishment for the failure. Good things.

She lifted her hand from his shoulder, the warmth and comfort now gone. Without saying anything further, she walked past him, her footsteps soon fading around a corner of the corridor.

It took great effort to scoop the sizable remains into a wheeled cart and dispose of them in the rubbish room down the hallway. Ennis then replaced the cart and shuffled back toward his work-rooms, making a clicking sound with his tongue as he moved. There were many prisoners to work on, and he'd already created a gifted this week. He could make more. But gifted were not what she wanted. Not really. She wanted more, and he would deliver, somehow.

When he reached his workroom, he felt along the high stone shelf, looking for something. When he found it, his hand grasped the cool bone handle and brought the tool down for closer inspection. His ceppit. A strange rune graced the handle, formed with silver scrollwork and ebony enamel. The blade was small, causing minimal trauma to his subjects. An important tool for an important job. And so beautiful.

"Thus begins another day," he said, gripping the ceppit in one hand as he stepped outside the chamber, looking right then left for a guard. He needed a fresh child to begin his work.

"Guard," he called down the hallway. Nobody appeared quickly enough to satisfy, however, and he clicked his tongue in frustration. "Guard!" Louder this time.

An older man appeared, a hand resting on the pommel of his sword as he ambled toward Ennis, his chain mail armor clinking with each step.

"There you are."

The man stopped and stood in place, waiting for Ennis' command.

Ennis' fingers fidgeted with the handle of the ceppit, his tongue clicking in anticipation. "This time, bring me a girl."

2

RUNNING

Nara darted across the meadows, beneath the trees, and over the hills, staying ahead of Mykel as he attempted to keep pace. The sun was high in the sky and most of the winter snow was gone, leaving only patches of white here and there. Most of the grass remained brown and dead, although some had turned green, and the birch trees did not yet bear leaves. Spring was waking from its long, cold slumber. Fresh scents of flowers and new grasses filled the air, nascent growth overcoming the barren mountain slopes. Hope welled in her heart, growing with every stride.

She and Mykel had left the cavern far behind this morning, running west for miles, larger mountains and peaks coming ever more into view. Flaring the health rune kept her from tiring, and the wind through her hair was exhilarating, bringing a sense of freedom that banished all worry. Right now, there was no Kayna in her thoughts, no fears for the people of the Great Land, and no questions about her destiny. There were only the wind and the sun.

Mykel burst ahead of her, laughing, bare feet pounding the grass and soil below, then he launched himself high overhead with a powerful leap, black hair flowing behind. The magic ivory staff was strapped to a small pack on his back, and his tunic flapped in the wind as he glided above, landing in a cloud of dirt and grass, then running and leaping again. Nara grinned, then flared speed to race ahead, moving well past him. The speed rune was relatively new for her, allowing her to mimic the powers of a racer, and Mykel could no longer keep up with her on runs. Not unless she let him. She would not let him today.

Only a few months since the battle at Fairmont Castle, since losing Bylo, and she had learned much in that time. Not just about magic but also about surviving loss. About growing up. About following Dei's will and embracing her part in His plan. She still missed Bylo, but she was getting stronger every day, and she imagined that he would have been proud to see her grow. She was no longer his little girl but a young woman embracing her role in the world, difficult as it was.

Nara had practiced much new magic. The most important was sight. And while she caught glimpses of what might happen in the upcoming hours or days, they were brief. More like flashes, with emotion and images intertwined.

"You'll get the hang of it," Anne told her. "It will take time. Keep practicing."

But Nara was tired of practicing. She wanted to run.

A few more minutes of speed pushed her far ahead of Mykel, but she slowed after reaching a high meadow that opened out over a broad valley, her breathing rapid from the exertion. A river flowed far below, winding between high peaks far in the distance. It was a beautiful sight, mountains still bearing their snow-capped peaks, drawing a clear transition between the landscape near Eastway and this stark mountainous terrain.

"I think we're just north of Took," Mykel said, catching up. "There should be villages along the river in that valley." He pointed south. "Rivers are the lifeblood of the interior, and there are always villages along them."

Mykel would know such things. His father taught him much about the native people of the Great Land and how they supported themselves in remote areas. "I wonder how they are faring," Nara said. "The people down there. I wonder if Fairmont— if my sister, rather, is treating them well."

"I can guess the answer to that question easily enough."

"We should check on them."

"We're supposed to stay hidden, Nara. You never know who'll be there. We can't risk a conflict, not until your training is complete. And you've just started."

He was right. She knew little, could grasp several new runes but wasn't skilled with them and wasted too much energy. She tried to be efficient, but she couldn't seem to ration her power. But these months had been enough waiting. Enough hiding. She wanted to get out in the world.

"So, we're just supposed to hide, to ignore everyone?" she said. "What if they need help? We're only a few days travel from Fairmont, and if things are going badly, they would be the first to feel it, wouldn't they?"

"I'm game, but Anne won't be happy."

"It's her job to help me learn, not to tell me what to do."

Mykel shrugged.

Nara stepped forward, passing the few trees that stood upon the high meadow, looking over the cliffs at the valley below. The cliffs wouldn't be easy to navigate, so she traveled along the edge until she found a rough pathway that served as a safer way down. Mykel followed and as they reached the base of the cliffs, the sounds of the river drifting up to them.

"The breakup of the ice and snow on the mountains has fed the river," Mykel said. "It's raging."

"I bet it's cold too," Nara said.

"No doubt." Mykel approached the river's edge, slipping between some large stones to dip a foot in a swirling pool. "Ooh! It's liquid ice!"

Nara joined him, slipping off a shoe and putting a foot in the water next to him. The chill rose up her leg, but she didn't withdraw. It was refreshing after the long run. "Feels good."

Mykel pulled his foot out of the pool and drew closer to her.

She sensed his intention and pulled her own foot out, turning to face him. He came even closer, grabbed her around the waist with his right arm, then lifted her chin with his other hand. She closed her eyes as his lips met hers. Softly. Just once. "You feel good," he said.

She smiled. "I love you."

"I love you too, Bitty."

She rested her head against his chest and held it there for a moment. His heart beat fast and loud, and she listened as it slowed. He was everything for her. And since Bylo's death, he was the only stable thing in her crazy world. Mykel had known her for her whole life, grown up with her in Dimmitt.

"We need to go back," she said, her head still pressed against his chest.

"To Dimmitt, yes. But not now. You're not ready. You've learned so little."

"I may not be ready to fight my sister, but we can get Sammy. At least that."

Mykel shook his head side to side. "I don't know. I want to, but–"

"Then it's decided. We'll tell Anne tonight when we get back."

"Nara, I–"

"It'll be fine. We'll avoid trouble, I promise." She smiled and hugged him even closer. It was a good idea, and she longed to see Dimmitt again. They could be there in a little more than a week. Less if they ran as they did today.

A few moments more and her heartbeat slowed, her breath no longer ragged, and she pulled away from him, slipped her shoe back on, then walked south. She didn't want to go back to the cavern. Not yet. This had been an escape from the training, from the pressure of what she knew was ahead, and it was refreshing. She couldn't let it go.

They walked for about an hour before several small shacks along the riverside came into view. When they approached, however, they found nobody within.

"Fish shacks," Mykel said. "There must be a Nupat village nearby."

As they opened the doors to a shack, Nara saw the carcasses of fish hanging on string within the structures. Flies gathered on the meat.

"Sheefish," Mykel continued. "Big ones too. But they've been hanging for a while. They should have preserved them already. Something is wrong."

Mykel's words sparked a touch of fear in her and Nara looked about for an enemy, scanning the riverside and the ridges above, but finding nothing.

They walked again for a time, finally coming upon a cluster of cottages on a rise overlooking the river. A well-worn path made their approach easy, but they heard no sounds. No children were playing, nobody was working, and there were no sounds of activity despite it being midday.

Nara picked up her pace as she approached the center of the small village. The cottages were empty and charred, and strange smells reached her nose. Burnt wood. And something else, something that wrinkled her nose and made her heart skip a beat.

She slowed her pace, fear growing with each step.

As she approached one of the blackened cottages, she saw items that lay scattered about the ground. A doll. A tiny wooden sword. And the horrible smell was so strong now.

"Wait, Nara," Mykel said, stepping in front of her and grabbing her shoulders with his hands. "This is bad. You don't want to see this."

She put a hand on his wrist and looked into his big brown eyes. "When I was afraid, Mykel, I wanted to run away. But people got hurt. Died. People I love. Fear won't stop me ever again."

She pushed past him and continued, approaching the dead husk of the structure. Three of the walls were still there, but the roof was fallen. A blackened stove, its chimney collapsed in pieces about it, stood in one corner. In the center of the home, she found multiple bodies in a pile. Burnt, blackened bodies. The empty husks of human beings gathered in one place. Husbands. Wives. Fathers. Mothers.

Six months before, she would have run from the cottage screaming and weeping. But she had seen pain up close, suffered herself, and it was no stranger anymore. It had a habit of following her. An unwelcome but familiar companion. This close to Fairmont, it was no great surprise that there would be suffering.

She counted the corpses—three, six, nine, maybe a couple more, but she couldn't tell because fallen pieces of roof blocked her view. She moved to lift the wreckage so she could continue, but Mykel moved past her, lifting charred beams out of the way so she could finish her macabre tally. Two of the bodies rolled away from the pile when he moved part of the collapsed wall, a crisp arm falling loose from a torso.

"I'm sorry, Nara, I—"

"There are eleven adults," she said. "But no children."

"Oh," Mykel said, looking back among the bodies as if he had just noticed that. "Where are they?"

"I don't know."

Nara moved to the other cottages, one by one, but found no other bodies. Still no children. She walked to a clearing in the center of the village where they likely gathered for group events. She found dark stains in the dirt there. Several, all collected in one area. She reached down to touch the stains, but they were hard and crusted. Blood.

Her heart seemed still, numb, and she shed no tears, somehow detached from the horror of the scene, as if a wall had gone up to protect her from falling apart. The protection was welcome, but while something held her emotions in check, her mind wandered on the circumstances of this slaughter. Were these people murdered quickly then burned afterward, or had someone burned them to death? She'd never heard of simple villagers being exterminated like this. Not in scripture. Nor the histories. Not anywhere. Who could have committed such acts, and why?

"We bury them, then go south," she said.

He waited before answering, his hands balled into tight fists. "Other villages," he said. His voice was low and angry. "Along this river."

"Yes."

Nara flared the earth rune to create graves on a hill above the village while Mykel carried the victims, one at a time, to their resting places. Angry at the senseless loss, Nara flared earth again to cover them over, the soil moving as she willed it. These murders were chilling but as horrible as they were, she couldn't help but focus on the missing children. Why would they take the children?

"It may not have been Fairmont," Mykel said, avoiding mention of the true villain's name. "Could be a local conflict."

"You don't believe that," she said. "And if that were true, it's no better."

"It's not your fault," he said.

But it was. She could have killed Kayna. There, in Fairmont castle, in the midst of the fury three months before. With the control of the king's armor and all the power it held, she could have ended it all. Prevented these deaths, saved the children. But she'd let the monster live. And now, with little training, no plan, and no magical armor to draw strength from, defeating her twin sister felt like an impossible task.

They moved south along the river to find a similar scene. Another village with only twenty homes, the burned corpses of the adults stacked in one cottage. Dried blood on the ground in the center of the village, and again, no children. Nightfall approached, and while they should have been getting back to the cavern, this was more important.

"We keep going," she said. Mykel didn't argue.

She had just finished burying the last of the bodies when she heard rustling nearby. From a bramble bush near one of the burnt cottages, two eyes stared at Nara. A child? She walked to close the distance, and a little one ran clumsily from the bush up a small hill but tripped on a root, falling.

"It's okay," Nara said. "I am here to help."

As Nara approached, the child rolled over, her face full of fear. It was a beautiful native girl, no more than four years old, with brown skin and coal-black hair. Her gaunt face showed that she hadn't eaten in days. Her clothes were dirty, and scratches covered her cheeks and forehead. Had she seen the horrors that occurred in the village? How long had she been alone?

Nara knelt, holding one hand out. "I won't hurt you. I promise."

The girl flinched as Nara touched her hand to the girl's cheek, then lurched forward, hugging Nara.

Oh, sweet dear, what have you suffered?

The wall she had been using to hold back the horrors came down, and tears came to Nara's eyes. She hugged the child, standing with her in her arms, patting her back and stroking her hair.

"I have you now, and I won't let anyone harm you."

She turned to see Mykel standing nearby, watching.

"What are we going to do with her?" he asked.

Nara shrugged and hugged tighter. "I don't know."

They walked south for the next few hours, the lights of Took looming closer in the distance. The girl refused to be put down, clinging to Nara as they approached the city. What would they find inside Took? If lights were lit, then people would be tending to the candles and lanterns. They wouldn't destroy an entire city, would they? As they approached, Nara heard the sounds of life—wagons and people moving about, and she exhaled a sigh of relief.

She stopped just outside the town wall, and Mykel came alongside her. Yet, instead of the sounds and smells of the vibrant city reaching her nose and her ears, all she could think of were the smells from the corpses earlier in the day. And the stillness, that horrible silence of the dead villages. She couldn't free herself of it.

Took was safe, but why? Because it was a larger town? A brisk wind brushed her face, blowing her hair back, and a seeing struck her. The suddenness of it forced her eyes open in surprise, unblinking. The images that came to her were of a village by the sea. Then she saw the mountain. The church. The harbor.

Dimmitt.

She saw images of soldiers with royal livery and someone in a red robe. Swords. Shields. Children were being gathered in the center of the town while screams from mothers echoed in the distance. Fathers bellowed and fought, wielding axes and sticks, struggling to defend themselves, their homes, and their families. But Nara fixed her attention on the children. Scared. So scared. Gathered together, they huddled in fear.

Then she saw fire and squeezed the child in her arms, trying to hold back her own screams.

3

YURY

I t was a clear, cool day as Gwyn crouched behind a tree in the forest, her eyes focused on a boy doing the same less than a hundred yards away. At Anne's direction, she had made the trek to this remote area in the northwestern area of the Great Land, far north of the Wastes and several days from Fairmont. Over a week of travel. To find a boy. And to save him. From what, Gwyn didn't know. Save him and wait for Anne—that's all she was told. It seemed foolish, but when an ancient seer tells you to find someone, you do it. Besides, spending endless days pacing about an old cavern had made Gwyn restless. She was a watcher, and she loved being on the move.

The boy was still, quiet, and well-skilled at woodcraft for one so young–he couldn't be more than fourteen years old. Gwyn slowed her pace more than usual to avoid alerting him to her presence. She had followed him since his departure early in the morning from Klaksha, the Roska village where he lived. He seemed to be easily distracted and a bit sloppy, rarely looking behind to assess other threats. At this moment, his focus was fixed on a creature in the clearing beyond.

Monsters such as these wandered about the woods and plains in this area, and Gwyn had heard of them in recent days but had never seen one. They began appearing several months ago and where they came from nobody claimed to know. But everyone feared them. And they should. This boy should fear them too, and he was far too close for comfort.

The creature had dark skin, bereft of clothing on its torso but with shredded, dirty fabric about its waist and legs. It moved while hunched over, walking mostly upon its legs, only occasionally using its arms upon the ground the way an animal would. Its eyes glowed in the near-darkness–orange, subtle, like embers from a dying fire.

It snarled and made sounds that were like words articulated through mangled teeth, though Gwyn couldn't make out what it said. More than an animal but less than a human, there was something fascinating about it, something that in a single moment was both magnetic and terrifying. Broken, monstrous, yet pitiable.

She looked at it with her special sight and marveled at what she saw. It wasn't just physically broken; its light was broken. Not brilliant and multicolored, like Nara's, nor bright and solid like that of a gifted. Instead, it flickered, bright one moment, then dull, dark, as if its soul was somehow damaged.

Curiosity must have overcome the boy's fear, fixing his sights upon the strange beast when he should have run away as fast as he could. Brave for such a young one. He was of average height and had a strong frame. He carried a long, thin knife in his right hand and his grip shifted nervously, betraying an eagerness to use the blade.

Anne had recently coached Gwyn in using her gift to look for subtle shifts that told so much more. The difference was often visible when the subject engaged in physical exertion, the light changing as the person labored. This boy would be gifted after his announcement. It wouldn't be an elemental power like that of a flamer. No, he was a racer, perhaps. Or a bear. Something physical, but it was hard to tell. But he had no cepp, no magic, and would need more than a knife to battle this beast. A lot more.

He stepped to one side, and the crack of the twig under his sole alerted the monster. A set of glowing eyes turned toward his hiding place. Caught.

The pounding of the boy's feet in a panicked retreat made it easy for Gwyn to follow him. Moving on a parallel course, the crashing of his pursuer among the bushes and branches helped to hide her own hurried footfalls. The boy would not outpace his adversary, and he must have known it because he slowed and turned, brandishing the knife and a scowl on his face. His shoulders were hunched, tense with anticipation. He intended to die facing the enemy, not running away. Brave lad.

The creature slowed when it saw the knife, then moved to circle its dinner. Gwyn stood less than fifty paces away, well-hidden by a large tree on a rise overlooking the clearing but intervening trees partially blocked her view of the conflict below. The creature pulled back its malformed lips, grinning hungrily and Gwyn could see long fangs that emerged from the creature's jaw. Long hair fell down its shoulders, but it sported no facial hair. It stopped circling and stood, fists upon the ground supported by massive arms and shoulders. Even hunched over, it towered over the boy. But Gwyn was now in a terrible spot; the boy was in the path of any arrow she could loose.

"Davay na menya, zver," the boy challenged in Roska.

Gwyn grabbed the bow on her back, nocked an arrow, and braced for an attack sure to come at any moment.

The monster stepped forward, its tongue slathering fangs with saliva, eager to devour its next meal. "Groshka," the beast yelled, then pounded its chest and growled, "Gnar." It pointed a long, clawed finger at the youth as it spoke in garbled words. "Gnar nack o'nit."

Gnar. Was that its name? And it spoke as if it were human. Disturbing. Gwyn couldn't understand what the monster said, but she moved to one side, looking for a clear shot at the beast.

Gnar lunged forward, sweeping a large claw within inches of the boy's nose. Although strong and fast, the beast was unwise, having chosen a simple, overextended attack for its opponent's face. The boy stepped to the left, avoiding the claws and moving the knife high then low as he passed, slicing its biceps on the upper attack, the hamstring on follow-up. The creature's howl betrayed its rage as it circled for another charge. This boy moved with surprising skill, and if he kept his wits and feet about him, he might live through the day.

Gnar's second attack was of a different sort. Instead of charging, the beast reared up on its hind legs, bellowed to the sky, and leaned forward, lungs heaving and eyes glowing brighter than before. Jaws opened, and a gout of fire shot out at the boy. It was a flamer! Though the lad tried to dodge the hot projectile, the surprise of it gave him little time, and as he spun midair, flame singed his shoulder.

Gwyn now had a clear target on the beast and her fingers relaxed on the bowstring, starting to release the arrow. Suddenly, the Roska boy launched himself toward the monster, directly in Gwyn's sightline, forcing her to abort the shot.

Long knife in hand, the boy was quickly underneath his opponent and the blade found a home in the monster's gut. Squatting, the boy wrapped his hands around the knife handle and thrust, cutting Gnar upward in a long gash from liver to lung.

The blood gushed forth, bathing the boy even as Gnar released another torrent of flames, scorching nearby trees and bushes.

The boy extracted himself from underneath the fatally wounded beast but no longer held his knife, having lost it in the close contact. Weaponless, he would have to evade the dying creature long enough for the monster's wound to overtake it, but by the look of the creature as it regained its feet and focused on the boy, Gwyn doubted the young warrior would succeed.

Gnar launched forward at its prey once again and Gwyn loosed her arrow. The fletching was soon visible in the side of the creature's head as it fell dead to one side.

The boy looked stunned at the sudden fall of the creature, breathing loudly. He looked about, eyes scanning the trees around him. "Thank you," he yelled to the empty woods in Landian, hardly a trace of his Roska accent detectable. Bilingual, then.

"More than you bargained for, today?" she asked, stepping out from behind her tree.

"Yeah. It was," he said, extending a bloody hand with a smile on his face. "I'm Yury."

She looked at his hand and gave him a glare.

He wiped his hand on the bark of a nearby tree, then on his own leg. "You're good with that thing," he said, pointing to the bow.

"I am."

"Who are you? Your name, I mean."

"Gwyn."

She moved to the side of the corpse, then kneeled to examine the beast up close. The body was twisted, with deformed joints that bent at odd angles. Patches of hair decorated its skin in an inconsistent, spotty pattern. She moved to the other side of the corpse and found an ornate rune on its back. Further inspection revealed a second design, mangled, with new flesh that obscured the pattern. Scarred. Had they burned it to mar the pattern?

"I've been following it all day," he said. "I first spied it this morning, scrounging about for berries and grubs. They sometimes move in small packs but rarely come close to Klaksha. We watch them to make sure they don't gather together and raid the village, then we pick them off when they are alone and we have the advantage."

"You should carry more than a knife," Gwyn said.

"I'm best with spear and shield, but it's hard to sneak through the woods carrying big weapons. I didn't plan on fighting but got sloppy, I guess. I didn't see you at all. How long were you following me?"

"A while."

"You're good," he said.

"That burn will need some salve."

"I'll be fine. I should go back," he said. "My sister will have dinner ready. Care to join us?"

"I think I will."

They spoke little as they walked for almost an hour before topping the final ridge between them and the Roska village. From that vantage point, they saw smoke rising from Klaksha. And fire.

Soldiers milled about the burning buildings. A lot of them. Yury ran, but Gwyn stood still. "Yury, stop!" she yelled, to no avail.

She should stay here. Charging into a village in chaos, with soldiers on a rampage doing Dei knows what–well, that was foolery. Gwyn was a survivor and didn't make mistakes like this. But her life was different now. She'd signed up for something risky when she left Fairmont. She'd decided to be a different person. A stupid one, apparently.

Her feet were moving almost before she'd decided to chase, and she reached for arrows, then sent them to find their homes in the necks or bellies of soldiers who tried to intercept. It was hard to keep up with Yury's vigorous pace, however. As she entered the village, the heat from the flaming huts beat against her face, and she almost lost track of the boy among the screaming as soldiers rounded up children and carried them off to carts.

"Ahna!" she heard Yury call from up ahead. She rounded a fiery stack of crates and saw him dash into an engulfed hut.

"She's gone," Yury said when he came out a moment later, hair steaming from the heat and a look of anger upon his face.

"Hey, you!" A man's voice from behind them startled her, and they both turned.

"Where's my sister?" Yury asked.

Yury dashed toward the man, his knife in hand, but he was unarmored and faced a soldier with sword and shield.

Gwyn loosed an arrow that passed a few inches above Yury's shoulder, but it bounced harmlessly off the soldier's shield a moment before Yury reached him. The arrow may have distracted the man, however, and Yury easily dodged a clumsy sword thrust.

Yury rained a flurry of knife thrusts and blows upon the soldier and they both fell, off balance, to the ground. The attacks soon overwhelmed the man and when Yury's fist crashed into the soldier's temple, he went still. Yury got to his feet, looking for another target.

"We must go," Gwyn said. "There are too many."

He looked at her a moment. "I have to find my sister. She's all I have." There was anguish in his voice and tears in his eyes.

Pain lanced up her arm. She looked down and saw an arrow had impaled her left forearm, forcing her to drop her bow. Her right hand went to the wound as she turned to see an archer and a soldier walking toward them down the otherwise empty street.

"Run," Gwyn said as she picked up the bow in her right hand and backed away from the threat, expecting Yury to follow. An arrow whizzed by her ear. She turned to see that Yury had left her, charging forward into the fray. An arrow now protruded from his thigh, and several soldiers surrounded him. With her wound, she couldn't use her bow. Only one thing left she could do.

She darted around another building, taking a moment to steel herself against the pain that now throbbed in her forearm. Sounds of soldiers approaching forced her to dash around another building, looking to escape.

Ahead, several horses were tied to a hitching post. She sprinted into action and a moment later, she was atop a black mare, galloping for the hills. As she left the area, she passed several wagons outside the village, nearby soldiers shouting at Gwyn as she galloped past. The wagons had cages. Children were inside. They looked at Gwyn with panic in their eyes. What did soldiers want with children, and why would they destroy an entire village to get them?

It took little time to evade the few who followed her on horseback, laden as they were with armor and gear. She found a vantage point to watch the scene from atop a high ridge, miles away, where she and the horse each caught their breath. The once-clear sky was becoming shrouded with the smoke from the village.

The wagon cages soon rolled to the east, followed by many soldiers. To Fairmont, probably.

Oh, Anne, what have you gotten me into now?

Hopefully, the boy would survive and get medical care before his leg wound festered. She looked at her own wound. The arrow had pierced the meat of her forearm but had not touched bone. She dismounted the horse and reached to the rear of the arrow, bracing the arrowhead against the saddle and breaking the shaft. Pain lanced up her forearm, but she didn't pause, immediately pulling the shaft free of the wound. As the blood flowed, she reached into her belt pack to retrieve some ground herbs from her pack. She mixed them with spit to form a paste that would prevent infection.

She wrapped the arm with bandages, and while it would likely heal, it would be useless for a time. But she had a horse and a task to perform. Save the boy. Yes, she could do that.

But where were they going?

4

INTERCEPT

The small city of Took hosted a home for children, but to call it an orphanage would have been generous, as small as it was. Even so, Nara was grateful for the elderly woman who met her and Mykel at the front door following their knock in the middle of the night.

"We found her in a village to the north," Mykel said. "Everyone was dead."

An anxious expression crossed the woman's face. Not of surprise, but more like fatigue. She sighed. "It's not the first village to fall," she said, "but they don't usually leave the children."

"This one hid," Nara said. "I found her in the bushes."

"I'll take care of her," the woman answered, rubbing her eyes then reaching for the girl who still clung tightly to Nara.

"It's okay, little one," Nara said. "She'll take care of you."

The girl relaxed, then reached out for the old woman, who received her.

"I don't know her name," Nara said. "And we don't have any money to give you."

"Thank you, dear. We'll be fine."

"Who is doing it?" Nara asked. "And why?"

"Nobody knows," the woman said, then closed the door.

As they walked away, Took began to quiet itself–shops closing and streets emptying. Nara also felt empty, as if she should have done more for the girl, or for the old woman. A subtle anger seethed within her. This horror was Kayna's for sure. Something must be done, but she couldn't act, not yet. She was needed elsewhere.

"We're not going back to the cavern," she said. "We don't have time. Dimmitt needs us now."

"Your vision could have been a mistake," Mykel said. "You're new at this stuff."

"They don't work like that."

"You're not ready," Mykel said.

"I know. Doesn't matter."

He shrugged. "We sleep. Then straight south?"

"Yes."

They spent the night under an abandoned wagon in a field on the south side of Took. Huddled up to Nara for warmth, Mykel fell asleep quickly, but Nara could not, troubled by thoughts of the vision and what it might mean. When the sun rose again, she couldn't remember having slept at all.

Running south from Took through the mountainous region was rough. The melting of the snows had created rivulets that crossed the road, eroding the dirt and crushed rock of the road under their feet. Nara twisted her ankle more than once with a misplaced step, yet she was undeterred, flaring health and continuing for hours, urgency spurring her on, Mykel following closely behind. They rarely stopped even to drink water from passing creeks, exchanged no words, and didn't slow when they passed merchants or travelers. How odd it must have been to see two young people sprinting at a supernatural pace toward them, passing by, then disappearing over the horizon.

At midday, they stopped for a long break at a creek to drink water and wash the sweat from their skin.

"This is going to take days," Mykel said.

"Then it will take days."

They didn't say anything else, and when they hit the road again, the urgency in Nara's heart had faded a touch, tempered by Mykel's words. It would indeed be days until they reached Dimmitt. They could not fly like birds, and many miles separated them from their home. This would be a marathon, not a sprint.

Though their pace didn't slow much, the second half of the day seemed to stretch forever. They passed several small villages that seemed unharmed, which was a great relief.

When darkness finally settled in, they slowed to a walk. The life in the bushes and grasses on the sides of the road could be seen in Nara's special vision, guiding her, the images in stark contrast to the dullness of the dirt and rocks on the road.

"We chase evil people," Mykel said, breaking the silence.

"Evil?" Nara asked. "Maybe."

"Maybe? Of course they are."

"I used to think that people could be evil, Mykel, I really did. I think that's what we want to believe. Makes it easier."

"How can you say that, after what you've seen?"

Nara took a deep breath.

"Anne used to believe in evil. A long time ago. But she changed her mind and decided that nobody's really evil."

"How's that?"

"Evil is a label. It's how we see actions that hurt others. Or actions that hurt us. But how many people deliberately hurt another simply to see the pain? To delight in another's torment? I agree; that would be evil, but nobody does that."

Did they really chase evil people? She kicked a rock to the side of the road and thought about Mykel's comment. It was hard to articulate what she was thinking because Nara only half-believed it herself. Anne had shared her thoughts on this matter, however, and they warranted consideration. As she thought about her sister and the conflict they were in, the topics of good and evil, right and wrong had often been on her mind.

"Kayna and the king," Nara said. "They did horrible things, but each with a purpose that served their own interests. It seems evil when you're a victim, or when someone you love suffers, but these are just horribly selfish actions. Some people take what they want and don't care about how it affects others. I don't know if evil is the best word. I like selfish much better."

"Maybe," he said. "Doesn't matter."

"I think it does." She stopped walking and Mykel turned to face her.

"Let's say Kayna ordered those soldiers to do what they did," Nara paused, taking a deep breath, then continued. "What if they defied her? Let's say they just told her, 'Hey, powerful magic Queen. I don't think I will.' What would have happened to them?"

"I don't know."

"I bet you can guess."

"Punishment," Mykel said. "Death, maybe. Or their families killed."

"Exactly. Family punishments are quite common for crimes in the Great Land. The soldiers who murdered those innocent villagers may have been thinking that they were saving their sweetheart, or a child, or a mother. If a soldier kills but thinks he has no choice or that he is actually saving someone, is he evil?"

"I didn't think of it that way."

"Or a warrior? When he fights in a war, he kills another man. Someone's son, perhaps. In the mind of the mother who loses a child in war, the other army is evil. Any warrior that puts a sword through her precious son's heart is evil, right?"

"I guess."

"And which side of the war is the evil side? Which warriors are righteous, and which are the dark ones? They can't both be, so which?"

"Sounds like you and Anne have been talking more than you've been training."

"We have," Nara said.

"I'm not good with words like you, but I think there are evil people. I really do. Kayna. The king. Those soldiers. What they are doing. I don't know what else to call it."

"Do you think I'm evil?"

"Of course not!"

"How you think Gretchen Wipp feels about me?"

Mykel's jaw went slack.

"'To her, I'm more than evil. I'm a monster. I'm the creature who sucked the life out of her sweet husband. A dark thing, a demon."

"But you didn't mean to. You didn't think you–"

"Exactly. When I did that terrible thing, I didn't think," she continued, her voice strained. "I just acted. Did what I wanted, without considering the cost, the risk, the bigger picture. I took Amos Dak's life to save you. To save me. I was so focused on our need that I didn't even realize I was harvesting the life of another person. Fear drove me. Panic. Selfishness. Not evil. At least,"–her voice quieted–"I hope not."

Mykel moved closer and put a hand on Nara's shoulder. "Bitty, I–"

Nara pulled away. "See what I mean? To Gretchen, I will always be a horrible thing. In her view, I'm as evil as evil gets."

"I see your point," he said. "Reminds me of Pop. He was a good man, folks say, until my mother died. Not evil. Just hurting. But killing innocents? Burning them? Stealing children? That's different."

They started walking again, not saying much as Nara thought on her own words. She believed them, sort of. There was wisdom in them, but she wondered if she repeated them to convince herself of something. That she was salvageable. Or perhaps having such thoughts invited hope for the future. Maybe these soldiers were really just good men dealing with bad times and wouldn't inflict their harsh orders on her precious town. Perhaps they would leave Dimmitt alone. A futile hope, perhaps. The vision of Dimmitt's doom was powerful, carrying a certainty and dread because she may not be able to do anything about it. Where was Dei in all of this? Didn't the God of this world care about the suffering of His creations?

The last light of the sun dropped over a mountain peak and Mykel slowed his pace.

"It's dark," he said. "I'm following the sound of your footsteps but can hardly see a thing."

"Use your staff. Or I can flare light if you want."

"We should rest, Nara."

"I want to keep going."

He was right. Flaring health all day long had drained them. They were tired and would travel faster if they could get a few hours of sleep. She sighed. "Okay."

Nara found a fallen tree, probably pushed over by a high autumn wind, and they made camp in the hollow below. At first, she worried that a fire would attract hostile attention, and her mind flashed to the ambush that nearly killed Mykel months ago. Then she dismissed the concern. They were no longer vulnerable to such things.

She found wood nearby and dragged the sticks and logs into a pile. She summoned the fire rune to her thoughts, extended her fingers and flared the rune. Flames leaped from her fingers, quickly setting the wood alight. As she moved to sit, she glanced at Mykel, his eyes wide.

"What?" she asked.

"Um, I just never saw you do that before."

"Oh."

Of course. He had been unconscious during the fight in the castle. He never saw her kill the king. What a shock it must be to see fire magic now.

"Gwyn told me what happened, but I never heard it from you," Mykel said. "You just said you killed him. But it was incredible, apparently. More than you let on."

She didn't respond, not wanting him to know how that happened, how she'd swelled up like a goddess with the power of the king's armor and used it to extinguish him like a gnat under her shoe. How the power of so much life energy felt as it coursed through her, delicious and unending. Delightful power. She had enjoyed the feeling, and even now she missed it. It helped her to understand why Kayna killed people, taking their magic, consuming the energy in their souls. It had felt good, and that was a horrible thing. Perhaps that was the purest evil of all.

She didn't want Mykel to know any of that. And she didn't want it to affect their relationship, though that was a silly wish. How could it not? Young men often sought to be stronger than the girls they loved, clinging to old notions about saving damsels in distress. Mykel might be the most powerful young man in the land, and no doubt he would have similar thoughts. Yet, just now, he looked at her with amazement. Or was it fear?

The wood crackled as they settled down on opposite sides of the flames. The shifting light from the fire illuminated Mykel's face in odd ways, shadows falling across his hair and nose, making him look like a very different person.

"I don't know what I'm doing, Mykel."

He didn't answer.

"We should have gone to Dimmitt long ago," she said.

"Anne said no. You've learned a lot, but you're not very good using the new runes. And gifted await us, out there. Racers, bears, and who knows what else?"

"Well-trained gifted. Big difference. And I tire when I use runes. 'Be efficient,' she keeps saying. Then I use strength or speed, and I fatigue so quickly. I'm exhausted right now. But Sammy needs us."

"Sammy is strong, Nara. And smart, for a kid. He should be okay."

"Nice try, but you are as worried as I am. Probably more."

There were no sounds of travelers pushing through the night on the road above them, only trickles from a nearby creek as it carried away the winter snows. Nara listened to the water and eventually, she was able to quiet her thoughts enough to sleep.

Hours later, Nara woke to see the sun barely peeking over the horizon. It dallied, coming late this time of year, rising slowly to cast its red blanket across the sleeping hills and mountains. Mykel snored across from her, smoke from the failed fire filling the hollow with its acrid odor.

She yawned and stretched, having rested far too little for the running her body had endured. But her mind was too busy to quiet itself again, so she rose and gathered more wood, then stoked the dying coals in an attempt to resurrect the fire. After a few moments, new flames began licking the logs. She reached into her pack and grabbed another biscuit, then took a bite as she watched the horizon, wondering what the day would bring. A few moments later, Mykel stirred.

"Good morning," Nara said.

He smiled.

"Sleep well?"

"Not at all," he said, rising and grabbing a biscuit. "We should get going."

Growing sounds from the road above interrupted their breakfast– sounds of horses moving closer, a wagon rolling, and men walking and talking.

Mykel smothered the flames with a few handfuls of dirt as Nara snuck up the incline to peek at the travelers.

Soldiers. Nara counted a dozen of them marching along the road, accompanied by two figures in robes, leading a wagon that bore an iron cage. Inside the cage were children.

"No," she muttered. "How dare they?"

Mykel joined her as they viewed the approaching group. The growing light would reveal them to the soldiers as they passed by in a few moments, but two travelers should be of little interest to such men. She could stand there and do nothing. No conflict. No screams. And the children would remain in that cold cage and be carried off to some terrible place, away from their village, away from their families. If they had any family left.

Mykel left her side and when he returned, he held the ivory staff.

"Don't kill them," Nara said.

He didn't respond.

"Please," she said.

She tore her eyes away from the cage and turned to Mykel. His lips were pursed, and his eyes held a harsh look.

"I mean it, Mykel. They're just following orders. They may have families."

Mykel stepped up onto the road and took a wide stance directly in the path of the oncoming soldiers. Nara joined him, standing at his side. As the entourage came closer, a soldier on horseback broke from the others and walked forward. A chain mail coif hung loosely about his neck, and in the dim light of dawn, Nara noticed dirt encrusted on his armor and fatigue in his eyes.

"What do you think you're doing?" he said with impatience as he stopped his horse a dozen paces away. The rest of his troop stopped behind him.

"What village did you steal them from?" Mykel asked.

"That's no business of yours," the man answered.

Nara flared the sound rune to amplify her voice–a trick Anne had shown her. Not very useful in combat, but it would make an impression. They would know she was gifted, and this might end without bloodshed. "Let them go," she said, her voice booming.

The soldier's face tightened in surprise, then he smiled. "Interesting trick, but you're two against twelve. Move aside." He gave his horse a gentle nudge in the ribs and it inched forward, but neither Mykel nor Nara moved. Nara sensed the anger rolling off Mykel in waves and she hoped he could restrain himself.

The soldier was only a few paces away when Mykel leaped forward, high into the air, and took the man off his horse with a single punch to the midsection. The stunned man fell to the ground, his armor impacting the dirt and rocks of the roadway, stirring all to surprise.

"Get them," another soldier yelled as half a dozen ran at Mykel.

In the next few moments, the ivory staff whirled, impacting legs and chests as Mykel delivered destruction. Nara had hardly advanced when the staff hit one man squarely in the temple. She sensed his life end as his skull collapsed under the blow.

"Stop!" she screamed, running forward and flaring protection in the event a sword came her way. "Mykel, stop it, now. Don't kill them!"

But he didn't stop. Three more fell in the seconds she had delayed. Others pulled swords and axes to engage with the warrior who waded through their ranks with his ancient weapon. Mykel wasn't listening to her–he was killing them all.

Anger rose at the senselessness of the destruction. There had to be a better way to save these children.

Nara flared the earth rune in her mind, holding it side by side in her vision with protection. The soil rose at her command, engulfing Mykel in dirt and rocks that solidified about his legs. Trapping him in place would prevent him from advancing on the others, at least for a moment.

His face whirled toward her, angry, streaked with the pain of betrayal. A sword flashed. Nara winced as Mykel took a cut across the midsection. The pain didn't seem to bother him, but he closed his eyes and flared protection and health, his wound closing. A fraction of a second later, he swung the staff to strike the sword-wielding soldier across his face, sending him to the ground in agony.

Half a dozen armed men lunged at Mykel, but he was immobilized and the fight would now be hers. She flared speed to confront the approaching attackers. Two were in the lead, carrying small axes and shields. She intercepted them, their movements slowing to a crawl as she accelerated. In an instant, she had grabbed the haft of the first soldier's axe, pried his thumb back, and seized the weapon. She then tossed it as far as she could over the side of the road. She whirled as she readjusted her path toward the second one, removed his axe, but kept this one for herself.

The soldiers continued toward Mykel in slow motion, surprise blooming on their faces as they realized that she had disarmed them. She positioned herself between them, flaring the motion rune and gesturing, focusing her thoughts, pushing them away from her. The soldiers flew into the air, landing thirty feet away, one on each side of the road. A sudden weakness came upon her, so much strength spent in using multiple runes at once.

"Gifted!" The voice carried fear, and the remaining soldiers slowed. She dropped the runes from her thoughts and stood in front of Mykel, axe still in hand, surveying the remaining combatants. One of the figures in the back of the entourage came forward, removing her robe to reveal herself as a young woman in a leather cuirass and breeches, a dagger in each hand and an angry expression on her face.

"We're on the queen's business," the woman said. Her short-cropped brown hair was tangled and her face dirty. "You have attacked soldiers on a royal mission. You are under arrest." Her voice sounded strained.

Nara heard a sound from behind her and looked to see Mykel step free of the earth and stone that had bound him, his strength rune still flaring hot in her vision.

"Leave the children and you'll be unharmed," Nara said.

The attack came so fast that neither Nara nor Mykel could react as the figure dashed toward them like a bolt of lightning. Nara lifted her right arm, still wielding the soldier's axe, just in time to feel a hot pain dance from her wrist to her elbow, forcing the weapon from her grip. Mykel touched his neck where a wound had appeared and blood now flowed.

A racer!

Nara flared speed just in time to brace for a second approach by the racer. The pain in her forearm distracted her focus, but she avoided many strikes from a second flurry exploding upon her. The racer retreated a dozen paces, slowly now that speed was again Nara's ally. Blood spilled from Nara's gut and left shoulder now. New wounds–and so fast!

She flared health and the wounds lessened, even as Mykel advanced on the deadly woman. He would be much slower than his opponent, but with the sight rune, he would know where she planned to strike. Nara searched with her vision for the woman's cepp, but the glow of energy from Mykel's staff made it difficult, as if searching for a candle in a room that held a blazing fire. Then she saw them–tiny bone rings, one on each hand, like those Gwyn carried. If she could siphon their magic, the racer would be powerless, but the young woman moved so fast that Nara's thoughts couldn't track them well enough. A fight was unavoidable.

Flaring protection and speed at once, she grabbed the fallen axe and stepped toward the racer, teeth gritted, and resolved to return the blinding attacks in kind. Maybe only violence would work with these people after all.

The woman's eyes widened with surprise at Nara, then she adjusted the grip on her daggers, both dripping with blood. The woman was faster than Nara and far more practiced with her gift.

But she was only a gifted, and Nara was more than that.

She flared sight for just a moment and knew what would happen next.

As the two women clashed, Nara's axe swung wide, missing the woman's shoulder by several inches as it whistled through the air. The racer's dagger, however, impacted Nara in her side, and the pain announced itself in outrageous fashion, causing her to buckle over. Nara let go of the axe and flared strength and speed with all her passion, forcing herself upright and grabbing the woman's arms with a rapidity and fierceness that took the racer by surprise.

Then Nara squeezed.

The bones in the woman's forearms snapped, an audible crack preceding her cry. A moment later, an agonizing sympathetic pain raced across Nara's own forearms, and she shuddered. She stopped flaring all her runes as an ivory staff came out of nowhere to crush the woman's skull, sending her the ground.

"No!" Nara screamed. "Mykel, no! She was beaten!"

Pain in Nara's side sapped her strength, forcing her to her knees. She stumbled to the racer's side, the crumpled form now devoid of movement, broken forearms askew, and blood spilling from the side of her skull.

"I told you no killing!" Nara screamed.

Silence fell. The remaining soldiers stood in place, clearly not knowing what to do.

"They deserve to die," Mykel said.

"Following orders. That's all they are doing!" Nara flared health to close her own wounds, then put a hand on the head of the fallen racer. She felt the softness in the woman's shattered skull, a sick, squishy feeling where there should have been hard bone. She recalled the knitting and sight runes that Anne had shown her, flaring them with what remained of her own strength, the designs popping alive in her vision. Images flooded her thoughts of the broken pieces of skull beneath her fingers. As she fed the knitting rune, the pieces of bone coalesced and fused but there was damage to the brain beneath, and Nara had run out of time. She had almost no practice in the repair of complex injuries and quickly lost hope. A final, raspy breath announced the woman's end.

She looked at Mykel, anger and frustration rising. "She was young, like us. Someone stabbed her hand with a ceppit, and her life changed." Nara stood, then took a step closer to him. "Maybe she wanted to be an artist or a baker. Or was in love and wanted to marry. Instead, she was drafted after an announcement ceremony. Forced to work with soldiers, kidnap children and kill their parents. She's a victim, Mykel. Like so many others. And you killed her!"

"You moved so fast," he replied. "Like lightning. I've never seen anything like it. Both of you. I couldn't see what was happening, so I trusted the staff. With it, I knew where to strike. Where to move, to protect you. It's my job, Nara."

"Don't trust the staff. Trust me!"

Blood on her hands, Nara turned toward the remaining soldiers who stood watching, awaiting their fate. The nervous movements of one of them betrayed his fear, an eagerness to run or perhaps to hide.

Standing among the soldiers was a figure in black robes; another gifted. He was in his mid-twenties, she guessed. A bone cepp dangled from a chain belt around his midsection, and fear hung in his eyes. He hadn't engaged in the fight and probably didn't know how. Perhaps he was a harvester, a mover of magic, not a warrior.

She understood Mykel's anger at these people; she had felt it herself. A moment ago, in the middle of the fight with the racer, she had tasted that fury. If she had kept her wits about her, she may have found a way to control the engagement better, but violence had seized her and she had embraced it, much like Mykel had.

"Open the cage," Nara said. A moment later, two soldiers complied, and half a dozen children spilled free onto the roadway. They were dirty, and their faces were haggard. She turned to the soldiers.

"Now go. To Fairmont. To your mistress." She needed to say something else, to convince them to end this craziness. Kidnapping children? Killing their parents? But what could she say? They knew the horror of their orders but followed them, anyway. "And be ashamed. To save yourselves punishment, you inflict it upon the innocent. There is little mercy in our hearts for you. If I see you again, I'll kill you!"

It wasn't true, but she wanted urgency in her words, to deter them from future wrongs. They didn't respond, heads hanging low and glancing occasionally in Nara's direction as they gathered their wounded and dead. They then mounted and spurred their horses on, leaving the six stolen children standing in the middle of the road.

Without turning to face him, she spoke to Mykel. "She was like one of these children once. Now she's dead."

Mykel came closer, putting a hand on Nara's shoulder. "She tried to kill you. It was her job. It's not fair, I agree, but if someone tries to kill you, I will put them down."

Nara didn't look at him, and Mykel dropped his hand.

"You're not like Kayna," he said. "Defending yourself won't make you any more so. Failing to defend yourself will end it all. Want to defeat her? Fight. You can't be everyone's friend and believing such nonsense will bring horrible things to this land. You're the only one who can stop her. If you won't make it happen, we're all in trouble. Be angry if you must. Yell at me. Cry. I don't care. But I'll protect you from these people until you get your head on straight. Get used to it."

Nara said nothing.

"And never use your magic on me again."

There was anger in his voice. And pain. She'd hurt him. It was a betrayal, and she knew it. She yearned to look into his eyes, to make him understand that she didn't want to be like her sister, and she didn't want him to, either. Killing was wrong. She wanted to heal. To protect, not destroy. Perhaps these battles would require sacrifices, but she couldn't bear to think of how she could deliver such destruction.

He was right, in so many ways. The mess of emotions running about her head made it hard to find the right words. By Dei, she didn't even know what she was feeling, so it was probably better not to say anything at all.

She approached the children. "Where are you from?"

"My house was burned," said a boy no more than twelve years old.

"They killed my mommy," this from a small girl, tears in her bright blue eyes. Nara moved to give her a hug, then realized she still had blood on her own hands and clothes. She knelt instead.

"What is the name of your village?" Nara asked. The little one didn't respond, hiding behind the leg of a taller girl.

"Keetna," the taller one said. She was about fourteen, with long black hair that needed care. "Through the pass, over there." She pointed to the southwest.

It would require a slight detour, after which they could continue to Dimmitt. A small inconvenience in order to return these children safely to their village, although there was no guarantee there would be anyone left alive to receive them.

"Keetna. Okay. Let's get you home."

5

EVIL THINGS

Ennis shuffled into the wet stone chamber, his tongue clicking as he held his freshly charged ceppit on the top of his palms. It was the same way that priests carried the relics during announcement ceremonies, so it was fitting. He enjoyed those ceremonies. The orderly ritual was comforting. With his recent experiments, he had been present at many recent announcements, with directions from the Queen to find out what they've been doing wrong all these years. To know everything about the gifted, and how to discover them. He took the job very seriously.

The young lady strapped onto the chamber's steel table was no more than twelve, and Ennis hadn't asked for a name. It was better not to know such things. He'd had many children on his table lately, and they had taught him much. It still seemed odd, however, to be using such young subjects, far younger than those he'd welcomed on his table before. But the Queen insisted, and it was her right. She was strong. He had learned long ago that strength determines authority, and he would not cross her.

Small ones cried more than the grown men he had worked on. They asked for their mothers or fathers, and they begged. He wasn't trying to break them, however. He was not eager for some secret missive they held in their hearts, or a reluctant confession. Finding magic was more difficult, however, and success often eluded him.

The process he currently used derived from a theory arisen from discussions with the Queen. Based on her own experiments, she envisioned human beings as containers. Containers with magic inside. Break them and the magic spills out. But if you can just stretch it, crack it, or maybe poke little holes, it comes out slowly, bit by bit, producing a gifted. Or a cursed, which was quite similar, actually, but far more valuable. There was merit in her theory, and there had been evidence to support it thus far, albeit in meager amounts.

"Don't worry, young thing," he said as he tested the tip of the ceppit with his finger. "It's sharp and has a very small blade. Smaller than most." He clicked his tongue several times. "This one is especially narrow. Works the same as others but doesn't do much damage. It will hurt, but only for a bit. Just like yesterday."

The girl started crying, then escalated to wracking sobs that shook her small frame. Ennis gripped her left hand, placing the tip of the ceppit over the soft flesh between thumb and forefinger. A quick thrust, the blade was through and she was howling, but strong straps held her in place.

"Let the magic sink in," he said. "Let it do its work."

Less than a minute later he removed the blade and set it on a nearby shelf, reaching for some bandages to staunch the bleeding before he began repairs. The girl no longer wriggled in place and Ennis checked her pulse at the carotid. Not dead. Fainted. All the better.

He grabbed her left hand in his own and reached to his belt with his other, finding the cool cepp that dangled under his loose smock. Tapping the power in the cepp, he worked his craft, knitting the tissues together, first the muscle, then the lower layers of skin, and finally the epidermis. Perfect.

With one hand healed, he moved to the other, dabbing it with the bandage. Soft footsteps in the hallway disturbed him, leather boots on the stone tiles differing greatly from the clanking and clunking that the soldiers usually made. A pleasant sound. Soft. Gentle. From a woman who was anything but. A knock preceded an opening door.

"Your majesty," he said, bowing his head.

"How goes the work, Ennis?" Her dark hair was back in a ponytail and she wore a simple, red silk shirt and dark trousers. And her smell. Sweet. Nothing like the damp, malodorous stone rooms that made up the nether regions of this dark dungeon.

"I was just finishing with this one, but she has no visible flaws and I didn't have much hope for her. The broken ones seem to be the easiest to work with and this method, although promising in theory, hasn't shown good results. Perhaps as a catalyst for my other plan? The revisions I proposed could be revolutionary. I was still hoping..."

"Hope no longer. I've considered your idea, and it has merit. We move forward."

He widened his eyes in surprise. Such an opportunity! He had expected she would refuse. They tried in recent months with little success. Some projects even escaped, and it would take so much effort from her to try again. But the search for a cursed had brought nothing but disaster, the experiments had been catastrophic, and the recent revisions were the best he could come up with.

"I will not disappoint, your majesty."

"More subjects will be here in a few days. Pick four. Then we begin."

She offered a smile, then looked to the unconscious child on the table.

"What will you do with this one, now that we're moving on?"

"I hadn't decided."

"Send her this afternoon."

"Of course."

Soft footsteps carried her from the room.

He shuffled about the chamber, clicking his tongue eagerly as he put away bandages and tools. The plan would go forward, and he still hadn't written out the script. Much to think on. There would be the science. Yes, he could test his theories much better now. And the protections must be in place. So dangerous. Much to plan. But manipulating the subject, oh that would be the hardest part. He had confidence in his own role, but could she pull it off? It wouldn't be useful to have their creation hate her as much as the last one did. Not useful at all.

Much to do! And he must not disappoint his Queen.

6

KEETNA

Fatigue from the previous battle weighed on Nara as she walked at the back of the group. Mykel led as they ascended the mountains around Keetna, avoiding boulders, loose rocks, and snowfields where they might be in danger of an avalanche. Keetna was not far out of the way of their original path, but slowing their pace to that of small children was a huge delay, and Nara bit her lip in frustration. The vision of Dimmitt in trouble could have been one from the future, warranting a rush to save the town. But it could have been from the past, and there was no way to know until they arrived.

The children were strangely quiet for most of the trip, and when they would complain from fatigue or cold, Nara or Mykel would carry them. For most of the day, Mykel held one in each of his arms, tirelessly moving forward without complaint. He was strong and good, his presence comforting not only to Nara but also to the others. Nara thought of the good father he could be, working hard for his family, helping others in trouble, defending those in danger. He would fight for justice in whatever place he eventually called home. She wondered if that would be her home too.

The day came to a close, and the sun began to slip behind a mountain peak.

"Let's camp here," Mykel said. He set down the girl he'd carried for the last hour and pointed to a stone depression on the southeast side of a descending slope. "Nara, would you make that into more of a shelter?"

She nodded and walked toward the stone depression. It was eroded by waters from above and loose rocks presented a challenge for her ankles as she navigated her way through the depression. The stone was dry, but with no bedrolls for the children, sleeping on the rocky surface would be uncomfortable.

She flared the earth rune in her thoughts and reached out with one hand to touch the stone of the mountain, calling it, coaxing it. She imagined how she wanted it to change, to shape itself. It responded. The depression receded into the mountain, becoming a cave thirty feet deep. Loose rocks on the ground near the entrance transformed to soil, then expanded, extending into the cave itself. Soft dirt, warm. Near the entrance, a stone pit revealed itself and eight circular, flat stones emerged from the soil beneath, rising, distributed around the pit. Seats for little children so they could warm themselves by a fire.

She broke the connection and looked about. It was dark in the cave, but there was no way to provide permanent lighting without opening the cave to rainfall from above. Yet the soil was much better for sleeping than hard rock would be, and she hoped that once a fire was crackling, they would be warm. It was a good place.

After deciding that the cave would suffice, she turned back to the group, only to find the oldest girl standing a dozen feet away, mouth open.

"Hello, Nilly," Nara said. Although they'd spoken little, she'd learned the girl's name during the trip. Nilly had been helpful in keeping the younger ones moving.

"How did you do that?"

"Um, it's kind of hard to explain."

The girl walked into the cave, knelt, and ran her hands across the rim of the fire pit and the stone seats. She turned back to Nara. "It's beautiful."

"Why, thank you," Nara said, smiling.

"Are you an angel?"

Nara smiled. What a sweet child. Perhaps 'child' wasn't the best word. She was only a couple of years younger than Nara. "No, I'm just a person. Like you."

"Not like me," Nilly said. "I could never do anything like this."

Nilly was right, she couldn't do this and never would. Nara felt oddly self-conscious at the realization. She cleared her throat before asking, perhaps too quickly, "Could you help me gather the little ones in here? We all need to rest."

A short time later, several children were asleep on the soft dirt of the cave floor. Nara started the fire with wood Mykel had collected, not bothering to hide her talent. Between the fight with the soldiers and earth-shaping, there seemed to be little point in secrecy. The questions came, as expected.

"I'm gifted, Nilly. So is Mykel. You're safe with us."

It wasn't enough of an explanation for the chaos these children had recently endured, but it would have to do. At least they didn't seem fearful. Perhaps being kidnapped from their homes was scarier than being protected by gifted strangers, and the magic brought them comfort. Or perhaps they simply knew that they had few options and were grateful for a warm cave and a crackling fire.

When Nara lay down for the night, most of the children had already fallen asleep. Mykel came and lay at her side.

"You did well today," she told him. "They like you."

"I did nothing. Other than biting my lip for miles, frustrated that I couldn't be running to Dimmitt."

"We couldn't leave them with the soldiers, Mykel. Or by themselves in the middle of nowhere."

"I know, but at what price? Your premonition is worrying me. We might have been able to prevent the attack on our home. If this delays us—"

"I know."

She stared at the cave's dark ceiling for a moment, the shadows from the flickering fire dancing across the stone's surface in a hypnotic pattern.

"The fight yesterday," Mykel said.

"Yes?"

"You did it again."

"Did what."

"Wasted too much energy."

"I got the job done."

"The way you moved afterward–you were tired, and it wasn't even a long battle. Be more efficient, or you won't last."

His tone was disapproving, and she didn't enjoy hearing it. As if she didn't already know her limitations. "I know."

"There will be battles, Nara. Maybe many. Your passion makes you strong. Stronger than me, even. But if you can't last–"

"I know. I'm trying!"

"Try harder. Kayna may have no such weakness. And she isn't slowed by compassion. She will crush us if you can't match her strength."

"She has armies! How could I ever match that? And do you expect me to just let children die?"

"No, but I expect you to end this all. Somehow. You're our only hope."

"No pressure," she scoffed.

"You told me to trust you. Okay, I will. But you need to be trustworthy. You can't just live in a pretend world of smiles and hugs, running around loving everyone, and expect to win a war against that evil woman."

Nara bit her lip but didn't respond because she had nothing to say. He was right. Having magic with no cepp was a boon compared to a normal gifted, but it required her to use the magic in her own spirit and when that ran low, she became vulnerable. Kayna had no such handicap. She just sucked the life out of other people and was probably more efficient with her magic as well.

Frustration with the problem and no clear solution kept Nara awake deep into the night. After a time, she rose to refuel the fire with fresh logs, then stood near the entrance to the cave, looking out at the dark valley below. Keetna was close, and the children would be back in their village soon. Or what remained of it.

She eventually found her way back to the soft soil that was her bed, only to find one of the little ones curled up next to Mykel, sleeping soundly. She joined them, hugging close, comforted by their warmth and the soothing sounds of their easy slumber. She closed her eyes and waited for the morning that would soon arrive.

With hardly an hour of sleep, Nara rose with the sun and collected berries to provide a meager breakfast for the children. There wasn't enough food for her and Mykel, but they would be fine, and the children needed the energy to finish the trek home. Mykel awoke a short time later to begin gathering the children. As they set out to leave, Nara wondered if she should cover up the cave.

"Leave it," Mykel said. "Who knows if travelers going through the pass might need shelter? It might save a life."

She smiled in agreement, picked up one of the smaller children, and walked down the hill. Someday a stranger might thank Dei for that little cave, and the pride she felt upon its creation came back to her in a small portion.

It took half a day to reach Keetna—or, rather, what remained of it. Blackened cottages lined the riverside that hosted the medium-sized village. It was much bigger than the destroyed villages they'd passed in recent days but no less damaged.

Fortunately, there were several people there, removing burnt timbers from the homes. As they approached, an elderly matron broke away from the others. She wore a torn, soot-stained dress and scurried to meet them. Several children ran to greet her while Nilly stayed by Nara's side.

"Mimi!" they screamed. "We missed you."

The woman was at least sixty years old but seemed to have more than her share of energy and enthusiasm for the little ones.

"Oh blessings," she said. "I thought I'd lost you all."

"She's like everyone's grandma," Nilly said, her voice cracking and tears on her cheeks.

"I'm glad," Nara said.

Nilly joined the children in Mimi's embrace, then grabbed her hand and led her to Nara and Mykel. Two of the children clung to the woman's legs, making it difficult for her to walk. A few moments later, two other women ran to greet the children, scooping several up into their arms and cheering. The remaining children just stood in a huddle, looking about for families that might never come.

"These are the people who saved us," Nilly said to Mimi.

Mimi gave a shallow bow and a wide grin. "Thank you," she said, then picked up one of the little ones who tugged on her dress.

"The soldiers," Mimi said. "How did you . . . ?"

"They fought them all," Nilly explained. "Just the two of them. They are gifted, Mimi."

"Then Dei has truly blessed us. Again, thank you."

Nara didn't know what to say. This woman was grateful for the return of the village's children, but the village had been razed, leaving few standing shelters and likely little means for the remaining villagers to feed themselves. Now there were more mouths to feed. Worst of all, there was no defense against royal soldiers coming back and doing it all again.

"How will you provide for yourselves?" Mykel asked. "How will you defend yourselves?"

"We'll manage," Mimi said. "There are farmers tending fields to the south. They were unharmed and still grow crops. Dei will provide."

Such faith in the face of calamity. Nara couldn't contemplate what strength of spirit she carried to endure in such circumstances. "What can we do to help?" Nara asked.

"You have done enough by returning our little treasures," she answered. "I'm sure you have more important things to do."

She was right. Dimmitt needed them, and they couldn't protect the entire Great Land at once.

Mykel put a hand on Nara's shoulder. "We should go."

Nilly stepped boldly up to Nara, her eyes focused, brows narrowed. "Take me with you."

"You are needed here."

"My family is gone."

"You are the oldest of the children," Nara said. "Almost a woman. They will need you to care for them. These little ones, and Mimi, they are your family now."

Nilly's demeanor relaxed, head dropping.

"I'll visit you," Nara said. "As soon as I can. To check on you."

Nilly looked up to give a grateful smile.

They said goodbye to each of the children, and to Mimi before setting out at a fast pace to the south. They had lost much time, and Dimmitt was still far away.

7

PUNISHMENT

S ammy crouched in the hollow, eyes fixed on the brown coney as it hopped toward the waiting snare a few yards ahead. Simon Tinny was at his side, and they both held their breath as the fuzzy creature inched toward the apple core that had been placed as bait.

A bent sapling strained against the round trigger that Sammy had crafted for the task, attached to a looped piece of string that served as the noose. He had sanded one side of the trigger to make it hold better, and it served him well–he'd already caught one coney yesterday. Sammy gave a thumbs-up to Simon, then nodded, confident it would work again today.

Several more moments passed as the coney nibbled at the treat. Testing. Tasting. Then it took a bite, pushing the apple as it did so, and the trigger slipped. The sapling came free, springing straight, pulling the string and catching both of the coney's rear feet in its tightened loop. It emitted a muffled squeal in surprise.

"Got it!" Simon stood, clapping. "Great job, Sam."

If only Mykel were here to see it. He had gotten much better with snares in the last few months and fashioned half a dozen triggers that worked almost every time. But Mykel had not come home.

Sammy liked to imagine that Mykel had survived the announcement and now lived in a faraway part of the Great Land, married to his sweet Nara. He thought of his brother wearing armor and carrying a sword, a powerful warrior who led armies. Other times he thought of Mykel as a simple farmer with a big field of potatoes he tended. Nara was his beautiful lady-wife, and she cared for their dozen children, some with black hair and some with red hair, little versions of Mykel and Nara running about and playing.

"Nonsense," Pop had told him. "Your brother is dead. He's cursed, and you're an idiot. Grow up."

But Sammy refused to believe it. Mykel still lived. He would come home someday.

As Sammy reached the panicked creature, he grabbed it by the neck and slipped the noose free from its feet. He looked it in the eyes as it struggled, trying to bite him, its eyes darting back and forth. So scared. Suffering. Sammy felt sorry for it, but he could understand. Sometimes he was scared too. With a quick motion from his other hand, he twisted and pulled the creature's head, snapping its neck.

"You can have this one, Simon," he said, handing the prize to his friend.

"Are you sure?"

"Pop and I ate one yesterday." He handed over the bounty, then knelt to untie the trigger and string. "And take these too. Now you know how it works, you can catch your own. Just don't take my spots!"

"I won't," Simon said as he received the valuable gifts. "I'll find new ones. Honest. Thanks, Sam. It will thrill Mama."

Sammy smiled. Simon was a good kid, and although he was eleven, just like Sammy, he seemed to be sweeter. Nicer. It was because he had a mama. She wore an apron and her hair was messy, but Sammy didn't care. Simon's mama was a kind lady and laughed a lot. It was a funny laugh, almost like a donkey, and it made Sammy laugh every time. Simon would blush when his mama laughed, but Sammy wouldn't have been ashamed at all. Sammy envied him. Living with a mama would be nice. She was someone to tuck you in at night and sing to you. She was someone who said nice things about you and rubbed your back when you cried about stuff. Sammy wished he had one.

He left Simon behind and headed toward the village. There was no food at home and he had given away the coney. Tonight would be a hungry one if he couldn't find scraps. Perhaps someone in town would have extra food.

His stomach growled as he approached the church. The stage remained outside, left over from the announcement a few months back. Some folks had commented on how it was cursed, just like Mykel, and nobody dared to touch it for fear of the curse spreading. Sammy slowed, wondering if it really was. He scaled the steps to the top, wood creaking under his bare feet. On reaching the top, he saw the boards where the blood had spilled. Blood from Nara, Finn Willy, and Gilbert Bonny. And Mykel. Cursed blood, they said.

He sat in the middle, crossing his legs and leaning forward, elbows on knees and chin resting on his hands. It didn't seem cursed. It just seemed like wood. But it was the last place he'd seen his brother before Nara's pop carried them both away.

The memory haunted Sammy, but being in this place comforted him, somehow bringing him closer to Mykel. He closed his eyes.

"Get off that stage," came a sudden voice.

Sammy looked to see Father Taylor waving through an open window in the church.

"Get off there this minute," he said again, then grumbled something Sammy couldn't make out.

Sammy frowned, then stood and descended the steps without a word and walked toward the docks. Father Taylor had been grumpier these last few months. The nice old man had become like a hermit and sometimes even canceled church services. Lots of folks had gone sad and talked about curses and how Dei didn't love them anymore. Some even moved away, to Junn or Fulsk.

Sammy wanted to move away, too. He knew how to paddle a boat but had never worked a sail, so he'd need to paddle the whole way to Junn. That would be hard, but he was getting stronger–and taller. He could do it. If he trapped enough coneys, sold both the meat and the hides, and didn't share the money with Pop, maybe he could buy a boat.

As he gazed out at the dock and the waves, he saw two boats come into view from the west. They didn't look like the boats that usually visited Dimmitt. These bore big sails, and a lot of men stood on board. As they came closer, he saw a man on the bow of the first boat wearing a black robe, two big white things dangling from a chain on his waist. That was odd. People on boats didn't wear robes; they wore trousers and aprons for cutting up fish and stuff. And they didn't hang white things on their belt.

Sammy sprinted from the docks and ducked behind the church, where he grabbed the rope to the bell tower and pulled it repeatedly. Gong! Gong! Gong!

"Boats!" he exclaimed as loudly as he could. "Big boats."

At first, nobody paid him any mind, but after he kept ringing the bell, some kids gathered around the docks. Kids were always the first to greet new people. Sammy stopped ringing the bell and joined the others, waiting at the entrance to the main pier but not walking on the planks. That would be rude. You never walked on the docks when important people were arriving–you might get in their way. Not unless someone asked for help. Then you could go all the way up to the boats and help tie them off. Or carry things.

The boats were even bigger than Sammy thought. Each bore two masts, but they tucked the sails long before docking. There were soldiers on the boats, but there were others too. Men who sat on benches and rowed.

"Oars up!" someone yelled, and the oars on the first boat rose. Mr. Fedgewick and some others stepped onto the docks and headed to the first boat as it approached the docking bay reserved for visitors. There was a skiff tied up there, and Mr. Fedgewick untied it and moved it out of the way.

The man in the black robe stepped off the first boat, accompanied by a man in armor. The two said something to Mr. Fedgewick, who then walked past Sammy, heading toward the church.

"What do they want?" Sammy asked, but Mr. Fedgewick didn't answer.

The man in the black robes walked past Sammy and the other kids, the soldiers following him. One, two, three, Sammy counted. He kept counting and made it all the way to twelve. They must have been cold, or maybe tired because none of them were smiling. Way down the dock, a man in a red robe held two white things that dangled from his belt. The robe wasn't a pretty red though. It was a dark red. Like it was dirty or old.

"Wow, a bunch of them," Simon said, coming alongside Sammy. Simon fidgeted with the string and trigger as he spoke. "Who are they?"

"Soldiers," Sammy said. "Pop told me about them. See the big swords on their belts? And that metal on their chest is their armor."

"Looks heavy."

"I bet they're so strong they don't even notice."

"Why so many?" Simon asked. "Are they on their way somewhere? Do they need to rest here a while?

"I don't know."

"What about those other men? In the robes."

"Dunno," Sammy said, scratching his chin nervously, as he often did. "But I think this is bad."

It didn't take long for the soldiers and the men in robes to gather the kids near the announcement stage. Lots of kids. Sammy was pushed up almost to the stage steps, with Simon next to him. Sammy wondered if he could sneak under the stage and run away.

He could do it without anybody seeing. Maybe he could make

it home to Pop. But Pop didn't even have a sword. And Sammy didn't want to leave Simon.

The adults gathered, and some argued with the man in black robes. But when soldiers came near, the men stopped talking. Some women were crying, including Simon's mama, but when Simon tried to go to her, a soldier stood in the way.

"Don't move, boy. Not a step." He spoke in a scary voice, deep and grumbly as if he was good at being angry. A crooked scar ran along his nose. He looked at the other children and held out a finger. "And none of you, either. Not a step."

"You're mean," said one of the kids. It was Simon's little brother, Dylin. He was six. "You should get a whoopin'."

The soldier laughed and turned away.

The man in the black robe stopped talking to the adults and pushed past the kids to walk the steps up to the stage. Father Taylor walked behind, taking a place on the stage. Father Taylor's head was bowed, but it didn't look like he was praying.

"The archbishop sent me to give this village its due. This is a reckoning," the man in the black robe said.

Since Sammy was close to the stage, he could see him well. The man wasn't old. He was kinda young. Older than Mykel, but not by a lot, with a little black beard covering only his lip and chin.

"What's a reckoning?" Simon whispered in Sammy's ear.

Sammy shrugged.

"This town, like many others, has defied the church," the man said, turning to Father Taylor, who didn't meet his gaze. "For years, you did not imbue your ceppit. You failed in your duty to the crown and the church. I am here to bring you to account."

Father Taylor stepped forward and spoke to the crowd. "I am to blame," he said. "I am sorry. Our coffers were empty, so I haven't filled the ceppit in years." He turned to the man in the robes in a quieter voice. "I never told them. It's not their fault. Punish me only. Please."

A nervous shuffling of feet spread through the crowd, and Sammy felt a chill. Punish?

"No," continued the man in the black robes. "Blame is shared. Not only did you harbor a cursed and fail to submit him to the church, but you also raised an enemy of the crown as your own. The girl with red hair, a demon in your midst. Dimmitt is a town of desolation. A den of iniquity that deserves no mercy."

Were they talking about Nara? They didn't know her very well.

The soldiers surrounded the gathered villagers, but some folks were missing. Kids that lived on other parts of the island, not in the village. And Lina wasn't here. Her parents, neither. Sammy was glad for that because the man said *punish*.

"The penalty will be harsh. First, we break your hearts," the man said, then cleared his throat and stretched his neck to the side. "You will lose someone precious, the cost of defying Dei."

A woman behind Sammy sobbed loudly.

"Then we'll break your bodies. We'll announce every adult in this town. Any gifted that result will be conscripted. For the rest of your life. No wages. No freedom."

A worried voice came from behind Sammy. "They can't announce adults. The church has already announced us."

Another voice said, "Apparently not. Taylor didn't fill the ceppit, that cur. They gonna do it again."

Were they going to announce the smaller kids too, like Sammy? He wondered how much it would hurt. But Mykel had done it, and Sammy was just as brave. Braver, maybe, though he wasn't as big.

The man in black reached under his robes and pulled out a knife with a white handle and a small blade. It was a ceppit, but different from Father Taylor's. "Submit a sacrifice to fill the ceppit," he said, looking at the crowd.

Nobody moved.

"Submit one, or we will choose."

It got quiet and Sammy looked around. Nobody moved.

"Fine, I'll pick one," the man said. He looked down at Sammy. And pointed.

"Me?" Sammy said, pointing to himself. Then he realized the

man wasn't pointing at him, he was pointing at Simon. Sammy turned to see that Simon's face was pale and he had stopped fiddling with the trigger and string.

"Come here," the man said to Simon.

"No!" came a voice from behind them. It was Simon's mama. "Not him!"

Simon put the trigger and string in his pocket and started toward the steps of the stage. Sammy watched Simon's mama pushing through the crowd. She reached Simon just as he put a foot on the first step.

"He's eleven," she said, crying.

Two soldiers and the man in red robes came forward. The soldiers pulled Simon's mama away. She fought them, but they were too strong.

"He's just a boy!" she pleaded.

Nobody helped her, not even Sammy. He wanted to, but his arms and legs didn't move.

Simon walked up the steps and stood in front of the man in black robes.

"Not a boy," Father Taylor said. "Please. Take me, instead. Please."

"You had your chance. Now you will witness the fruits of your heresy."

"This isn't about Dei. This isn't His way at all," Father Taylor said. "You know nothing of Him."

A soldier walked up and whispered something to the man in black robes.

"Absolutely not," the man said. "This is Dimmitt. We need to make an example of this place. *She* insisted."

The soldier said nothing else. He turned and grabbed Father Taylor's arm and led him off the stage.

The man in red robes went up the steps next. He gripped one of the white things on his belt, and flames came out of his hand, streaming high into the air. Sammy could feel the heat on his face.

"Don't come near the stage," said the red-robed man. The flames disappeared as his hand dropped to his side.

Nobody moved, but there was a lot of crying. Sammy squeezed his fists tightly, trying to beat back the fear that was swelling inside his chest.

"We're just a poor town. Please!" someone shouted.

Then the man in black robes, still holding the ceppit, put his hand on Simon's head. More people cried. A moment later, the man in robes thrust the blade of the ceppit into Simon's heart. Simon screamed, fell to his knees, and his skin began to change. His mama was screaming. Then Sammy realized that he was screaming, too.

Sammy had seen this before. They had all seen it when Mykel fell. But Nara had run to him, and Nara's pop carried them away. Sammy looked around, but there was nobody to help today. Nobody to carry Simon away.

Simon's skin turned black as he fell to his side, then curled up into a ball like a sleeping kitten. His skin dried up, and cracks appeared all over his face, blood oozing out of them. Simon's eyes were open, but they weren't looking at anything. Simon was dead.

The man in robes pulled the knife out of Simon's chest and rose to his feet. A big soldier went up the steps to the stage, then lifted Simon's body and carried him down the steps to the grass below. Simon's mama ran to him, but Sammy didn't. Sammy didn't move at all.

A bunch of adults were directed to the stage after that and got their hands stabbed. Some cried. Others fell. Some had trouble breathing afterward. Sammy didn't understand what was happening, and the confusion seemed to go on forever. He could hear his heartbeat in his head, and he was sweating.

A soldier spoke about someone making trouble. When Sammy looked across the church field, he saw Pop fighting with soldiers. Sammy tried to push through the crowd to reach him, but couldn't find his way through. People were screaming and crying and everything was confusing. He finally made his way to the edge of the group and could see again. Pop carried a big stick. He knocked over two of the soldiers, but then they hit him with swords. Pop never cried, but he fell. Sammy tried again to run to Pop, but strong hands around his shoulders kept him from leaving the others. The soldiers hit Pop with their swords again, and he didn't get up.

Mykel was gone. And Simon. Now Pop was gone too. Sammy was really alone, now.

They put some adults into the post office building. They carried Simon in there. The man in red robes lit the building on fire. Soldiers stood around while it burned. When people tried to come out of the windows, the soldiers stabbed at them with swords.

Then they made all the kids take their clothes off.

"Look for defects," said the man in black robes. "Anything. Curved spines, extra fingers or toes, any defects at all. Separate the broken ones from the others."

Gilbert Bonny's little sister, Ellin, had a clubbed foot, and they pulled her aside. She was screaming and crying out loud, so loud that it hurt Sammy's ears.

"It'll be okay, Ellin," Sammy tried to say, but she didn't hear him. It wouldn't be okay, though. It wouldn't be okay at all.

Sammy spent the night in the church with the other kids and a bunch of soldiers. It smelled bad, and there was lots of crying. The next morning, they got on the boats. The sails were raised, and the wind took Sammy away from home.

8

DIMMITT

Even at a breakneck pace, it took Nara and Mykel three more days to arrive in Junn, fatigue held at bay by the health runes that were ever present in their thoughts. The journey left them haggard, dirty, thin, and, for Nara, barefoot. The endless miles had destroyed her shoes and was a curse at first, but aided by the health rune, her soles had developed a thick, leathery layer of protection in a very short time. Even so, she missed her shoes.

Junn was just as busy as they remembered from their last visit, months before, and Nara was again fascinated with the wealth displayed in the third-largest city in the Great Land. Bells jangled on the doors of shops as customers came in and out, workers pushed carts of goods, and children played in the spring sunshine.

"These people have no idea what is happening in the surrounding villages, do they?" Nara asked.

"Probably not. Kayna is picking on the easy prey but she may come here, eventually."

Upon arrival at the docks, Mykel picked a small dingy with a short mast, low boom, and a sail. Nobody was near, so he tossed his pack and the staff inside, then untied the craft from its mooring. He motioned Nara to join him. She looked about, fearfully, then stepped down the center of the boat to keep it from tipping.

Mykel pushed off, settling upon the aft seat even as Nara settled in the middle, grabbing the oars.

"We return it when we come back," Nara said.

"Okay." Mykel turned, eyes scanning the docks as they left the harbor. The boat was empty of everything but oars and a sail, and Nara wondered who owned it. She dismissed the curiosity and rowed for a while, fatigue from the long runs deadening the feeling in her arms as she powered them out of the port. They hadn't eaten a meal for days, and she was weak from the toll on her body. She wouldn't be able to keep this up forever, and neither would Mykel. She flared the health rune repeatedly as she rowed, knowing it would be magic alone that would get them to Dimmitt.

Once they left the harbor, Mykel set the sail, and they tacked against the wind toward Dimmitt. Nara seemed to know the general direction and directed Mykel accordingly. The wind was light, but it might be enough. Darkness was growing, however, in more ways than one.

"What are you thinking about?" she asked.

"Nothing."

She waited, hoping he would say more. He didn't.

"I'm worried about them too," she said.

Mykel gave a brief, almost painful smile in her direction and turned back to fiddle with the tiller.

The sail occasionally went slack and Mykel adjusted, Nara ducking under the swinging boom as he tacked back and forth. She then rowed to realign the boat as it caught the breeze again. Long moments passed.

"We had to do it," Mykel finally said. "The children. Keetna. I don't blame you."

Another silence.

"Can you make this go faster?" he asked.

"I'm terrible at summoning air. Maybe we just take turns rowing?"

She grabbed the oars again, the strength in her arms threatening to leave her. Flaring health, she felt vigor return anew.

The boat surged forward with her efforts, moving in good time. Despite the spiritual exhaustion, using the magic, along with the vigor it brought, felt good. At least she was in control of something, simple as it was. After what seemed like forever, exhaustion again came over her and she let Mykel take over, switching positions carefully in the unstable boat.

As Nara sat at the stern, Mykel tied up the sail and grabbed the oars, the craft bolting forward as if in a race.

"It's still a long way," she said. "Might want to pace yourself."

He continued with the vigorous rowing.

She scanned the horizon, the faint outline of trees visible only to her in the now complete darkness. Mykel rowed and rowed, and she only occasionally needed to guide his efforts.

"We'll stop on one of the northern beaches," she said.

"Yes."

They could run faster than they could row and travel on foot would be far quicker than rowing around to the southern harbor. But with the fervor in Mykel's efforts, she wondered if he would have anything left for such a run.

What would have taken all night via sail ended up being only a few hours under Mykel's oars when they pulled into a lagoon. They dragged the boat well above the high tide line, grabbed their gear, and ran.

Nara led, but Mykel was holding the staff and found his way through the dark woods with its help. In less than an hour, they passed the trail to the mountain's peak and entered the outskirts of the village. Nara slowed to a walk. The numbness in her feet and thighs made it difficult to control her gait and she almost stumbled on the uneven terrain of the forest path.

The sun started to rise over the distant horizon, and a clearing opened up. The northwest side of town and a few cottages came into view. No, not cottages. Burned husks.

Dei, no.

A long moment passed. "We're too late," Mykel said.

He burst into a sprint toward the east side of town. Nara

followed. They passed the church, which was one of few buildings still standing, but Mykel ran ever faster and Nara couldn't keep up. Little strength remained for flaring runes to sustain herself, but she knew where he was going.

She fell several times as she followed after him, struggling to run in the half-darkness, through the fatigue and the tears that wouldn't stop. She heard crying from some cottages that still stood, muffled crying that was soon accompanied by her own sobs. Her legs were almost numb, and her skin was cold. She slowed to a walk, afraid to reach her destination. Afraid of what she would find.

When she came to the unburned cottage, Mykel said in a quiet, sterile tone, "One grave in the back. Pop. Not Sammy."

"How do you know?"

"It's not Sammy!"

Even in the weak light of dawn, she could see that his eyes were hard, a wave of sudden anger his voice. It wasn't Sammy. It couldn't be. Like Mykel, she chose not to believe it. It must be Mykel's pop. Sammy would have been taken, like so many other children.

"Mykel," she said, and he turned toward her. She wanted to say she was sorry about his father, or she was sorry they hadn't gotten here sooner, but she found no words.

He turned away and strode off, then stopped, whirling, anger and confusion on his face. "I don't know what to do. Where do I look?"

"If Lina is here, she might know."

Mykel bolted down the path toward the Tibbins' house. Moments later, they approached the area above the docks in Dimmitt, near the church. They could see several adults going through the remains of the burned cottages, salvaging what they could. The Fedgewicks' home next to the smithy was still standing, but Gilbert Bonny's house was gone, and his mom was crying on the remains of her doorstep.

When they got to Lina's house, they found it burned as well.

Her pop was using a straight bar to pry charred timbers apart. Mykel stepped up into the husk of the home.

"Mykel Aragos." Mr. Tibbins' shoulders drooped, and his eyes were tired. "I never thought we would see you again." He turned to Nara and scowled. "And you. The cause of all this. I'd welcome you home, but," he turned, arms out, gesturing toward the destruction, "there's not much left."

Mr. Tibbins' scowl felt like a stab through the heart. This was her doing. She'd started it all, and now these people suffered.

"It's not her fault," Mykel said.

Mr. Tibbins returned to using the straight bar, having trouble with the timbers.

"Is Lina here?" Mykel asked.

"With her mother. Next door." He pointed to a cottage on the same side of the street.

So, they didn't take all the kids. There was hope.

Mykel walked the short distance to the cottage, then stopped on the front step and knocked. It was more like a storage shed, with the door half-falling off its hinges and many openings in the weathered wood where air would leak in. A makeshift home for a family with nothing else.

The door creaked inward, and the face of a very sad woman met them.

"Mrs. Tibbins," Nara said, "we are looking for Sammy. Mr. Tibbins said Lina was here, and we were hoping—"

A young face suddenly peered out at them from behind the woman's legs. Lina. Recognition dawned in the girl's eyes. "Mykel! Nara!" She darted out to grab Nara's hand, then gave her a hug. A moment later, still holding Nara's hand, she turned to her mother.

"Mom, can they come in?"

Mrs. Tibbins said nothing, instead just opening the door further so they could enter. As they did, Nara saw three bedrolls on the floor. Lina had two brothers and a sister, so there should have been six. Lina sat on a bedroll, pulling Nara with her and directing her to do the same. Mykel remained standing.

"Where is Sammy?" Mykel asked.

"Um, they took most of the kids away," she said, still holding Nara's hand. "A few of us were hiding, and they didn't find us."

"Who took them?"

"Soldiers. With swords and armor. Some in robes."

"Did they take Sammy too?" Mykel asked.

Lina averted her eyes from Mykel and let go of Nara. "I don't think so."

Nara didn't want to hear what came next.

"Tell me," Mykel said.

Lina sighed, fidgeting with her fingers. "I was hiding under the porch of the old Carsten house. You know, the broken-down house on the hill above the church? Sam and I play there a lot, and you can see a lot of the town from there."

"Go on," he said.

"They gathered all the kids, and many grownups, in front of the stage. Down by the church. They said we were in trouble. They would make us pay." She looked at Nara. "Pay for you. They were mad at you, Nara. They called you a demon. But I don't think so. Really."

Lina swallowed, pausing, her eyes growing soft, reluctant to continue. She turned to Mrs. Tibbins, who said nothing but nodded, urging Lina on.

"Sammy and Simon were up front," Lina said, looking again at Mykel. "Standing near the stage. I couldn't see well, but I know they were both there."

"What happened?" Mykel asked.

"They took one of them—I'm not sure which—up onto the stage." Lina choked up, tears flowing. "I'm sorry, I can't."

Nara put a hand on Lina's knee. "Keep going."

Lina wiped her eyes on her sleeves and tried to continue but couldn't.

Nara turned to Mrs. Tibbins. Her face was wet with tears.

"They killed one of the boys," she said. "Sucked the life right out of him. To fill the ceppit. Punishment, they told us. To break our hearts or something. Lina saw it all. Mr. Tibbins and I were foraging near the creek, so we missed it. Heard it all from Lina when we got back. They announced some adults and took the children. All they could find. Most of the kids are gone. And they killed many of the adults. The Tinnys. Abel and Meera Trinck. Bran Fedgewick." Mrs. Tibbins sobbed. "Bran used to live just a few doors down. Helped with the house sometimes, when Mr. Tibbins was away on fishing trips. We would have them over for dinner." She cried again and Nara found herself crying along with her.

"Where are the bodies?" Mykel asked. "The ones they killed."

Mrs. Tibbins wiped her eyes. "Post office building."

Mykel left without another word and Nara was close behind. It was a short walk, filled with anticipation and dread. When they got there, Mykel dropped the staff and tore open the front doors of the half-burned building, sending them flying back so fast, Nara had to move to avoid being hit. He tossed aside burned timbers like toothpicks at first but slowed as he got closer to the buried pile of bodies.

The familiar smell of charred corpses hung in the air, triggering dark images of the villages they'd seen in a similar state. But this was Dimmitt. Their home. A numbness started in Nara's legs, then moved up to her torso, a dead blanket over her heart. She was not ready for what was coming next.

It didn't take long for Mykel to find a little boy in the pile. He held the body close as he carried it to the street before setting it down. Several people came by, but they kept their distance. With the way they abandoned these bodies in the post office, unburied and ignored, there didn't seem to be much courage left in Dimmitt. Kayna had broken the spirit of this town.

Mykel was on his knees, looking down at the dead child. It didn't look like Sammy. Or like Simon. It almost didn't look like a human being at all. Blackened, twisted. Part of the fabric on the pants was unburned. Perhaps a body had covered it, protecting the garment from fire. With hesitation, Mykel reached inside each of the front trouser pockets.

He seemed to find something, and as he pulled it out, recognition turned Mykel's face to horror. He collapsed on the body, sobs racking his large frame. "No, no, no, Sammy." His voice was weak, broken, grieving beyond imagination. "I wasn't here. I wasn't here."

In Mykel's hand was a piece of string, partially burned by fire. A snare. Attached to the string was a round trigger.

Nara collapsed on Mykel, holding him as he cried, joining in the grief. Just a little boy. A darling boy. He was good, kind, and hardworking. Memories of his smile came back to her. His laugh. The way his long black bangs always got in his eyes. The way he scratched his chin when someone teased him.

And now he was gone. It was too much to bear.

Nara cried for both Sammy and Mykel—and for her own guilt in allowing this horror to come to pass. They should have run the whole way from Took. Saving the children, taking the detour to Keetna—it had taken too long, and the delay made all the difference. She should have heeded the vision, running nonstop from the moment she'd seen it. Sammy was dead because of her. Because she tried to help others and did not heed Mykel's warnings.

They cried for a long time, and when there were no more tears, Mykel gathered up his brother's body and carried it home. He set it on the ground next to his father's grave and retrieved a shovel from the shed.

It didn't take Mykel long to dig the grave and put the body inside. Nara tried to say something, anything, but her tongue was as heavy as her heart. She could barely bring herself to even look at Mykel. Eventually, Mykel covered Sammy's corpse with dirt and sat still again.

They sat on the ground next to the graves for hours, and nobody came by to offer condolences. The remaining villagers had their own suffering to occupy them.

Mykel did nothing but sit near the graves, a faraway look in his eyes. Eventually, numb in both her body and her mind, Nara found her way into the cottage and lay down on a cot, begging for peace from this nightmare. As she lay there, something changed inside her heart. Or maybe something broke. Who she thought she was, or maybe how she saw the world around her. Her faith had been based on the idea that Dei guided things, operated the world in a way that was, in the end, fair. Just. She believed if she did the right things, followed the rules, and was kind to people, it would all work out. She was wrong. About everything. And the price for her foolishness was being paid by others.

I tried to do the right thing, Dei, she prayed. *Tried to be the help that you send to the Great Land. No matter what I do, I find nothing but destruction. Now this? Sammy? You break our hearts. You should heal, but instead, You hurt. You should save us but instead bring pain. You aren't Dei. You aren't a God of love and salvation. You are Kai. You allow death and pain. You allow evil.*

The anger and sorrow welled up inside her, bursting with fury and hopelessness. Images from the announcement ceremony flooded her mind, the ambush that almost killed Mykel, the battle on the plateau, the confrontation at Fairmont Castle, and now the murder of an innocent boy. It was too much.

And I am done with you.

9

———

LAST LOOKS

Anne checked her pack one last time, fingers searching until they found the cool bone handle of her ceppit. She hoped that she wouldn't need it.

She filled a wooden bowl with imbued ink from a pool, then walked across the cavern and down the tunnel that led to the exit. Arriving at the door, she turned carefully, holding the bowl gingerly in one hand as she stepped to the water rune, tracing the design with an inked finger. Rushing water preceded a grinding sound as stone slid on stone.

As the cavern sealed shut, she retrieved two vials from her pack and filled them with the remainder of the bowl's ink. After replacing the stoppers, she dropped the vials into her pocket, hearing a clinking sound as one bumped the engraver she'd placed there earlier. She patted her pocket. Ready to go at last.

As she tucked the bowl into her pack, she thought about Gwyn. Two weeks had passed since she'd sent the watcher west. "To find a certain boy," Anne told her. "You'll know him when you see him. He'll get into some trouble. Save him, then I'll find you."

Gwyn had not argued, nor asked for direction beyond that, knowing that none would be given. She was trusting, that one. Or obedient. There was little difference between the two.

"How long before the babes come back?" she asked the sky.

They were the first words she had spoken since Nara and Mykel left two days before. Intending to go only on a long run, they were now caught up in their story again, and Anne would not see them for a while. Her ability to see their next steps was clouded. An unusual thing.

"You're not showing me much, lately," she said to the empty wood. Aided by her walking stick, she worked through the birch and spruce trees that swayed in the afternoon breeze. "Found someone else to do your work?"

As was often the case, no answer came. No matter. She was finally playing the role she'd waited for, and there was peace in it, even without knowing what exactly came next.

Making her way to the top of the plateau, her gaze rested on Eastway. She had not attended to the abbey grounds for months and never said goodbye. A monk had likely visited in early winter, but she had been in the cavern with the others and the tiny cabin was boarded up. They likely thought she had abandoned them. In truth, hadn't she done exactly that? She turned to the northwest, to Fairmont. The Twins stood proud, one a peaked mountain, the other a plateau, both disappearing into the cloud cover above. She adjusted her backpack and took a few steps but then stopped, turning to look about. Cold rocks and sticks scattered the area, and the birch trees atop the flat rise had not yet responded to nature's command to produce new leaves. No squirrels danced about their bare branches, and the wind whistled through the sleeping sentinels unnoticed by living things. Unnoticed by any except her. But Anne was leaving, and these trees, this plateau, and the cabin below would be lonely. She lingered a moment, reluctant to say goodbye. For many years she had spent time here, praying, thinking, sometimes even sleeping. But that was over, and this was her last look.

She harrumphed at her melancholy and turned again to the west. Nara had run off with little training. She knew many runes but was skilled with few. She had missed a critical lesson and, without it, she would find no victory. But there was another way to deliver it, a way prepared long ago. Anne started down the plateau, avoiding rocks on the path to prevent injury.

She looked up to the sky. "To Veneti," she said. "I go where You send me."

But He didn't answer.

10

CAGED

Sammy didn't like being at the bottom of the boat. It was dark, and he didn't like the dark. Not at all. Sometimes they opened the door above, and when light came down the stairs, he could see the faces of the others who were with him, huddling together to stay warm. The air was wet and cold, though. That was almost as bad as the dark.

When the kids first came into the boat, a soldier gave them blankets, but there weren't enough to go around. Sammy wanted a blanket for himself, but there were smaller kids who needed them more, so he shivered alone. After a while of shivering, someone came over and sat next to him with her blanket. He couldn't see her face in the dark but was pretty sure it was Serah Willy. She always smelled like onions, and her voice was very soft.

"Are you cold?" she asked in a soft, oniony voice. Definitely Serah. He wondered how she knew it was him. She couldn't see him either, but maybe he smelled like something too. Or maybe she had seen him when they opened the door. He hoped that was it.

"I'm fine."

She moved her blanket to cover his legs, then leaned against him. She was warm, and it felt nice.

"Where are they taking us?" Serah asked.

"Dunno."

"I'm scared."

Sammy was also scared, but wouldn't say it. Not in front of a girl, anyway. He wasn't the oldest boy here. That was Clive Anders, thirteen and sitting alone with his very own blanket. But Sammy was older than most of them and would be brave for them, even if he was just pretending.

"We'll be okay. They won't hurt kids."

"They killed Simon."

That was true. Sammy had tried to put that out of his mind, but it came back now, and his eyes tried to cry. Sammy scrunched up his forehead, but a tear came out, anyway. At least it was dark and Serah couldn't see. She wiggled around, then leaned on Sammy, putting her head on his shoulder.

"Why did they take us?" she asked.

Did Serah think Sammy knew these things? After a while, she fell asleep. He could tell because she stopped moving around, and her breathing got slow.

But Sammy couldn't sleep. He kept thinking of Pop, and how he fought the soldiers. He thought about the post office on fire, and the screaming. He thought about Simon but stopped because it would make him cry again. Crying was for babies and he would be brave. At least until Mykel could save him.

But Mykel was gone and had been for a long time. And Mykel couldn't save him because he didn't know they were on a boat. Even if Mykel came home to Dimmitt, he wouldn't know where the soldiers took Sammy and wouldn't be able to find him at all.

He scrunched up his eyes again, but he couldn't stop the tears this time. Lots of them came rolling down his cheeks. He leaned his head against Serah's and let the tears flow.

A long time passed on the boat before the men opened the door at the top of the stairs and let Sammy and the other kids out. Sammy waited behind, shielding his eyes from the daylight with his hands.

The deep voice of a soldier yelling made Sammy move, and he walked up the steps behind the other kids. They walked in a line to the edge of the boat near a big plank. The plank had little wood strips you put your feet on so you wouldn't slip on the wet wood, but Serah slipped anyway and almost fell.

They stood on the dock for a while before two wagons arrived. Wagons with cages. The soldiers forced them into the cages, then put a lock on the outside. The wagon ride was long, and it rained sometimes. They were given wet biscuits and they huddled together because the sun didn't keep them very warm. Sometimes, they stopped to pee, but the soldiers yelled a lot because the kids didn't move very fast. At night, they stopped in the middle of the road and the soldiers slept in shifts, but the kids stayed in the cages. It was mean to put kids in cages. He remembered what the man in black robes said about punishment, but the kids had done nothing wrong, and they shouldn't be punished.

After several days on the road, Sammy saw hills. Another day and he saw mountains, big ones, way bigger than Dimmitt's, and with snow all over the top. It was even colder in the mountains, but it was beautiful, too.

When the wagons stopped for good, it had been many days, maybe ten or twelve or more. The kids all got out, and when he walked, Sammy's legs hurt. His back hurt too.

"Follow me," one soldier said. He was a short soldier, but still taller than most of the kids. He led them into a big red brick building, with every brick lined up perfectly. Even cold, scared, and with sore legs, Sammy could appreciate those bricks. Maybe he would be a bricklayer when he grew up.

Inside the building was another cage, big enough for all the kids. There were pillows inside, enough for every kid to have one.

Some kids ran to pick the best pillow they could. Sammy grabbed one as well, hugging it tightly. Then he wrapped himself in his wet blanket and closed his eyes, pretending he was home in Dimmitt.

11

GRAVEYARD

Nara heard a sound and opened her eyes to see Mykel enter the cottage. His eyes were dry, and he carried purpose in his posture as he stopped in the middle of the room.

She rose from the cot and went over to him. "You okay?" she asked.

"We need to bury the rest."

"Where?"

"A new graveyard. Near town."

"Easy to visit. So nobody forgets."

"Yes."

Mykel decided on a clearing several hundred yards to the west of town, a flat piece of land on higher terrain. Nara stood at the edge of the area, overlooking the southern Dimmitt coast from atop the small cliff. Waves crashed on rocks below and she squinted, barely able to make out the large island to the south where one would find the Village of Fulsk. Dimmitt felt so different now, and it wasn't just because of the murders or losing Sammy. The last time she stood here, she was a silly girl with no idea what her future would hold, ignorant to the darkness that was coming for her.

She turned away from the seascape to see that several villagers stood near the entrance, watching Mykel. Lina and her mother were among them. Nara began to watch Mykel as well. One by one, he would reach his arms around a tree and lift, tearing it from the soil below, then drop it with a crash. He then broke away the roots by hand, eventually dragging the tree off to a pile on one side, then returning to pull the roots from their home in the soil. It was violent, and even with his magic, Mykel seemed to strain with the effort, skin reddening and muscles taut with the effort.

It took over two hours, the trees and brush now cleared away, but the earth was profoundly disturbed from Mykel's efforts, piles of dirt and broken branches scattered about. More villagers came, and a dozen stood together, watching in amazement.

His work complete, Mykel walked over to Nara, shoulders slumped, his shirt and skin dirty and scratched, eyes tired, exhaustion apparent on his face.

"Good job," she said.

He said nothing, instead moving to the cliff's edge where he sat and stared out at the ocean.

It was her turn, now.

She moved to the center of the clearing, sat cross-legged, and placed her hands on the ground. Closing her eyes, she summoned the earth rune, the soil seeming to come alive in her mind. She told it what she wanted, and it moved to obey, swallowing the debris, smoothing out the rough patches, and forming nineteen individual graves. She summoned up a pile of soft dirt next to each of them, ready for the villagers to cover their loved ones. To say goodbye.

Headstones rose from the earth, each with slightly different shapes. The faces were blank, and Nara imagined someone would chip names into the stones. Too many names.

Cobblestone paths soon wound through the graveyard, small, multicolored stones set closely together to guide those who would come to visit. Large lumps of disturbed earth transformed into stone benches, simple but strong enough to last many years. Two raised basins appeared, each with room to hold rainwater for birds to drink. Or perhaps for visitors. One was lower and could be reached by small children, while the other was taller. A single stone arch rose at the entrance to the area. Simple. Strong. A symbol to those who would enter, reminding them that this was a different sort of place.

That was enough for now. Maybe someday she would come back, plant trees or flowers and lots of grass. Or maybe the villagers would do that for her. She suspected that once she left Dimmitt again, she wouldn't be back for a very long time.

Nara rose and walked over to the group of villagers.

"It's beautiful," Lina's mother said through tears and hugged Nara. "Thank you."

"You're both gifted," Mr. Tibbins said. "But what I've seen today, I, uh . . . I've never heard of anything like it. Gifted don't do this."

She understood what he was saying. Gifted go to war. They destroy. They don't create. When Mykel cleared the area, Nara wondered at the wisdom of showing their magic openly, old habits of hiding the truth coming to mind. Habits that served no purpose here.

"No more secrets," she said.

"Are they going to come after you?" Mr. Tibbins asked, his eyes shifting to Mykel, who was still looking out over the sea.

"Probably."

"What will you do?"

"We'll fight," Nara said.

"You will need more people."

"Yes. We will need an army."

12

A NEW PLAN

I t was cold in the castle today, and as the minister approached her on the throne, Kayna wrapped the fur stole around her shoulders more tightly.

"Your Majesty, we have a concern," he said. It was Jayho something—she couldn't remember his last name, nor did she care. He was nothing but a bureaucratic fool who spent his days shuffling parchment, counting numbers, and dwelling on uninteresting things. Oh, how Papa had loved to agonize over such minutia. She loathed it all.

"Things aren't going well," he continued. The man's voice sounded weak. Submissive. An appropriate tone for one who was failing so miserably.

Kayna raised an eyebrow.

"Um . . . the people. I'm talking about the people. They aren't paying their taxes as they should. Or delivering goods on time. Even the indentured ones seem to be slow in fulfilling their normal duties."

"Well, you're the minister of lands, are you not? If they aren't paying their leases or fulfilling their contracts, wouldn't that be your fault?"

"Yes, perhaps. Perhaps you're right. I mean, of course you are right. But there are rumors. Children missing. Villages destroyed. It has them quite upset, and I . . . um . . ."

"Spit it out, Jayho."

"Would it be possible for you to interact with the people more? I mean, go to them, be visible, provide a sense of security or something? If they saw you, perhaps they–"

"You want me to hang out with peasants?" Her harsh tone hung in the air, and he faltered.

"Um, no, not really that. I would never presume. But since the unfortunate death of your father, they have seen little of their monarch. With all these rumors there just doesn't seem to be much incentive for them. To obey, I mean."

She had indeed been reclusive since taking the throne, and the people saw little of her. Perhaps a big show would jolt them into action; it would not do for the royal coffers to run out of coins.

"Very well. Get with my steward and plan a ceremony. One week from today. Invite the people to visit their queen, and I will receive them with open arms."

Oh, how revolting to be near those people. Some worked in stables or pig yards and didn't even bathe! Yet she could just crack a peasant's skull and that wonderful, tasty life energy would leave their bodies and find its home in her own spirit. An enigma of grand proportions, for sure. It mattered not at all if they were children or old people, criminals or clergy. They all tasted delicious.

Which reminded her of Ennis' ongoing research into the manufacture of a cursed. Perhaps a visit to his rooms down below the castle was in order. He was a detestable creature himself, with his sores and such. But he was brilliant, and, thankfully, he didn't smell like dung.

It didn't take long to return to her spacious chambers, get into something more comfortable, and make her way down to the damp, cold dungeon halls. The screams that welcomed her made it clear that Ennis was hard at work.

"Any luck today?" she asked. Ennis looked up from the subject he was working on: an adult male, spread-eagled, both hands and a forearm bleeding profusely. His eyes were closed, and he wasn't moving.

"Fainted?"

"Yes," Ennis said. "It happens a lot. The pain, you know."

"Of course. So?"

Ennis clicked his tongue as he shuffled over to a shelf and placed the bloody ceppit in a tin container. "Not so much success here, but I have worked out the details of our plan."

"Go on."

"Well, the compound is nearly complete."

"That was quick."

"I made sure that the construction crews were well motivated."

"Good work."

"A central large building serves as the initial receiving area, quarters for the guards and staff, as well as administrative offices. We have four project buildings, each with cells in an area below, where the real work happens. We can progress with four simultaneous trials."

"And the process?"

Ennis cleared his throat. "It will be as with all the others, but much slower. Less damage, I'm hoping. Or controlled damage, perhaps." He shuffled back over to the unconscious subject on his table, gesturing over the young man like he was a prop. "We still require you to stretch the container, creating flaws in the shell that let the magic seep out. They will suffer as before. There is no other way. If we slow down, however, we will manage it better."

"How will we prevent them from hating me? Causing all that pain when they know I'm the one doing it? They need to have someone to hate, you said."

"Yes, of course. But you won't be you, Your Majesty. You'll be someone entirely different."

"And who is that?"

"You'll be *her*."

It took a moment to sink in. "Oh, that's good," she said in a flat tone. "They will be driven by both hatred and loyalty. Turn the process around. Make the flaw work in our favor."

He smiled. "There is only one problem."

"What's that?"

"Some from the latest group came from Dimmitt. Quite a few, actually."

"Yes, I heard. Finally. That town needed to learn its lesson, but —" She paused. "Oh. Curses. They know her."

"I think it will still be okay. We start the grooming and take advantage of the first level of damage."

"Amnesia."

"Yes."

"*Then* you play the role."

She nodded. This man might look like a troll, but he possessed the practiced strategy of a field tactician. "You would have done well in the army. Or politics."

"I'm happy to serve right here, Your Majesty."

PART TWO

The sounds of creation are a mournful thing, voices of beauty that rise and ring.

From bird to beast, from child to stone, every pretty thing fears being alone.

— *Poems of the Ages, Lady Bess Amwater, 565 PB*

13

FIRST STRIKE

It wasn't dark yet, but twilight neared as they looked upon Junn's walled fort and its soldiers milling about. It had taken little time to find this outpost on the outskirts of town, and they now lay quietly in the woods atop a small rise, looking down upon the fortification. A constant rain found its way through the trees, dripping from the leaves and branches above. Nara and Mykel hid in the wet foliage, prone, elbows propped as they surveyed the fortification ahead. Nara's bare feet dug into the muddy soil, toes fidgeting in anticipation of what she and Mykel were planning.

"Shift change, I think," Mykel said.

Some soldiers were leaving, several were talking with one another, and only a couple appeared to be serious about guarding the place.

"What do they keep in there?" Nara asked.

"Who knows? Armor. Weapons, probably. Maybe some horses."

"Cages on wagons, I'd wager."

"Yeah."

"Maybe some kidnapped kids?"

"I doubt it," he said. "Probably sent those north right away."

"We'll know soon."

There were several buildings in the middle of the outpost, including one very large one, and a tall tower with a single guard in it. The guard was sitting, eating something. From this perspective, it looked like no one was working.

"At night we'll have the advantage," Mykel said. "They can't see much."

They would have even more of an advantage with no light at all. "The torches," Nara said. "I'll take care of the ones on the outside first."

"Yes. But there will still be a lot of them. Some soldiers are leaving, but I bet they'll still have plenty. When they wake—"

"Don't kill them if you don't have to."

"Yup." He didn't sound convincing.

"Is it stupid to attack them, then hope they'll join us?" she asked.

"I don't know."

Nara shrugged. "I guess we're about to find out."

If they held any hope of getting these men to follow her, to be part of an effort to resist Kayna, killing them would not be a great move. But some would probably die. Junn was close to Dimmitt, and some of these very soldiers could have been responsible for Sammy's death. Mykel wanted justice, and so did she. It was a new feeling for her, this bitterness. It was at once sweet and foul. It disturbed her, but not enough to change her mind. This outpost would fall, regardless of the cost.

"Leave the gifted to me, if there are any," she said. "If we're going to build an army to stand against my sister, we will need more than bullies with swords."

She'd changed her tune, talking like this. Accepting that there would be deaths was a big shift for her. Mykel hadn't commented on her change of heart. Not on the boat ride from Dimmitt, nor as he stole backpacks from an outfitter's shop and bread from a bakery. They would need to break the rules to keep going, and Nara had not stopped him. Too much had happened. So much that it was hard to talk about, even with the person who was closest to her in the whole world. She wanted to say something kind, to comfort him, or maybe just to reach out and ask him to hold her, but she didn't know how to start. Instead, she lay on the forest floor and waited, watching.

Two hours later, the sun finally disappeared over the horizon and many soldiers dispersed, heading inside one of the larger buildings. A barracks, then. No surprise.

"You ready?" Mykel asked, standing and gripping the ivory staff at his side.

Nara nodded, getting to her feet to join him. She hung her pack on a tree branch above her and stepped out of the damp foliage. A breeze brought a chill to her skin, and she balled her hands into fists, clenching them.

"How do you want to play this?" he asked.

Nara thought about the question as she looked around. There might be something she could do to make it easier for these soldiers to switch allegiances.

"Stay here," she said.

"Where are you going?" The concern in his voice was clear.

She put her palm on his chest, pushing gently, hoping to better make her point. "Stay here. Please. I mean it. I want to make them an offer."

"What kind of offer?"

"I want to give them a chance to give up. Do the right thing."

"Not alone you don't."

"Trust me," she said, holding up her hand.

She turned toward the high walls of the outpost, then walked down the slope of wet weeds and bushes. The ground became irregular as she descended, uneven, with divots and mounds where trees had been removed, probably when they cleared this area, years before. At the bottom, she came to a large flat area with spotty patches of grass, and a packed-dirt road that led to the main gate. Rain fell in increasing frequency upon the ground as she walked. The sun was long gone, but the road grew brighter as she approached the gate, lit up by the many torches on the wall, each set in a sconce with a lid to prevent water from extinguishing the flame.

"Ho, there!" someone called from on the wall above the gate.

"Hello," she answered. "Open up, please."

"Nobody enters. This is an outpost of the Queen's army. Piss off, child."

"I am not a child," she said. She cleared her throat. "I bring a message of warning. And of invitation."

The soldier laughed, and a couple more appeared on the wall, looking down.

"What's this, Derg?"

"Some idiot girl who has let the water seep into her skull," said the first.

"My name is Nara Dall, of Dimmitt. I am the Queen's enemy, and I bring you a message. Surrender. All of you. Join me right now against the witch who holds the throne, and I will spare you. I'll see that you get fed. And that you no longer have to do her bidding. No kidnapping of children. No murdering of innocents. One chance. Right here. Throw open your gates."

The laughter from atop the wall was delayed, but when it came, it was raucous. She wasn't surprised. A moment later, after their guffaws ran out of steam, one spoke. "How about I make you a counteroffer, Neera. I open the gate, and you give us all a good time for a few hours. I have ale and a warm fire, and we know ways to keep young ladies entertained."

Her nose wrinkled in disgust. "I gave you a chance," she said, then turned and walked away.

A few moments later, she was back with Mykel near their hiding place atop the rise.

"That was foolish of you."

"We'll see. Now they know I am not unreasonable. Nobody willingly follows a tyrant. I will be different from her, Mykel."

They stood for a moment, looking at the scene.

"It would be nice not to have to fight them all at once," he said.

"That might be hard to do. Once we're inside, it will be chaos.

We won't even know where they are all coming from. There will be the one in the tower and those on the walls, but once the soldiers in the barracks come out, we'll be in the middle, surrounded."

"I could take twenty myself. More, probably. But I'd rather they came a few at a time."

"Unless something goes wrong. They may have gifted," Nara said. She engaged her vision to look for sources of magic, cepps or gifted who were using their talents. She saw nothing. "I'll take care of the torches. Once it's dark, we go in."

"Over the gate or through it?"

She smiled. Yes, Mykel could bash that gate in, and probably wanted to, but that would give the entire outpost warning and such overconfidence was probably unwise in battle planning. She remembered Anne's words on the matter. 'Be efficient with your energy, girl. When you run out, you die. Or someone else does.'

That advice should apply to Mykel as well.

"We go over," Nara said. "Surprise is safer. We are two against many, and we must be smart about it."

Nara made her way down quietly to the front left edge of the outpost wall, avoiding the brightly lit areas near the torches. She peeked out from behind a large rock, focusing on the closest torch. Closing her eyes, she summoned the motion rune, then held it in her vision as she concentrated on the sconce. Feeding it just a breath of energy, she pushed on the lid of the sconce, deforming it, bending it out of the way so it no longer protected the torch from the steady rain.

She stepped back from the wall, hiding behind a fairly large rock, and looked at the torch. She could hear the sizzle of rain-water as it spattered the flames and evaporated. The torch was dimming. Her plan was working. She moved around the left side of the wall and saw several more torches. A sentry walked the top of the wall but didn't seem very attentive, looking mostly at the inside of the outpost. She disabled the sconces on the two torches she could see, then skulked her way through the rocks and mounds until she reached the torches on the back side. In this way, she encircled the entire outpost, never getting so close to the wall that she could be seen, but close enough to disable their exterior lighting. It wouldn't take them long to notice.

Finally finished with the torches, she was walking back toward Mykel when she heard something from a sentry on the front wall.

"Is the old woman still awake?" The man was shouting down inside the walls to someone Nara couldn't see. "Torches are going out. Wake that wench and send her out to light new ones."

There were civilians in there.

A few moments later, Nara met Mykel near a fallen tree. "Be mindful of the innocents," Nara said.

"Is anyone who serves Kayna innocent?"

"Yes."

Mykel sighed, then nodded.

Nara led him to the left side of the outpost.

"Jump or climb?" Mykel asked.

 "You can do what you want, but let me get close before you blow our cover. I'm climbing."

Just then, a creaking sound revealed the front gate swinging open. A middle-aged woman in a sopping-wet overcoat made her way toward a sconce holding a sputtering torch in one hand and two unlit torches in the other.

"An open front door," Nara whispered. "Even better." She dashed toward the gate in the near darkness.

"Who's there?" the woman asked as Nara approached.

In a burst from the shadows behind the woman, Nara grabbed the woman's torch and threw it into the rocks far beyond.

"Wha . . . ?"

"Run away, good woman," Nara said, whispering into her ear. "This outpost will be a dangerous place tonight. Don't scream. Just run."

"What's going on down there?" came from the wall above.

"Uh . . . nothing," the woman answered, then promptly dropped her other torches, lifted her skirts, and ran away.

With the exterior torches now extinguished, it was time to pick the fight. Nara flared earth, and the bottom of the gate became trapped on either side by stone. It would move nowhere now, and only one person could come through at a time.

"Brilllanl," Mykel said. "But they'll have archers on the wall in no time once this starts."

"I can handle them."

Nara retreated to the left side of the fort, watching for archers while Mykel moved to the roadway in front of the gate. He would be in plain view once the soldiers found some light. Several moments of shouting and frustrated voices inside the fort were followed by three soldiers bearing torches, exiting through the gate, one at a time. Two tried to push on the gate to open it further.

"It's stuck," one said. "A bunch of rock down here blocking it."

"I believe we're to blame for that," Mykel bellowed, quickly grabbing their attention.

The soldiers turned toward him, holding their torches high in an effort to see him. The rain made hissing sounds as it hit the flames.

The soldiers pulled swords from scabbards as they snapped into action. Once they got close enough to see it was a single unarmored man with a staff, they seemed to relax.

"You're under arrest," said one. They were the only words spoken before Mykel moved. In a few heartbeats, all three were on the ground in various stages of discomfort. A sword lay broken, along with a leg, an arm, and several ribs. One man remained conscious, whimpering softly. A moment later, a loud bell rang and more soldiers streamed out of the front gate. Several appeared on the wall, and Nara saw an archer. It was her turn.

The archer nocked an arrow, aiming at Mykel. Nara flared motion and pulled. Or pushed, actually, from the opposite direction. That was how the motion rune worked—you always had to push. But her aim was way off, and the archer launched off the wall as if a catapult had thrown him way too hard, and in Mykel's direction. She changed perspectives in her mind, imagined being below him, and gently pushed upward to slow his fall, but his sideways momentum was so great that if the fall didn't kill him, an impact with a tree or a rock surely would have. She switched perspectives again to counter his lateral momentum but was too late. He hit the ground hard in front of the outpost, bouncing and rolling, his bow flying off to one side. When he came to a stop, he didn't move. She hoped she hadn't just killed the man.

More soldiers poured out of the gate. "Surrender now and you'll live," Mykel said, but he didn't give them long to consider before engaging them, whirling with his staff and flinging the men to the ground in short order.

Two more archers reached the top of the wall, and Nara focused on a bow this time, flaring motion and pushing it out of his hands. That was way easier. She pushed on the second bow, but the archer was holding so tightly, he almost came with it, and barely kept himself from falling from the wall. Disarming them was a much better strategy. She would have to learn to be smarter about these things.

Mykel had now defeated a dozen soldiers, each lying in various degrees of consciousness on the ground. Nara heard a sound near the front gate. They were stacking crates to bar the entrance. Smart play. They were changing the confrontation, probably directed by a commander within. She would need to get to him somehow.

She flared protection and approached the gate again.

"Nara, stay back," Mykel said.

"I've got protection up. I'll be fine." She walked up to the gate and yelled. "I repeat my offer. My name is Nara Dall. Surrender. All of you. No harm will come to you. Follow me against the Queen and—"

An arrow fired through the doorway hit her in the chest. Even with protection up, it hurt. A lot. Her temper flared, and all thought of restraint abandoned her. These men had killed Sammy and so many others in Dimmit. Burned her town. She'd shown

patience, but they refused her offer of leniency. They understood force and nothing else. She would learn to speak their language.

Flaring earth, she commanded the ground to erupt below the gate, dislodging it to one side with a horrendous snapping sound. She flared strength and leaped through the now wide-open gate, soaring through the air at least thirty feet. The inside of the fort was plain, with several buildings against the inner walls and a tower in the middle. More than a dozen soldiers stood about, eyes wide in surprise at her entry.

Several soldiers screamed, "Gifted!"

She flared speed and felled two soldiers in the middle with strength-enhanced punches to their chests, knocking them back, one into the wall of a building, the other into a hitching post near a horse that whinnied in surprise. Several more emerged from the barracks with swords, running straight at her. She flared earth and their feet became one with the dirt, stopping them abruptly.

Several arrows whizzed by her without striking, luckily, as she realized that she'd dropped protection when she leaped in through the door. She flared protection and speed, then turned toward three archers atop a smaller building. They launched arrows at her again; she dodged two and caught the third in her right hand, spun around, preserving part of its momentum and flared strength to throw it right back at the archer. It sank into the archer's leg just above the knee, dropping him instantly with a howl of pain.

More soldiers streamed out of the barracks, but now Mykel was inside the fort. Finally. Under the power of the speed rune, her sense of timing was wildly distorted, and it was easy to forget how slowly other people moved. Mykel battled several near the barracks, then disappeared inside, sounds of conflict continuing.

Nara's eyes darted across the scene, seeing that some soldiers were now retreating in the face of a superior threat. But where was their commander? As if in answer to her query, a door on one of the larger buildings opened and a single figure emerged in silver armor. Royal livery was emblazoned on his breast—a gold dragon rampant on a red background. The man carried a sword at his side but didn't draw it. He shouted for the soldiers to stop fighting.

As she looked at him, the first enemy figure of authority she'd met, she experienced an odd feeling. It was a combination of anger she held for these people and the power she felt at having them before her, unable to defend themselves in any significant way. But the need to turn their allegiances in a different direction tempered her desire for justice.

I really don't know what I'm doing.

The leader approached, a man in his mid-thirties who had far too much grey hair for his age. He stopped about twenty feet away, then motioned to his soldiers to stay further back. They obeyed. The sounds of fighting in the barracks ceased, and Nara turned to see Mykel emerge, seemingly uninjured. He walked to her side, nobody barring his way.

Nara turned back to the commander.

"So you're her," he said, matter-of-factly.

"I am."

"They warned me about you. Even put a price on your head."

"How much?"

"Ten thousand crowns. And five for him."

"Is that a lot?"

"Yes."

"You won't beat me," she said. "Not ever."

"Oh, I know that. They won't even give me gifted to fight with. Too precious, apparently. Only for rounding up little kids and torching their parents. How they expect me to earn a bounty for capturing the likes of you with only these few brave men, I have no idea." He gestured to the soldiers as he spoke.

"Brave men who kidnap children and murder their families, you mean."

"True. But when one's life is threatened, or one's family is at risk, brave men will do what they are told. Killing them won't stop the horrors."

"Maybe we kill you instead," Mykel said.

"Yeah, that would work. For a while. Until they replace me and it all starts again. I don't like it any more than you, but if you want to stop this madness, you will have to get to the heart of the problem. And she's not here."

"We're not yet ready to attack Fairmont," Nara said.

"You command the earth," he said. "Ripped the gate right off my outpost."

"Yes."

"Never even heard of that before. And you are a bear. And a steelskin. Arrows bounce right off you."

They still hurt, though. He didn't know that. "Yes."

"You move like a racer and have fire, too. Used it to kill the king. Right in the middle of his throne room, I hear."

Mykel stepped forward. "She can do even more," he said. "Far more."

"I don't doubt it." He paused for a moment. "My name is Captain Ander Jahmai," he said. "I saw the king single-handedly rout an entire barbarian army. Most amazing feat I ever witnessed. If you killed him, then I'd rather be with you than against you. And we've been waiting for someone to stand up against Fairmont. Others will feel the same."

Was this man offering, right here, to lead his men against Kayna?

Another man stepped forward. He was tall, wearing the same uniform and with a thick beard. "I'm Lieutenant Martel. I'll join. Many of us are sickened by what we've done. But not all will come. Many have families. You will get maybe one in three from this outpost."

"That would be more than we have now," Mykel said.

"How many follow you?" Jahmai asked, looking about.

"None," Nara said. "Still willing?"

Jahmai didn't look so sure, then gave a resigned expression and sighed. "Yes."

"I don't want you to follow because you fear me," Nara said. "I won't fight with those who will stab me in the back when they get the chance. And I won't lead those who fight only to preserve themselves. We're doing something bigger than that."

"How about fighting with those who have something to atone for?" Jahmai asked. "With those who are ashamed at what they've done and want nothing more to do with a Queen who has no heart? That woman cares nothing for her people. We'll fight, and we'll fight hard. But it will be out of guilt and a fair measure of fear, at least for a while."

She surveyed the men before her. Their faces looked tired, and they had given up easily, which didn't say much for their ability to endure in a protracted conflict. Clearly, their spirits were broken, but she didn't have a lot of options. "I suppose it will have to do," Nara said. "But don't expect sympathy. With what you've been part of, what you've inflicted on others–" She didn't know how to describe her anger. "I'm furious. I came here fully accepting that I might destroy you all. And I'm not convinced that I still won't."

"That would be justice. I hope you won't deliver it."

"Prove yourselves useful in the conflict ahead, and I won't have to."

"Fair enough."

"Where are the children you took from Dimmitt?" she asked.

"Not us. That detail came directly from Fairmont. Queen's special decree. Very irregular. She has a sweet tooth for that backwater town, for some reason."

"Where do you think they are?"

"The kids? Fairmont. All are taken to Fairmont. No idea what she's doing with them."

A long pause ensued, and Nara was in no rush to fill it. In truth, she didn't know what to say. She looked over at Mykel, who shrugged.

"You'll need to feed us," Jahmai said. "And pay us. That will take money."

"I have none," Nara said.

"That's okay," he said, glancing at Martel, then back at Nara. "I know where we can find some."

14

THE COMPOUND

G wyn followed on horseback, trailing the soldiers and their rolling cages. When her horse showed signs of hunger, however, she unstrapped the saddle and set it to wander free. She carried no food for the animal, and it would do better on its own. A shame. If a scout or wandering patrol surprised her, it would have been nice to make a quick escape on horseback.

After a second day following them, Gwyn saw the kidnappers arrive at their destination, a fenced compound just outside of Fairmont. She could see the twin peaks of Mount Fi to the southeast and a road heading toward the capital. The tall spires of Fairmont Castle reached high above the city, as if presenting a warning to any who defied the crown.

The north gate of the compound opened, and the soldiers led the wagons into a wide staging area that was equally suitable for practicing swordsmanship and archery; dummies on posts lined the perimeter of the area. A western gate, smaller than the main one on the north side, was also visible. Recently broken ground outside the fenced area showed evidence of excavation in recent months, with piles of dirt unaffected by rainwater runoff or erosion.

Five brick buildings stood inside the high wood fences. The

largest of the buildings was several stories high, positioned near the south end of the fort, with some high windows and two guards pacing on the roof. Four smaller buildings were closer to the walls. The fresh color of the bricks made it clear that the buildings were recently-built. This was a new fort.

She climbed a tall tree to get a higher viewing angle and was able to see activity near the tall brick building in the southernmost part of the compound. She was too far away to get a good look, but the soldiers might have been guiding the children inside a ground-level door of that building.

She considered the fences again. Tall, so they would be difficult to climb over, but not that sturdy. They would not repel any well-supplied invaders, but that wouldn't be necessary this close to Fairmont, where they had plenty of resources for defense. No, these walls and buildings were hastily built, intended to keep whatever was going on inside from the citizens of the Great Land. To hide secrets.

She waited in the woods until dark; sneaking around was always better at night. She wished she could take a closer peek from a nearby hill or high trees, but there were no hills nearby— they'd carefully chosen this location to avoid easy spying into the compound. The trees were gone as well, cleared for several hundred yards on every side. She would have to cross a wide, flat area to approach the compound. Fortunately, there were still plenty of dirt piles and discarded tree stumps littering the land-scape that might hide her approach.

Once the sun had set, Gwyn placed her traveling pack down near a bush. She grabbed her bow and tested her grip as she pulled back the bowstring, the pain in her forearm making her wince. That arrow may not have hit the bone, but the muscles refused to be very useful. Perhaps in the heat of battle, adrenaline would help her with this. She removed the quiver from her back. Only nine arrows left, but hopefully she wouldn't need any of them. She tucked four arrows into leather slits inside the quiver, equidistant around the inside perimeter so they wouldn't move about. She placed the extra arrows inside the bush for later retrieval. It wouldn't do to have loose arrows rattling about.

She then replaced the quiver over her shoulder and sat on the edge of a fallen tree to remove her walking boots so she could extract the linings. The layer of soft leather served as insulation from cold and would be perfect for softening footfalls when sneaking around secret compounds. She used string from inside her pack to fasten a boot lining around each foot, then dropped the pack onto the ground.

She then did a noise check—at least, that's what she liked to call it. She wiggled back and forth, hoping to find anything that jingled or rattled. The quiver was tight, the arrows secure. No noise. A strap on her back was loose, however, and she secured it with a tug. Silence must be her ally tonight.

As she made her way through the cleared area, the soft leather of her boots made almost no sound on the disturbed earth, allowing her to approach undetected. Using her own special vision, she looked for sources of life in the darkness ahead, noting three sentries on raised platforms behind the high fences and two on the roof of the tall brick building. She hoped that none of them were watchers, and spent long moments tucked behind tree stumps and dirt mounds as she got closer, each time gauging the reactions of those who were glancing in her direction. If they spotted her, they'd call out, allowing a retreat long before they could pursue. But none reacted, and she got within a hundred paces of the western wall without incident.

One problem remained—getting inside. The western gate would be latched from the inside, and they would likely notice an attempt to climb unless she could create a diversion. But that would also call the sentries to attention. Stealth required patience. She would wait. It wasn't cold. No wind stirred, and heat from the spring sun still lingered in the air.

After several hours of watching from behind a pile of dirt, she heard a noise. Horses pulling a carriage. She moved north far enough to see the carriage as it moved toward the compound along the road from Fairmont, illuminated by the northern gate's exterior torchlight. It was a new carriage with royal markings, flanked by two mounted soldiers on each side. A sentry in a platform behind the north fence shouted something, and a latch disengaged, then the main gate opened. She looked up at the sentry platforms on the western wall—only one sentry maintained his post, facing northward, watching the carriage as it entered. Both of the sentries on the top of the building had also left their posts. Now was her chance.

Gwyn sprinted straight south as far as she dared, as quietly as possible, hoping that the noise of the carriage and the distraction it provided would cover her footfalls. Just as she passed the western gate, she turned eastward, slowing her pace so as not to alert the one remaining sentry. As she approached the wall, she slung the bow over her shoulder and reached as high as she could, jamming a fist between the rough wooden logs that made up the fence. Her forearm screamed, and she grimaced as she sought a place for her foot on the log to launch herself upward. Her other hand found its way into a hold and she alternated hand over hand, cramming her toes between the logs as she made her way toward the top of the fence, her left forearm screaming in protest. It would bleed again, but she could deal with that later.

As she reached the top, she peeked over to survey the interior of the fort. The roof of the tall brick building was still absent its sentries, but a sentry walked along the ground toward his post not thirty feet away from her.

She hung there on the outside of the wall, toes and fists crammed between the upright logs, waiting for a chance to leap over and launch herself onto the nearest small brick building. Her hands were complaining, her forearm was on fire, and even her toes were now begging for release. The sentry climbed the ladder to his post and, upon reaching the top, opened a small pack he dropped onto the platform. He turned slightly away from her, rummaged through his pack, then pulled out what looked like bread and cheese.

Gwyn took that moment to launch herself over the fence, hoping his focus on the food would cover her noise. Her feet landed on a beam that supported the vertical logs, then launched her through the air toward the nearby roof. She landed firmly and performed a forward somersault to disperse the energy of the fall. A moment later, she was on the ground, her back against the south wall of the small brick building, shadows shielding her from the torchlight.

She drew her bow, nocked an arrow, and waited for the man to call out. Nothing happened. She leaned around the side of the building to look up at the platform, but he was still busying himself with something in his pack.

She relaxed the bowstring and replaced the arrow in her quiver, then retreated to the south of the one-story building, staying close the wall to remain in shadow. The sound of a door opening in the distance drew her attention to the south end of the tall building. Two figures emerged in the near-darkness.

"Make it quick," said a large man carrying a torch, following a smaller figure toward the southwest corner of the compound. A child. They were being kept in the tall building. So, what were the smaller buildings for?

An odor reached her nose—the smell of waste. She followed the figures as they approached an outhouse. The child opened the squeaky door and entered.

The outhouse was mounted on boards that straddled a trench alongside another trench dug in parallel. A field latrine. She'd seen them many times at hastily constructed outposts without septic systems. The latrine would be moved along periodically until they filled the trench with waste, then covered it with dirt. It served as a simple but malodorous way of managing the needs of many soldiers or, in this case, of both soldiers and children.

"Hurry," said the man. A few moments later, the child came out of the outhouse, heading back toward the large building. The man cuffed the child on the back of the head with his palm, and she yelped in pain. "Next time, go before bedtime, you little rat."

Gwyn hated bullies. If there was a fight, she hoped to have that one in her sights. Men like these should never have power over children, and they now had many in their clutches. Not only were Yury and his sister inside, but there were others.

Once the man and the child were inside, she maneuvered around the trenches, close to the fence, breathing through her mouth to avoid the stench. Around the south side of the building, she saw a single air intake at ground level and a door with no handle. There were no windows on the bottom story; in fact, there were few windows on the entire structure.

She glanced back and forth for guards, finding none—although a skirmish with a guard might be preferable to hanging out near that awful trench any longer. Skirting the shadows between sources of torchlight, she arrived at an air vent on the large building. It was a metal grate, firmly grouted into the brick wall, serving as ventilation, probably.

Holding there, quiet as a mouse, she heard the voices of two men. She looked to the nearby door. No exterior lock, not even a handle. It must be bolted from inside.

The children probably slumbered inside this building, but she didn't know how to free Yury or his sister. She didn't even know what Yury's sister looked like. Anne said to save the boy, and it was clear she'd found the right one. But now what? There would be no breaking into that brick building. She'd have to watch and find another way

Moments later, she was across the yard, up and over the wall, and across the cleared area. A few more visits and she might learn something useful. As long as she wasn't caught.

MONEY

Nara was reluctant to take part in today's robbery, although Jahmai had provided a simple and compelling plan.

Accustomed to light clothing and, recently, the absence of footwear, she now marched alongside a large wagon in heavy boots, along with six of their soldiers. More had wanted to come, but this wasn't to be an all-out assault. Mykel steered four horses that pulled the wagon from the driver's seat, with a little guidance from Jahmai, while she walked alongside in bulky chainmail that made it difficult to walk without tripping. As if to add to her discomfort, she had agreed to conduct this brazen act in the middle of the day. An illegal act. It was something she had never expected to be part of, but she didn't know another way of raising funds for a fight against Fairmont. This plan carried the added benefit that it would strike a blow against her enemy's resources.

The Royal Bank of Junn was a tall, lavishly built stone edifice in the center of the city, surrounded by a series of smaller buildings that made up the financial district. It was now the noon hour in the middle of the week, and bankers, brokers, salesmen, and royal officials scurried about their daily business conducting transactions, meeting clients, and arranging for taxes to be delivered to Fairmont. As they did so, none took notice of the routine passage of a wagon filled with crates as it pulled up to the dock at the bank's rear, flanked by soldiers. Mykel pulled the reins to stop the horses.

"Ho, there," said a guard on the dock. He wore the typical garb of a royal soldier of rank and held his hand up in greeting. "Deliveries don't come till the afternoon—why are you early?"

General Jahmai, dressed in the captain's regalia from his former station, walked up the steps to greet the man. "Our arrival is timely, good soldier, as we have no intention of making a delivery. We were thinking of making a withdrawal."

Just then, Mykel grabbed his staff from its hiding place at his feet and leaped more than twenty feet, landing next to the guard, staff brandished in a threatening gesture. The guard pulled his sword.

"I wouldn't do that if I were you," Jahmai said. "Last night, that young man took out twenty of my soldiers without breaking a sweat." Jahmai motioned for the other guards to climb the steps to the dock platform.

"I . . . uh . . . don't understand," the guard said. "You're robbing the Royal Bank of Junn?"

"Yup," Nara answered as she climbed the stairs, armor clanking as she walked. "My sister has too much money. We will relieve her of it. What's your name?"

"Dylan," the guard answered, lowering his blade and stepping back from Nara as she approached within his comfort zone. He was soon backed up against a stone wall with nowhere to go, his sword arm dropping the tip of the blade to the ground.

"Dylan, you look like a smart lad," Nara said. "We're able to fight, having brought nine of us. But you have more—am I right?"

He looked scared. This man should have chosen a different profession. "At least a dozen on site, another forty at the garrison down the street."

More than fifty. Maybe they should have been sneakier. Just then, she turned to see ten guards stream out the back of the bank and form up at the other end of the platform. Drat. Maybe she could scare them into submission. It would be nice to recruit a few of these. If not today, then at some later point. That would be more difficult if Mykel crushed their skulls.

Nara left Dylan and walked straight at the ten guards. She must have looked ridiculous in her sloppy, oversized chain-mail. It was difficult to walk in, and would be even harder to fight in, but it didn't affect her magic.

"You," she said, approaching the dozen soldiers with her finger pointed. "We serve a noble purpose but have no desire to kill you. Surrender and live."

They walked toward her, eyes wide and swords drawn, in a pyramid formation of sorts.

Nara dropped to her knees and placed her hands on the stone platform. She flared the earth rune, and both the platform and nearby stairway to the street rumbled, then collapsed under the soldiers who were about to attack. They dropped to the ground below in a pile of dirt, debris, and bruised limbs.

"Gifted!" one of them shouted. Several of the others ran, with the rest rising to face their foes, albeit from a lower elevation. With one end of the platform crushed, they would have to fight their way through Jahmai and his men to make it to the only remaining stairway if they were to reach Mykel or Nara.

"I warned you," Nara said, then motioned with her head to Mykel and Jahmai. With Mykel leading the effort, the skirmish lasted only a few moments, and though none were killed, one was unconscious and two more had fled, including Dylan.

As Jahmai and the others tied up the defeated guards, Nara wriggled out of the chain mail with the aid of flared strength. She removed the boots as well, happy to put her bare feet on the cool platform.

She turned to Jahmai. "How long before the rest of them find us? And the forty from the garrison?"

"We've made a lot of noise, but it's midday," he answered. "I'm hoping they are eating their lunch. We have a few minutes."

"Shall we?" Mykel asked, nodding to the building's rear entrance double doors.

As Nara entered the royal bank, followed by the rest of her team, she gaped at the polished marble floors, giant candelabras, and torches that filled the spacious entry lobby with expansive light. Well-dressed patrons and important-looking officials were situated at desks and tables.

"Over here," Jahmai directed. Nara followed him up a wide stairway without incident.

"And just what do you think you are doing?"

They'd reached the top, and a short, balding man holding a sheaf of papers and a quill stopped in front of Jahmai. "Royal guards and employees only, sir. I don't care what your military rank is."

Jahmai knocked the papers out of the man's grip and pushed him back with a firm hand. Nara would have felt sorry for him, but she thought of how rich these people were while so many others suffered. She was a criminal now, and her sense of right and wrong was in turmoil. What would Anne think of this? Or Bylo? She decided not to care. Given her few options and the recent loss of Sammy, her anger pressed her to strike back in whatever way she could.

"Show us the tax collections," Jahmai said, prodding the man onward.

They kept walking until they reached the end of a short hallway where two sets of thick metal bars blocked their passage into what appeared to be large vaults.

"Here," the banker said, pointing to the vault on the right with a shaky finger. "The other vault is for customer accounts."

"Who has the key?" one soldier asked.

"Mykel does," Jahmai answered.

With that, Mykel handed Nara the staff and stepped forward. He gripped the bars near the latch on one side, placed his foot on the stone wall, and pulled. As he paused, the sharp intake of breath from some soldiers filled the silence, then the sound of metal bending and a loud pop was followed by the stone wall shattering as the latch and the bars slid to the left.

"I figured it would be easier for everyone if I moved the bars out of the way rather than just bend some to squeeze through," Mykel said.

"Smart," Nara said, smiling, then tossed the staff back to Mykel. She turned to look at the men. They were frozen in awe at Mykel's feat. It would take time for them to get used to the new normal of their lives.

"Stop gawking and work," Jahmai said to his men as he stormed into the vault.

Nara stepped away from the vault and looked over the balcony into the bank lobby. Few patrons remained, and two guards entered the front doors from the street, presumably the first of those from the garrison down the street. It wouldn't take long for the rest to follow, she surmised, but they would be too late.

From this height, the earth was harder for her to reach with her magic, and the distance required more energy than usual to direct a wall of rock to block the bottom of the stairwell. It mattered not if the enemy brought forty men or a hundred. They'd have to find another way up, and the robbery would be over by then. Nara and her men would escape out the back of the building via a stone ramp that she would summon in a few moments.

She walked over to the banker-looking man with papers that Jahmai had first confronted. He had since gathered his documents and now sat on a chair at the top of the stairway, watching with wide eyes as they stole Fairmont's tax revenue.

"What's your name?" Nara asked.

"Wha-what do you mean?" His stuttering revealed his fear — no doubt over what would happen to him when the Queen learned of the robbery.

"Your name, sir. What is it?"

"Able. Able Wileman." He adjusted his spectacles and fidgeted with his papers.

"Pleased to meet you, Able. My name is Nara Dall. From Dimmitt."

"Hel—" He coughed and scratched his balding head. "Hello, Miss Dall."

"What do you do, here?"

"Manager of accounts."

"What's that?"

"I'm a banker, miss."

"Thought so. How much is in there?" She pointed to the tax vault.

"Um. Twenty thousand, give or take."

"Gold crowns?" she asked, trying to understand the scale of that much wealth. She'd never even seen a single gold crown. Just iron pennies and copper bits.

"Yes."

"Queen Kayna is my sister. I'm taking her money. All of it. I will put it to good use. Tell her that."

"She'll have my head."

"Then maybe you should run."

"I have nowhere to go."

He probably didn't. Especially after this. She wondered what his punishment would look like.

"I assume that you are good with figures? Paying people, purchasing things?"

He fidgeted with his papers, distressed and not knowing what to do with himself. "Um, I suppose so."

Noise from below prompted Nara to look over the balcony to see several more soldiers as they entered the front of the bank. The first two were now positioning a ladder at the bottom of the stairwell to scale the barrier she had summoned. She turned back to the banker.

"Maybe you can be useful, then. Follow, if you dare."

He nodded but didn't move.

"Your choice." She returned to the tax vault. More than a dozen large sacks, each bulging with coins, now sat on the floor, Mykel standing beside them.

"More soldiers are coming," she told him. "Time to go."

Nara went over to the back wall of the bank and placed a hand on the stone. She flared earth and the wall turned to dirt, then flowed like sand, forming a narrow stone ramp to the ground below. She peered over the edge to see the platform, the wagon, and the horses.

"Down we go," she said and stepped down the ramp to the waiting wagon.

It took only moments for them to toss the empty crates out of the wagon and load the money, soldiers, and one fearful banker. Jahmai spurred the horses into action, and they were on their way.

As they raced through the city streets, Nara looked back at the bank from the crowded bed of the wagon.

Mykel leaned close to her. "Even if they tried to pursue us—"

"They won't," she said. "They're afraid. We're criminals now. Powerful ones."

"We had a good reason."

"Does it matter?" she asked. "It's still wrong. It's just not as wrong as what she is doing."

"Do you regret it?"

"I'm not sure. But Jahmai suggested it, and I couldn't think of any other way. Maybe I'm not smart enough to lead a revolution."

Mykel patted her on the back. "I think you're doing great."

The wagon bounced hard on a pothole, and she grabbed for a handhold but found a sack of money instead. She opened it, reached inside, and pulled out a handful of tiny metal coins. Gold.

"We were innocent before," she said. "On the run from the church and the crown but having done no wrong. Can't say that anymore."

"There is no other way. To fight an army, you need an army. Armies need food and wages."

"Perhaps. But doesn't every selfish leader say such things to get what they want? What if Fairmont says we stole from the people, not the crown? They could just move the other money to the tax vault—money from merchants or farmers. Or they could double the taxes to fill their coffers again. Put an even greater burden on the poor folks to replace what we took."

He shrugged his shoulders. "I'm open to suggestions if you have a better idea."

But she didn't. She was neither politician nor bureaucrat, just a village girl out of her depth.

She put the coins back in the bag and looked at the road ahead, wondering where this conflict would take them next.

"We'll need a base. A place to gather strength," she said. "Any ideas?"

"How about the hills near Keetna? A week or two of good marching from here."

"Right in the middle of the Great Land, far from the big cities. And Keetna has flatland to the south. Farmers. Food we could buy."

"And they know us there," Mykel said.

"Yes," Nara agreed, eager to see Nilly. And Mimi. Familiar faces in the middle of the chaos.

"We'll need you to build a place for us," Mykel said.

He was right. These soldiers had no place to lay their heads, and once they returned to the outpost to collect the others, they'd be leaving Junn. Scarcely more than a dozen men—hardly an army. But they would build an army to take on Fairmont, and it would require a headquarters.

She thought about what such a fortification would look like. It would have to be underground, as the high walls of a fort would attract attention. The hilly region north of Keetna would be perfect for that. Many tunnels for entry, for easy defense, and for escape. Yes, Keetna would work.

She nodded. "Keetna it is."

16

THE PROJECT

Sammy woke to rough hands pulling him out of the cage and a deep voice yelling.

"Move, runt!" the soldier said.

He wondered where he was going. They took two kids from the big cage yesterday, a boy and a girl, but they never came back. As Sammy walked outside the building and across a bumpy, flat area, the soldier pushed at his shoulder to get him to walk faster. It was bright outside, and he squinted his eyes. He saw a high fence surrounding some brick buildings, and the soldier directed Sammy into a door of a building, then down a stairway to a basement. The basement had a dirt floor, dirt walls, and two cages.

The soldier pushed Sammy into a cage and closed the steel door, the sound of the metal ringing in his ears. He was in jail again, but he had done nothing wrong. And now he was alone. That wasn't fair, and it made him mad and scared him too. People shouldn't be able to put kids in jail, and he wished Serah were here.

After a little while, Sammy's eyes started to adjust to the light. A cot rested in the corner of his jail cell, so he sat on it. On the other side of the bars, he heard something move.

"Hello," he said. He peered through the bars, but it was very dark, and he couldn't see much. "Is anyone there?"

He heard soft footsteps as someone came near. He thought it was a woman, but he couldn't tell for sure. It was too dark to see her face.

"Hello," a voice said. It *was* a woman.

She reached through the bars and pressed her hand on Sammy's hand. It was warm and soft and he shook her hand, then held onto it for a long time. She finally pulled her hand away.

"What did you do?" Sammy asked.

"Nothing," she said. "Nothing at all."

"Me neither."

"Where are you from?"

"Dimmitt."

"Where is that?"

"Um. I don't really know. It's on an island. We go fishing. And trap coneys. I go to school too." Talking about Dimmitt made him sad. He wanted to tell her about Mykel and Nara and Simon, and maybe even about Lina. But he couldn't say the words. He was alone and talking about them would just make him even sadder.

"I miss my home too," she said.

The way she spoke was soft and fancy. He wondered where her home was but didn't ask. It was weird, sitting in the dark and talking to someone he couldn't see. He wanted to ask lots of questions, but this wasn't like a normal conversation. People talked when running around the woods or playing soldier and robber. You should talk when you are doing things with someone, or quiet in whispers at church, or maybe in class. But they were in jail, and it was dark, and he didn't know what to say.

The woman moved back into the darkness, and his cell felt colder. Then he heard a bad scraping sound. She was moving a cot, and it clanged when it hit the bars between them. Then he heard her lie down on the cot, and her warm hand touched his hand again. He laid his head on his cot, still holding her hand.

"I'm Sammy," he said. "What's your name?"

"Pleased to meet you, Sammy. My name is Kayna."

17

VENETI

The hard seat of the wagon had been unkind over the many miles, and Anne's lower back ached as the driver steered the horses to avoid yet another pothole in the old road.

"It's just up around the bend here," the driver said. "Market day today. You can find some good root vegetables sold by the monks hereabouts. But they have no cabbages."

The man's voice was deep and unsteady. Age was unkind to hardworking farmers, evidence he bore in his slouched posture and deeply wrinkled face.

"It would have been a much longer trip without your help," she said. "Thank you, Armen."

"My pleasure, ma'am," he said. "It was good to have the company."

The journey west had begun with many footsteps and several nights spent camping in the cool spring air, but men like Armen had been kind with the occasional rides.

The wagon rounded the bend, and the village of Veneti came into view. It was much bigger than the last time she was here, but still modest compared to many other villages. Sharply-sloped roofs adorned most of the homes and buildings, designed to shed the snow load that accumulated in these mountainous regions west of Fairmont.

Shoeless children played in the rivulets of water that danced across the old roadway, enjoying the snow runoff from the higher peaks that surrounded the village. The true blessing in this place, however, was the grand edifice on the side of the mountain behind Veneti. High stone walls surrounded the monastery that had stood for many years as a center of service, learning and study. And of faith. It had been the home of her dear friend Bylo, long before he knew his role in this world. But Veneti had been more than that to Anne.

Armen pulled to a stop. "Well, that's it for me," he said, getting out.

She carefully stepped down, one hand on the small of her back as she straightened herself. Her shoes touched the ground and she paused a moment. Long wagon rides were not part of her normal routine, and although she was grateful for the lift, she would be sore for several days.

She walked to the back of the wagon and retrieved her pack, slung it over one shoulder, and approached Armen, who was removing the wood posts that would make a canopy for his stand. Cabbages filled much of the wagon, stuffed into more than a dozen baskets.

"Setting up so far from the market?"

"I like to get the out-of-town folks as they come in." He pointed back down the road. "Before they spend all their money. They like cabbages. Use them in their caribou soup."

"Sounds delicious. I'd like to buy one if you don't mind."

Armen raised his eyebrows briefly, then reached for the nearest cabbage. "It's on the house," he said, smiling as he offered the cabbage with a largely toothless grin.

"Why, thank you, sir," Anne said, taking it. "I pray that you earn many coins today."

"Thank you, ma'am."

As she walked into Veneti, she passed a bakery where a boy

stood in the doorway eating a biscuit. The smells of fresh bread and rolls made her stomach grumble. She looked up as she walked, seeing a raven staring down from atop a nearby shop building, eyeing her cabbage, most likely. She looked to her left and saw a young lady approaching on the opposite side of the street. A puppy with an odd pattern of black-and-brown fur strained against a leash in the girl's hand, but the girl held it fast as it bounced about, splashing in the street puddles as they walked. This was it! The young man she was looking for was nearby, but she didn't want to turn to look at him for fear of missing this opportunity. It had to be just right.

"Come here," Anne said to the young girl.

The girl slowed, looked both ways, then crossed the street. The puppy followed reluctantly at first, then lurched forward, pulling at the leash as Anne knelt to greet the girl, still holding the cabbage in one hand.

"Does your mama make caribou soup?"

"No. But my grandmama does." The girl's voice was squeaky, delightful, and Anne suppressed a smile. Though she had foreseen this meeting and knew what the girl would look like, she always wondered how the child would sound. What a doll.

"It's yours," Anne said, handing the cabbage to the girl. "Got it special, just for you."

The raven overhead cawed loudly and flapped its wings. Anne turned to the left. At the edge of the road was a young man holding a basket of bread. His jaw went slack, eyes wide in aston-ishment.

"You're her," he said.

Anne walked over to him. "Was it close?"

"The tapestry! You're the old woman."

"Tell me. Was it close? The girl is perfect, I'm sure. I spent a lot of time on her. But the raven. The puppy. Did I get them right?"

"Holy Dei! I gotta tell Papa. He won't believe this!"

"What's your name?" Anne asked.

"Gabriel," he said. He was in his mid-twenties, with a scruffy face and high eyebrows. "My grandpapa told me about you, old woman. Almost every night at bedtime. Said you would come back someday."

"I'm not such a big deal."

"Papa said he was crazy. Said they all were. 'Nobody lives that long,' he always told me. But grandpapa was sure—and said as much every day till he died. And I always believed. My sister too."

"You're a gem, Gabriel. But, please, take me to it."

"Oh. Um, okay." There was hesitation in his voice.

"What happened?"

"I'll have to show you."

As a seer, Anne was accustomed to seeing things that had not yet happened, but those visions were often accidental. Or sent by Him. This one had been different. She had done this one on purpose. *For* a purpose. But now she worried.

"Papa and I worked at the monastery for years, cleaning along with the monks. Papa even cooked for them. Family tradition. Grandpapa worked there. And his papa did too. Way back for generations. But the church dismissed most of us." Gabriel sighed. "I rarely get work anymore. I move things into storage as monks move out, or when they pass. 'You're young and strong,' they say. So, I carry cots and chests into storage. Where they stay. Forever, it seems."

From a distance, the monastery walls looked the same as they always did, but such was true of stone. The structure had not changed, and nobody would know from a glance that it was nearly vacant.

"A shame," Anne said. "Places of prayer should be filled with people. Nobody in the town worships with the monks anymore?"

"There's a church in town, but lots of people have moved away. Ever since the waters changed, that is. They're not like they used to be, some say.

The walk didn't take long, and they avoided the city center where the growing market crowd would have slowed them, instead skirting the edge of the town along the small river that rushed along.

"Do you want me to carry that pack for you?" Gabriel asked.

"Nah, I'm fine," Anne said. She looked over at the river and smiled. "At least, the river still runs strong."

"It used to have a blue tint. Long ago. From the glacier that feeds it, I think." Gabriel pointed high above the monastery to a field of ice and snow. "Freshest, cleanest water in all the Great Land. People used to come from miles around to drink it, even carry it back home. Healing properties, they thought. It's why so many people lived here."

They passed an open cave in the side of a rock face to the right. An old man was kneeling in front of a pile of sticks, striking flint to spark a fire. Beyond the cave, the road opened into a large, flat area, where several fields had once been. Potatoes and grain had been grown here, but now weeds had overtaken the soil.

"No potato fields anymore?" Anne asked.

"Not enough monks to care for them. Easier to just buy them at market."

"Sad," Anne said. "I used to enjoy digging in the dirt here. Work is good for the soul."

"It is."

"How often do they have you working in the monastery, Gabriel?"

"Couple of times a month, maybe. They don't even have an abbot anymore. Brother Makin runs things, but he's often sick in bed."

It was sad to hear that the monastery had been largely abandoned, but not surprising. Places of worship required money to support, and greedy regimes often spent those funds on something other than supporting the faithful.

The trail from Veneti to the monastery was overgrown, with potholes even worse than the ones on the main road into town. Weeds sprouted in the middle of the path and overgrown bushes and birch saplings intruded on the walking area. There was still enough room to walk or ride a horse, but it didn't seem as if many wagons had been making the trip.

The monastery gates were open, and Gabriel led Anne straight into the main yard, where pools of water covered many of the worn stone tiles. Mortar crumbled in many of the grooves between the stones that formed the walls, and moss accumulated in shadowed areas. Weeds and loose gravel cluttered the space; added to that were crates and trash stacked in odd places.

"How many monks still serve?"

"A dozen maybe."

"Do they still have a library?"

"Of sorts. Most of the books are gone. I helped crate them up a few years ago. Off to Fairmont they went."

"A shame."

"So why are you here, old woman? I'm sorry, I don't know what to call you. They never told us your name."

"Call me Anne. And take me to the library. I don't know my way around here anymore."

"Okay. This way."

Gabriel led Anne down a long passageway. They passed a monk in sandals and a long tattered robe pushing an empty cart; he paid them no attention as he passed. At the end of the passageway was a dark stairway. Gabriel grabbed a torch from a wall sconce and led the way, holding the torch high to spread the light ahead.

Dust billowed up with their footsteps, and Anne coughed as she covered her mouth. At the bottom of the stairs, they turned right. The passage continued into a large, dark chamber that would have to be directly under the yard above. Boxes, crates, and discarded furniture were scattered about with little organization and around the perimeter of the room, one could see empty bookcases bolted to the stone walls in places. No books adorned the shelves.

"It's over here," Gabriel said. After about twenty paces, he turned back to Anne and offered the torch. "Hold this, please."

For the next few minutes, he moved boxes, rolled rugs, then a huge pile of trash to create a path. He turned back to Anne, and she returned the torch to him.

"It's in the same place it's always been," he said. "This way. Right where you left it."

"This used to be a grand studio," she said as they walked. "While reading the books, one could also gaze upon paintings and sculptures. Tapestries and mosaics on the walls. Beauty and learning, in one grand room. Now it's a trash heap."

Like so many old things, this monastery was dying. But it wasn't just the decaying building that weighed on her heart. She remembered this monastery's charity efforts. Here they gathered to feed the poor, teach trade skills to the young, and provide medical care. This place wasn't just about prayer and seeking the divine; it was about serving the living. Humility. Sacrifice. No, the pathos of a failing monastery was not about crumbling mortar and empty rooms. It was a symptom of a nation that was losing its faith… and its heart.

"I'm sorry," Gabriel said. "This is what I meant. They used to treasure the work in here and display it proudly. But the room is dry, so I put everything here, on orders from Brother Makin. They haven't maintained the rest of the structures, so now the other roofs leak. This is the only safe place."

"It's okay, son. I expected as much."

They came to a wall where a tapestry hung, nearly twenty feet tall and twice as wide, dusty, faded, and old.

"Took me fifteen years," she said. "I was never skilled at weaving. Kept making mistakes."

"Grandpapa used to sit here as a boy when his papa was sweeping the room and dusting the shelves. When I was little, he would tell me the story, passed down from ages ago. About how you came and served alongside the monks of old. How you weaved this every day, and how it seemed to take forever. You told them to keep it right here. Never to move it. We may have let the rest of this place go to dust, but we didn't move it. Not an inch. I swear."

"You did well, Gabriel. And your grandfather too. I think I was close, wouldn't you say? Maybe the color of the cobblestones is off —they have faded. And that building on the left. Too tall."

Gabriel held the torch closer, and the shapes depicted in the tapestry became clearer. Shops lined a roadway filled with people on their way to market or home. A tailor adjusted a gown in a display window, and a boy sat in front of a bakery, nibbling on a roll. An old woman in the street knelt, offering a cabbage to a little girl who held a puppy on a leash. The woman had a patch over one eye and a pack on her back. On a roof above, a raven flapped its wings, and one could imagine it cawing in protest. In the fore-ground was the silhouette of a young man carrying a basket of bread.

"It's perfect," Gabriel said. "But why did you come back, after all these years? And why did you make it in the first place?"

"To hide what's behind it, of course. Why else?"

18

DERIK

Mykel, Nara and the soldiers walked at an agonizingly slow pace for three days. Traveling with over two dozen men from Junn to Keetna was taking forever, and Mykel was having trouble keeping his patience in check. Jahmai insisted that they were making good time, but Mykel disagreed.

With the staff strapped to his back, Mykel walked in the middle of the road. The wagons jostled and shook on the uneven terrain. Quiet conversations between soldiers could be heard, but there were few other sounds. No birds, no animals, and no children. This was a different experience, walking among these men as they were, armed and armored. Perhaps this was the life of a soldier, but it seemed menial and uninteresting, without the excitement he always imagined a martial lifestyle would bring.

As they encountered other travelers, they were given a wide berth, merchants and couriers stopping as the soldiers passed, or stepping into the trees to avoid them entirely. It was a journey in stark contrast to the exhilarating run he and Nara had experienced when passing through these parts just days before. Worst of all, the monotony of the march allowed too much time for his thoughts to wander.

He thought of Pop and of Sammy. Of how they would rest in

the earth for all time. Sammy would never grow up to have a family of his own, never catch another coney. Never laugh again. Never cry. The loss of his sweet brother would go unpunished if the effort against Kayna failed, and that task seemed all too daunting right now. He thought of how he now marched alongside men who were responsible for crimes against boys like Sammy. And against other villages. These men were the unwitting stooges of powerful people, perhaps, but they still had blood on their hands, and he was their ally. It felt like a betrayal.

He thought about Nara. His friend was changing. She was no longer the enthusiastic young lady he knew in Dimmitt; neither was she the frightened companion overwhelmed with her circumstances. She was giving orders. Fighting. And she was powerful. Fast like a racer. Strong like a bear. A leader and a thief. A very different person than she had been just months before. It reminded him of Anne's words so long ago, when she said that Nara wasn't ready to love him. Not like he wanted. It made sense now. There were bigger things on her mind, and a grand weight on her shoulders.

He looked ahead to see her. She walked at the front of the group, alone, carrying a pack on her back when she could easily have tossed it into a wagon. What was she thinking right now? He figured the weight of her new responsibilities must have lain heavy on her, and he could do little to lighten it. His job was to protect her, and he would do that to the best of his ability, but how much protection did she really need? She could do everything he could—and much more.

Mykel glanced at the wagon in front of him. In the wagon's bed rested an archer who had suffered an arrow shot to his leg so severe that he could not walk. Yet the man still wanted to accompany them to Keetna. It surprised him that Jahmai had allowed it.

Mykel veered to the side of the road to speak with another soldier. "Will he recover?" Mykel asked, referring to the injured archer.

"Who, Derik? Dunno." The man scratched the hair on his head, which was meager and graying over the ears. "Jahmai's nephew, that one. Took him to a knitter, but he said the wound was deep. Hit the bone hard. May not walk again. May not even live."

"Why did he want to come?"

"Same as the rest of us, I s'pose," he said. "Do something good for a change. Maybe you should ask him."

Mykel kept walking, but after a few moments, he hopped up into the bed of the wagon. Derik winced as the bed of the wagon lurched.

"Sorry. Hurts, eh?"

"Yeah. Bumps are the worst."

Derik was young, no more than twenty. Probably closer to eighteen, actually. Mykel's age. They'd wrapped and splinted his leg to restrict movement, but the erratic motion of the wagon surely aggravated the injury beyond bearing. He shouldn't be moving at all.

"Arrow, I hear," Mykel said.

"I deserved it."

"How so?"

"I'm an archer. I shoot arrows all the time. Now I get to know what it feels like to take one. It hurts more than I thought."

"Only hurts if you survive it, my friend. Pain means you're still breathing."

"True."

Mykel untied the staff from his back and sat cross-legged next to Derik.

"Tell me about yourself." He hoped the conversation might distract the man from the pain.

"What do you want to know?"

"Brothers? Sisters? Where you from?"

"Little town outside Junn. Uglas. No brothers or sisters."

"Fishing?"

"For fun and for dinner, but not for money. My dad would never have approved. He always told me to work and work hard. He was a logger. Cut big trees. Huge shoulders, always sharpening his saws, moving, lifting. Couldn't sit still. He worked at a mill for a while, with my uncle." He pointed back over his shoulder, then winced with the movement. "Captain Jahmai. He's my uncle. He quit the mill and joined the army when my parents died."

"How did they die?"

"Rockslide took 'em. Mom liked picking berries in the fall. Wrong spot that year, I guess."

"Sorry to hear that."

"It's okay. Uncle kept food on the table when I was young, but he left a lot. Long trips. Months, sometimes."

"Yet, you still wanted to be a soldier. Like him."

The wagon lurched when a wheel hit a pothole, and Derik winced, then breathed hard for a moment.

"You're hurt," Mykel said. "You should be in a hospital. Why are you here?"

"Same as anyone. I want to matter," Derik said. "Cutting trees like my pop—well, that might feed me, but I wanted to do something more. It didn't work out as I hoped. When you two showed up, well, I thought we were all dead. Then I thought maybe I'd join up, get my chance to do something different. Something better." He looked down at his leg. "That may not happen."

"It might heal," Mykel said.

"I'm hopin'."

"Knitter worked on it, right?"

"Yeah, but he's bad at fixing bone, so he just did the muscle and skin. Bone is broke. Broke bad. Hurts a lot."

Mykel nodded. "Wish I could help."

"It's okay. Your girl, though. Wow. She's the fastest thing I've ever seen. I've heard of racers and what they can do, but I've never heard of that. Caught my arrow and threw it back even harder than my bow. More than a blessed, they say. Dei must really love her."

"She doesn't think so."

Derik's eyes went wide. "What? Why not?"

"She lost her pop," Mykel said. "Um . . . and someone else. Someone special. We both did."

"Heck, I lost my parents, but that doesn't mean Dei did it. He's magnificent," Derik said, looking around at the mountains on either side of the road. "Look at what he created!"

It surprised Mykel to see the faith of this man, but it also puzzled him he would have taken part in such crimes against the people of the Great Land. What made good people do bad things? This soldier wasn't a villain—or didn't seem like one. It put Mykel at ease, experiencing a feeling he almost didn't recognize. Hope.

"She's gonna fight the Queen, eh?"

"Yes."

"Can she beat her?"

"Maybe."

"She has you, though. And you can fight." Derik glanced at the staff lying on the floor of the wagon bed.

"Yes, I can. I hope I'm enough."

"Couple dozen of us here to help, but you don't even need us."

"If we get a hundred of you, that'll help."

"They'll come," Derik said. "I know they will. When they hear. More soldiers. Farmers too. Simple folks. What the Queen is doing, it ain't right. People are mad. That'll bring a bunch. Not the family folks—no, they won't come. But younger ones like me and you." He smirked. "Well, not like you."

"I hope so, Derik. I really do."

The wagon lurched on a dip in the road, and Derik winced again.

Mykel leaned over to speak with the driver. "Can we take a break? This soldier is having a rough time with his leg and could use a rest. Just a few minutes."

The driver whistled and Jahmai came near, pacing alongside the wagon from atop his horse. He spoke with the driver and then raised his hand to call a halt.

"Take a break. Right here."

Mykel looked down at Derik.

"Thank you," Derik said, smiling.

Mykel nodded. "Heal up, Soldier. We'll need you at fighting strength. And soon."

"Yes, sir."

Nara sat on the side of a high hill, looking down on the soldiers who rested on the road below. Mykel took a seat next to her.

"How's he doing?" she asked.

"He's hurt bad. Shouldn't be traveling at all."

"Femur?"

"I dunno. The big leg bone," he said, tapping his leg. "Arrow."

"I know—I was aiming for his heart." She couldn't believe that she just said that. What was happening to her?

"Can you heal him?" Mykel asked.

"Probably."

She didn't move.

"You don't want to?"

"He deserves the pain."

"Wow," Mykel said, shaking his head.

"I'm still angry."

"I can see that."

"Aren't you?"

"Of course I am. But these aren't the men who attacked Dimmitt. Once I got that through my head, it was easier. And if you talk to them, they don't seem like monsters. They're just men. Maybe you're right about evil and selfishness. I don't see evil here."

"Mykel, they've done terrible things, and they are every bit as bad as those who killed Sammy. You know they are."

"And they know it too. Trust me. They are down there, hating themselves just as much as you hate them from up here."

A breeze picked up, not a warm one, but it wasn't cold, either.

Snows were still melting, and the cool wind was a reminder that summer wasn't here. Not yet. But it was coming. Time marched on, and there was much to do. Although they now carried stolen coins from the bank and two dozen men to start their push against Fairmont, it didn't seem as if they were making enough progress. Nor fast enough. And now they were being delayed by a slow entourage and a wounded man who should have stayed behind.

Nara's hair fluttered in the breeze as she considered healing the soldier. He shouldn't be traveling at all, but letting him sit in the back of the wagon, bumping with each jolt, that wasn't good either. It must have been torture, and she was allowing it. It wasn't like her. Not at all. Punishing that man would do nothing to reverse the pain Kayna was bringing, wouldn't bring back Sammy, and said more about Nara's character than it did about that of the soldier.

"I'm horrible," she said. "What's his name?"

"Derik. He's Jahmai's nephew."

"Okay."

She stood and walked down to the wagon where the soldier rested. Not tall enough to see over the side, she climbed up into the bed. Standing over him, she spoke. "Derik, right?"

"Yes, miss." His eyes were wide, fearful, but she didn't blame him. She had been caught up the fervor of battle and must have looked fearsome when she tried to kill this man. She had very nearly done so. Without further care, he might still die.

"You tired of the pain?"

He nodded, but his eyes widened further and he seemed to draw back as she crouched in front of him.

"Relax, I'm not going to put you out of your misery. I would like to fix your leg."

"Oh. You, uh, you can do that?"

"If you want."

He nodded again, smiling, and his eyes grew teary. "Would you?" he asked, his voice cracking. "Please?"

Nara felt terrible, the man's tears melting her heart. Despite the things he had been part of, his pain defied reason. Pain she should have stopped. Maybe he had deserved the wound, but this ongoing suffering was her responsibility. It would have horrified Bylo to see his little girl acting this way.

"Don't move," she ordered. "This will take a moment and I'm no expert, but if it's as bad as I think, I can't make it any worse."

Nara turned to two nearby soldiers. "Hold him down. This will hurt."

As the soldiers climbed into the wagon and grabbed Derik by each shoulder, she dropped to one knee and placed her left hand low on his leg, the other hand higher. Moving her right hand along the femur, she closed her eyes, summoning both the knitting rune and the sight rune. With sight, she didn't need to memorize the biology, the organs, the structures—she could *see* them. In fact, Anne said sight would make her a supreme knitter in a short time if she practiced.

She visualized the skin under the bandage. It was intact, so this was not a compound fracture. The muscle was almost completely healed, but the fracture itself was a mess. The impact of the arrow had done terrible damage, shattering the lower part of the bone. Marrow leaked and blood pooled around the injury, deep inside. Nara flared the knitting rune, and, ever so slowly, the pieces of bone came together. Derik screamed.

"Stop moving," Nara ordered. "Not a muscle!"

Again, she flared the knitting rune, and the chips fused further, the fracture healed, and the femur became a single bone once again. She lifted her hands from the leg and opened her eyes.

Derik had passed out. Good. She turned to see that the other soldiers had gathered around to watch. All of them, even Jahmai. Mykel was behind, standing on the side of the hill and grinning.

"It's not done," Nara said. "Blood has pooled inside, so it'll bruise and swell yet. Probably for a long time. I doubt he'll be able to walk for a week, but the bone is whole."

They still stared at her, wide-eyed.

Jahmai moved to the side of the wagon and reached in and

placed his hand affectionately on Derik's head. He looked at Nara. "Thank you."

"You're an angel straight from Dei," another soldier said.

"Hardly," Nara said, then hopped down from the wagon and started walking back toward Mykel. "I'm no better than the rest of you."

19

THE GRAND SQUARE

The Grand Square of Fairmont was a beautiful, open area between the Chancery and Fairmont's central park district. The square was constructed from thousands of stone tiles, a beautiful checkered pattern of granite and slate that must have looked interesting to the ravens that passed above, flying back and forth as they searched for food among the throngs of people below.

Kayna looked upon the attendees from her throne atop a tall stage that rolled along behind eight horses. Purple velvet covered the stage, and two stone gargoyles guarded the front corners. She wore a fine white gown, a modest silver circlet on her head and carried an ornate scepter in her left hand.

A ring of soldiers made their way forward, covered in polished plate armor, directing the many citizens back to allow for the Queen's entry to the square. From behind Kayna, a blaring of trumpets made her arrival official, the noise so loud that she almost covered her ears to shield them from the noise.

The entourage came to a halt, and the trumpets ended their painful tribute.

"Behold, Queen Kayna, liberator of the Great Land. Champion over the barbarian hordes, and bringer of justice," the royal crier announced. With his strong voice, the people could surely hear his well-articulated words across much of the square. "We revere her above all. She is our light and our salvation, blessed by Dei to protect her people."

She wished he would get on with it. There were things to do.

"She comes among us to show her love. To shower you with gifts of her affection and to declare undying loyalty to our nation."

Many servants came forward into the square at that moment, each bearing baskets full of bread that they distributed among the people in the crowd. Kayna stood and smiled, arms out wide, scepter held high in a gesture of generosity.

"Thank you, my Queen," she heard from not too far away. "Thank you, Majesty," from someone over to her left. "Bless you, milady," from another.

But handing out bread and showing off her wealth would not be enough. They would forget this within a week and be grumbling again. More was required, and more would be done. She proceeded according to the plan, placing the scepter on the throne, and leaped into the air over the crowd. The air caught her and propelled her higher as she directed herself over the middle of the square.

"This is your Queen," said the crier.

Kayna flared the light rune, becoming a blinding, scintillating beacon rising ever higher above the crowd, now fifty feet.

"Behold," yelled the crier, "an angel of Dei!"

With that, Kayna extinguished the light rune, summoned fire, and shot it out to the sides, turning as she did, the flames heating the air in a circle around her. The crowd below her gasped in awe. Some ran away. Others were transfixed. She held there for a long time, sending the fire, then flaring light again, turning, basking in the air and the heat and the colors.

She imagined what it must be like for those below. Hungry, misbehaving people who sought only their own comfort. They now saw a deity above them; pure power they could never comprehend. Scriptures talked about miraculous healings and signs of wonder, but simple people rarely witnessed such acts.

What stood as an annoying interruption in her schedule would be, for many of these, the most memorable event of their lives. The contrast was interesting and further showed that she was in her rightful place above them.

She extinguished the flames and the light, then commanded the air to lower her to the square. The crowd moved back in response, leaving a wide, open area where she landed gracefully, her long black hair and dress billowing in the breeze that lingered.

The people fell to their knees and gushed with exclamations and prayers, overwhelmed by the display.

"Praise Dei," said one.

"Our angel," said another. "Thank you, Lord."

"Dei bless the Great Land."

Some were prone, babbling in shock, while others were silent. Staring.

It was time for her to speak. "I am the hand that feeds you," she said, hands held out, palms up. She took two gentle steps toward them. "I am the flame that guides you."

She licked her lips, which were now dry from the wind and the heat.

"I am the dawn. I am the way. Follow me, and my light will take you into Dei's favor." She looked up at the sky. "Into Dei's love."

Kayna then looked down, cleared her throat, intending to deepen her voice. She narrowed her eyes as she delivered the next words. "Never cross me." She lifted a hand and pointed at the crowd, her brow furrowing and a scowl appearing. She turned slowly, her finger directed at all as she completed a circle. "For I will hand my enemies over to darkness. My foes will taste pain and torment. I will deliver their souls to Kai and they will never be seen again!"

Her hands fell to her sides as she held the pose, brow still furrowed. After a moment, she erased the scowl from her face, replacing it with a bright smile. She lifted her hands in a gesture of blessing. "I bless you, my people. May your crops grow rich, your children healthy, and your hearts full." She stepped toward them again, hands still raised. "I love you all. With all my strength. From the depths of my gentle heart. Now until the end of the age."

With that, she flared the light rune, blinding the crowd again, then flared strength, launching herself with a great leap into the air, where the wind took her into the sky and far from the Grand Square.

Several hours after the display in the square, the minister of lands knelt before Kayna in the middle of the throne room.

"That should help your efforts, Jayho," she said. "Don't you think?"

"Yes, Majesty." He wasn't displaying any of his former frustration, instead shaking in place like a child caught stealing a cookie. She almost expected him to wet himself. Hopefully, the rest of today's attendees were experiencing similar emotions.

"I will hear no more about unpaid leases. You will solve your own problems or be punished."

"Yes, Majesty."

"On your way out, tell the page to send in the next one."

He nodded, then scuttled out of the room. General Jordan Almit followed thereafter, then took a knee before her.

"Yes?" she asked.

"We have a problem," he said, rising.

"And?"

"A caravan from Keetna, carrying prisoners back to Fairmont, was struck by two ruffians on the road. They took the prisoners."

"Don't you have gifted in every village detail?"

"Yes, Majesty, and few left for the army because of it."

"Stop whining and state the problem."

"One attacker moved like a racer and had other gifts. She had red hair, Majesty. Her companion used a staff. They killed one of our racers."

Kayna's heart skipped a beat. Nara was attacking? She had expected to have more time to prepare, to build cursed and then go looking for her sister. She needed months, or maybe even a year to do this right, but that little witch was on the offensive?

The man fidgeted with one of his sleeves as he cleared his throat. "Majesty, that's not all."

"What else?"

"We haven't heard from our outpost in Junn."

PEP TALK

Nara directed Jahmai and several others to resupply in Keetna, but she and Mykel never showed their faces in town, despite her desire to check in on Mimi and Nilly. Instead, they took the rest of the soldiers and one wagon to the nearby hills, where there was work to do.

Derik's leg fared well, and when given the chance, he got to his feet, strutting awkwardly but with a smile on his face, saying thank you to Nara whenever he could. The enthusiasm was encouraging, as there was little to be found in the rest of the troops, many of whom were tired of travel and eager for action.

Nara directed the group to a wooded area replete with game trails. Mykel directed the others to cover the wagon with tree branches.

"I'd hate for some kids from Keetna to find this here and alert the rest of the village," Derik said.

"They will know eventually," Nara said, irritated. "But I'd like to have a defensible position before our enemy learns of our whereabouts."

"We should fill our bellies and rest. It would be nice to have moose for dinner," Mykel said as they finished covering the wagon. "There is plenty of game sign on these trails. While you build us some shelter, maybe others could go hunting. They'd enjoy the sport, I'm sure, and while Derik is laid up, Ferron can manage a bow just fine."

"I hope you're right, but he may prefer hunting humans."

"They're hungry, nothing more. We all are. Nobody is hunting humans today."

Nara was surprised at her own negativity. These men had followed her, far from their homes, yet she still harbored dark thoughts where they were concerned. Maybe she should do something for them, as much for her own attitude as anything else. "I'm heading uphill. This slope would be perfect for a cave. Until I can make something more permanent."

"I wish I knew more about soldiering," Mykel said. "We'll have to pick Jahmai's brain. Combat. Fortresses."

"For now, just a cave. I have enough on my mind."

The snark in her voice prompted an odd look from Mykel, and he frowned before heading off to talk with the soldiers. Nara regretted her harshness. Maybe she needed a nap.

She wandered for a while before finding a stream that trickled down from the snowmelt above that would provide plenty of water for their needs. Close to the stream, she happened upon a level area that butted up against a cliff face rising almost a hundred feet. There was little evidence of a rockfall from above, and, with some massaging, it might provide a good area for staging supplies, sparring, or just milling about in the open daylight. Both the ground and the cliff were rocky, with little moss or foliage. Ideal for making a cave, as it would be far faster than trying to convert large amounts of soil.

She took her time, savoring how the earth magic moved with her thoughts. It took almost an hour for her to finish, but the cave was even larger than the first one she had made and more open, with room for many. She crafted three fire pits to accommodate them all. As she finished, she pictured the soldiers, absent their armor and weapons, eating a meal around the fires. Perhaps they would sing, and Mykel could join them. She'd heard him sing at church from time to time, long ago. A beautiful voice, deep, solid and happy. She'd like to hear that again.

She sat on one of the stone seats. Moving earth was getting easier with practice, and the joy of working with the magic eased a headache she hadn't noticed was bothering her. She would have to apologize to Mykel.

Footsteps approached, and Mykel came into view. "Better now?"

"Yeah," she said, motioning to the cave. "Making this helped."

"I figured." He dropped a pack and the staff near one of the dirt sleeping pads. "Dibs on this one."

He lay down, hands behind his head on the dirt, and closed his eyes. "Derik saw Jahmai and the others. Way down in the valley, heading this way. Should be here soon."

"Good. He can pick a more permanent spot for us. Hopefully not too far from here."

"Yup."

"Mykel?"

He didn't move, still resting with eyes closed. "Yeah?"

"What are we doing?"

He didn't answer right away, and the question hung there for a moment. He sat up and looked at Nara straight on. "I want to say we're saving the world. Fighting for justice. But I'm not sure that's it."

"What is it, then?"

"She killed Sammy. We're angry, and we don't know what to do. So, we do the only thing we can. Maybe stop another kid from dying."

"In Dimmitt, when I snuck into the church and filled the ceppit, I thought the same thing. I was sure it was the right thing to do, but it was foolishness. People died. You almost died. Now we attack soldiers. Rob banks. It's out of control. What makes us any different? What makes fighting the right choice?"

"I don't know. But I have no better ideas."

"Me either."

"You want to stop?"

"Is it that simple?"

"It's very simple. Either we fight or we don't. If we fight, we need help, and we are getting it. We have money. You'll build us a place to gather. We get more help. It's as simple as it gets."

Nara bit her lip in frustration. Indecision was something she had left behind, or so she thought, but the cost to others would be profound in the days ahead.

"We'll need more men."

"Yes. There are places we can go."

"Go? Do you mean raid? An outpost or two we can destroy, and some soldiers we can convince to join us or die. Like that?"

"It worked in Junn."

"Yes, it did."

"Nara, I'm a simple thinker. We fight, or we don't. We get help, or we don't. You make things complicated when you second-guess yourself like this. They killed my brother and my pop. I want payback. If I can stop it from happening to another family, to some other town, I'm happy with that." He grabbed the staff and stood. "Dei gave me this." He slammed the staff on the stone, the thunderous impact cracking the stone, chips of rock exploding outward.

The shock of it prompted Nara to take a step back.

"He gave me strength. Protection. The ability to heal from wounds. Aside from you, I may be the most powerful warrior in centuries! You want me to sit by and let Fairmont walk all over the people of this land? You want me to tie my hands and do nothing? I'd have a hard time with that."

Wow, he was worked up. Her fault. "No, I don't want that."

"Then stop talking and act! Build us a fortress. Or a simple hidey-hole in one of these mountains where we can plan, train, defend ourselves, and launch a war. Maybe we'll just use this cave. It's enough. Let me take Jahmai, get more soldiers, and we'll march on Fairmont. Heck, I'd go with a hundred. If we hit them hard and fast, with both you and me, it might be enough. I'm half ready to go north with what we have right now. These men—they'll come. They think you're a goddess and will follow you anywhere."

She didn't know what to say.

"And so will I," Mykel said. "Anywhere. Just name it. But don't say you will stop. Not now. We can do this. We really can."

"You're looking violent, today, Mykel Aragos," she said, smiling. "Maybe you need a good dinner and a long nap."

He chuckled and looked at the shattered stone under his feet. "Yeah, maybe so."

"Thanks for the chat. I'm good, now. I'm hungry, though. What do you say I go look for some game? Probably find it faster than a few tired soldiers."

"Good idea."

She got up to leave.

"Nara?"

She turned, still smiling. Mykel looked sheepish from his outburst, examining the damage he caused.

"Sorry I broke your cave."

21

OLD PLACES

Anne found the port in the wall and busied herself with the sharp engraver, chipping at the mortar that she had used to fill it so long ago.

"Is that a defect in the wall?" Gabriel asked. The odd gap between two of the stone blocks showed what appeared to be a measurement error by the builder who constructed the wall.

"I put it here on purpose. Hold the torch closer," Anne said. "I've only got one good eye."

"I don't want to get it too close to the tapestry," Gabriel said. "It's wool. Would burn fast and I don't think we pinned it up high enough."

"Who cares? It's done its job. If you light up that old rug, maybe I'd be able to see what I'm doing!"

His sharp intake of air made it clear that Anne had horrified him. He doesn't see the big picture, but how could he? "That should be enough," she said, then blew the gap free of dust.

"What now?"

"Just watch."

She reached into her pocket and retrieved one of the vials of blue liquid she'd carried from Eastway, then removed the stopper and poured it into the wall defect. She tapped the edge of the vial on the stone, using every drop, then replaced the stopper and dropped the vial back into her pocket.

"Nothing's happening," he said after a moment.

"Just wait. Takes a while to drip down into the rune."

"Rune? What rune?"

She didn't answer, instead holding up one finger and cocking her head, moving an ear close to the wall. "Here it comes."

A rushing sound of water from behind the wall began, then grew louder.

"It still works. Ha! I worried for a moment."

Rock vibrated and Gabriel stepped back, a terrified look on his face. Then the mortar around more than a dozen stones burst from the seams as a huge section of the wall receded, revealing a dark passageway. Anne clapped her hands together.

She took two steps, then turned to see Gabriel standing still, awestruck.

"You coming? If not, you better gimme that torch."

The dark passageway led at a slight downward angle, taking them deep into the mountain behind the monastery several hundred paces. Light runes could be seen high on the walls, but there was no life in them. This place died many years before.

"Move faster, boy. Nothing in here to bite you."

The tunnel opened into a large cavern, a dried-up hollow to the right where a lagoon once was, the torchlight inadequate to reveal the ceiling or the far walls.

"This place used to be full of life. People living. Teaching. Learning." She pointed to the lagoon. "I learned to swim over there."

"Amazing," Gabriel said. "Right under the monastery. Nobody knew. All this time."

"I pulled the wool over your eyes, eh?"

The joke elicited a loud cackle from Gabriel. Excellent. That should push his fear back.

They walked across a wide, flat area, passing stone tables,

benches and fire pits until they reached the entrance to some far rooms.

"This one," she said, veering to the left, waving Gabriel to follow.

They entered the room, the torchlight revealing a good-sized chamber with many desks and chairs, all fixed into the stone—or, rather, grown from it. On one wall was a stone lectern with an old wooden table on either side. A variety of objects rested on the near table, crafted from metal, stone, and wood. High on the walls near the ceiling, many runes were visible, engraved in the stone.

"A classroom?" Gabriel asked.

"Yup. Spent many days in here. First as a child, then as a teacher," her voice cracked with the emotions of the memory. "It's a good room."

She approached the first table, directing Gabriel to illuminate it with the torchlight. Covered in dust, some of the wooden objects had long since rotted away. Several long, thin stones bore markings on them. "These were rulers. Used to teach basic measurements." She picked up a stone mortar, blew the dust off, then stifled a sneeze. "Where's the pestle?"

Gabriel moved the torch closer and pointed it out, near the edge of the table.

"There you are," she said, grabbing it and placing it inside the mortar. She tipped it, displaying the rune carved on the side so that Gabriel could see. "Grind all kinds of stuff in this one. Then we'd set it in a water bath. Would stay fresh forever. We used bigger ones, too." She tapped the rune. "As long as it sits in the water, this design keeps the rot away. Well, not just any water, I suppose. But that's not why we're here."

She set down the mortar and pestle and moved to the other table. "There it is." She reached for an old metal chalice that sat all alone in the middle of the table, covered in cobwebs. She blew the dust off, being careful not to inhale the subsequent cloud this time. Holding it high, she turned it reverently in the light. "Been here the whole time. Even when we studied. Teacher's cup. Not just mine, but every teacher before me." She turned to look at Gabriel. "It was a big deal back then. Represented knowledge. Patience. Care for the students. It was a badge of honor we often carried with us."

"What does it do?"

"Do? It's just a cup. It does nothing. 'Cept maybe hold water. Wine. A good ale."

The look on Gabriel's face was priceless. An ancient wool tapestry that held an almost religious significance in his family's life for centuries had covered a hidden passageway to an ancient cavern. When an epic figure arrives to reveal solemn secrets, leading the frightened young man to a reverent place of learning, she retrieves an ancient chalice so she could.... get a drink of water? Anne laughed loudly—a long, steady chortle that surely convinced her companion she was cracked.

"It's okay, young man," she said, wiping away an errant tear. "It's not what it does. It's what it *will* do, for someone very important to me."

She went to the wall and looked up at the designs near the ceiling. "Hold the torch higher."

The oblique lighting made the outlines of the runes stand out clearly and she moved around the room until she found what she was looking for. "This is the one. It's not that complicated, but much is riding on this, so I wanted to be sure. Keep the torch close."

She reached into her pocket for her engraver, touching the tip to a flat area on the cup and beginning the inscription. She looked back and forth at the rune several times before finishing, then blew the metal shavings free from the cup.

"Done." She handed the engraver to Gabriel. "A souvenir for you."

"Thank you?" He looked perplexed as he took the engraver from her.

"We leave now."

"That's it?"

"Yup. I have another vial to close things up."

"What happens next?"

"I have some guesses, son, but I don't know for sure. In any case, I'm leaving, and you're staying in your little town. You'll have a story to tell, eventually. Just keep this secret for a little while. Maybe a year."

He nodded.

"Promise?" she asked.

"I promise."

22

LOSING

Mykel had risen at dawn to help the soldiers train. Eight men now surrounded him, each armed and in full attack. Sweat dotted his brow and with eyes closed and staff in hand, he dodged several of the strikes but took a hard hit to his head. It stung, despite having the protection rune up, but he was grateful that they were only using wood training sticks as the blows rained down. He flared health, and the bruises faded.

"Keep in formation," Jahmai bellowed. "Don't let the gifted escape the circle. And don't pull your blows!"

They practiced eight at a time, learning techniques for fighting gifted opponents that Jahmai taught years ago at the military academy in Fairmont. This particular drill was for fighting a steelskin, one of the more common gifts found in clashes among infantry. And the least threatening. The goal was twofold. First, they must learn to prevent this type of gifted to fight one on one, but they must also deny them the ability to shield an advancing line of troops.

After all had practiced the formation, Jahmai called a break and stepped up to Mykel. "Thank you again, this is a fantastic opportunity," he said. "Most steelskins can only go a few rounds before they need to break for days to heal. But you can keep going forever!"

Mykel half smiled. He couldn't go on forever, but no need to tell Jahmai that. Better they think him invincible. "Happy to help. But I was wondering, how do you counter a racer?" Mykel asked.

Jahmai smiled. "That's a tough one, those boogers give us fits. It often takes a racer to beat a racer. No other way around it."

Mykel snorted. "I know. Nara and I encountered one recently. Even with the staff, it was difficult. Two racers might be the end of me."

"Nah, you're a different thing altogether. You'd take a racer, easy. Maybe two, with a bear thrown on top. Not that I've ever seen more than a few gifted together in any battle. But the way the Queen is pouring money into her army and all these extra announcements, who knows how many we'll face? But they may be new. Untrained. At least, I hope that's the case."

"Not much of a comfort. Facing a bunch of scared, magic-wielding kids in battle?"

Jahmai shrugged. "Yeah. Tough circumstances."

"I'm out for a while. Going to check on Nara."

"It's midday, anyway. I'll call for chow." Jahmai marched off.

Mykel stepped into the southernmost traveler cave they had used for shelter the past few nights, entering the darkness in the back. A passageway greeted him there, and he wondered how she would make a door. Maybe they'd just have to put a big rock in place to bar the entrance, but for now, it was open, smooth stone that led to a long tunnel. The passage was unlit and as he stepped into the darkness, losing the last bit of daylight that streamed in from the front of the cave, he closed his eyes and moved the staff back and forth a few times, activating the sight rune so that he could find his way in the darkness.

The tunnel floor rose on a slight incline, and, after perhaps a hundred paces, it widened. At first, it was only three feet wide, but it had now become twice that. As he moved forward, it opened further, ten feet wide, then twenty. A light at the end of the passageway grew as he approached, and he dismissed the sight rune. The wide tunnel opened into a grand cave with an open roof, light streaming down from above; the dome of the mountain was simply gone. Two more tunnel entrances could be seen, equally spaced and just as wide as the first, heading off to destinations unknown.

"What do you think so far?"

Mykel looked to see Nara sitting on the stone floor nearby. Cross-legged, she was fidgeting with two small stones, tossing them back and forth between her fingers.

"It's amazing! So big. How long have you been at this?"

"I got up early, but I think I'm done for today."

"Tell me about the tunnels."

Nara hopped up and grabbed Mykel by the hand, pulling him back into the tunnel from which he had emerged. "You know how Jahmai said that when the soldiers fight, they like to field greater numbers in every skirmish?"

"Of course," Mykel said. "That's what small unit tactics are all about. Even if the opponent has a larger overall army, if you can move your troops in such a way to battle twenty against fifteen, or a hundred against eighty, you'll always have an advantage."

Nara nodded. "Exactly. I guess that's essentially what a fortification helps with. It creates a number advantage. Walls and barriers delay attackers, allowing defenders to move and respond quickly."

"Defenders can move quickly to a flank when the enemy attacks from a different direction. Maximizing their numbers."

"Yes. When I picked this mountain, I thought of how it would be to defend this place. What if you and I weren't here? How could they hold against a much larger force?"

Mykel's eyes widened at the implication. "Ever-widening tunnels. Nara, you're a genius." He could have kissed her right then, and he would have, but she continued.

"No matter how many men they bring against us, they will only be able to trickle them in, and they will always fight in a more narrow area than our soldiers. The tunnels keep widening and even if they advance, they still have less room."

"One enemy will always face two of ours. Two will always face three. We'll always have the advantage."

She grinned. "Yes, and if they want to attack from a different direction, they have to retreat in that same narrowing tunnel, then run around outside to attack from a different tunnel. Long delays."

"What if they storm up the outside of the dome and shoot arrows down?"

"Well, they can jump to their deaths, or we could just shelter in the tunnels. Besides, I could handle them if they concentrate in one place like that."

"Of course. This is great. I doubt many have thought to put a fortress under a mountain or had the ability to do so." Mykel glanced up at the open dome. "Brings in lots of light, but lots of rain, too."

"I have a plan for that. I'll put a big pillar in the middle, and a huge, flat area up about fifty feet. It will block out some light, but the flat area will slope in the center and the rain will run down a central pipe. Not a pipe, really. Just a hole in the middle of the rock. It will come out the bottom and flow into a channel I'll send off somewhere down there." She pointed off to one side where there was nothing but a sheer rock wall. "Maybe I'll make a pool for bathing. But it will be cold. Rainwater, you know."

"Wow, you have it all planned out. Defenses, water... light."

"Not exactly. Tunnels will still be dark. No light runes, or any way to maintain them. This is far from a Breshi cavern."

"I don't care. It's what we need. I'll say it again–you're a genius."

He moved toward her and her expression changed, grin fading. Wrapping his arms around her and drawing her close, he leaned in to kiss her, but before he could, she put a hand over his lips.

"What's wrong?" he asked, confused. "What did I do?"

"I don't feel very lovable right now. I... I'm sorry." She

squeezed his hand, then broke from the embrace, turning to walk several paces away.

"What do you mean? You are saving the Great Land. You designed this incredible cave. The soldiers who follow us think you're amazing." He faltered a half second. "I think you're amazing."

Still facing away from him, she lifted her arms in exasperation. "This is all so rewarding, Mykel. Moving, crafting, building. The stone feels alive under my hands. Full of power and potential." She turned around quickly, taking a rapid step toward him and twisting her hands together. "But it's wrong."

"What is it now?" He heard the coldness in his own tone. Hadn't they already talked about this, again and again? When would she finally get it?

"Here's the point," she said, speaking quickly. "This is a fortress for killing. It's designed to slaughter our enemies. They'd have little chance against us, and we could defend against much greater numbers." She sighed, then began again, this time slower, and with softness in her voice. "I'm proud of my vision for fresh water and bathing areas. I even planned out chimneys for bonfires, so we don't smoke ourselves out. But this place, it's not about preserving life. It's a place for welcoming death. Earthshaping should be for building shelters for peaceful people. Families. Mothers. Men who carry their children about, not those who carry swords. I should travel around the Great Land healing. Guiding. Eliminating poverty and sickness. Being a light in this dark world. And there's more." She looked away. "I don't feel the pain anymore."

"What pain? The headaches?" he asked.

"No, I still have those. But flaring the earth rune reduces them, so it's manageable. I'm talking about the pain I feel from others. When Derik was suffering in the back of that wagon, it didn't bother me at all. The agony of his injury, bouncing along that terrible road day after day... I didn't feel a thing. All of this fighting is changing me. I'm becoming like her. That's what I was thinking about when you came in." She nervously fiddled with a loose string that dangled from her sleeve.

How could he make her understand? How could he show her how different she was from Kayna? How different she was from all the other girls? How precious she was to him? He took a deep breath. "You'll never be like her. And after she is dead, you can build all the homes you want. Guide rivers to where they are most needed. Heal injuries. Whatever you like. But you can't right now. She would destroy everything you started."

Nara said nothing but turned away, dropping her arms to her sides and looking up to the open dome of the cave. What else could he tell her? She wasn't wrong. They shouldn't have to do this. This cave shouldn't need to exist. They were just two kids pretending to be generals in a game far too grand for them.

"Are you going to finish it?" he asked quietly.

"I don't know," she said, stepping towards one of the nearby walls. "I need to be alone. I'm sorry."

The wall opened as she drew close, its stone peeling apart like the petals of a blooming flower. Nara didn't even slow down as she walked into the opening. In reflex, Mykel reached towards her, vainly swiping the air in front of him, but it was too late. The entrance had closed behind her just as quickly as it had opened, and she was gone.

"Holy Dei," he said, shocked at the ease with which she had just moved the earth. The ease with which she had left him.

Conflicting emotions raced through him, and he felt almost dizzy. Despite the epic struggle they were in, he had always looked at her as his young, vibrant friend. The girl he had known from childhood in their sweet little coastal village. But so much had happened since then. Nara was changing. She was becoming someone he did not know–a powerful figure destined for something far greater. All she had shared with him about Bylo's study of scripture and how her own destiny was supposedly foretold by Dei now came to the front of his mind. She was not gifted, and she was not blessed. She was something else entirely. Something far greater.

In the past, he had feared losing her in a battle. At the palace with the king, on the road with the racer, or at the compound with the soldiers, there had been many risks taken. But a new fear crept into Mykel's heart. It wasn't a fear of her dying.

He was losing her in a very different way.

23

REPORT

They took him from his cage and strapped him to a table. Again. The red-haired demon held a hand on each side of his face, squeezing him like a vice so he couldn't bite her. Her strength was incredible and as she squeezed, his head felt like it would cave in. She never spoke. And she never said why. She just hurt him.

The pain in his chest began again, deep down. It felt as if his soul was stretching and tearing. Sharp spikes of agony grew hot and then became an excruciating sensation of pulling, twisting. Then came dizziness. And panic. He felt weak but so angry. He wanted to bite her, to scratch her, or to put his fingers into her eye sockets and push until he ran out of strength. Screams and curses came forth from his mouth. Foul curses at her beautiful face. Furious screams at her long, red hair and the evil smile she wore. She used to be a friend, this demon, which confused him and made the pain worse because it made no sense. He searched through his memories, but they were scattered, distant, and he couldn't find her name. Or even his own.

Dei save me.

But there was no Dei. Only the demon. And the pain.

As he suffered, he tried to think of the only blessing in his life.

The angel in the dark who had held his hand like a mother and whispered words of comfort into his ear. The sweet lady who loved him.

It was morning and Ennis shuffled down the hallway toward the stairs. Although it was cool in the project buildings each morning, particularly in the cages below ground, it had warmed in recent days. Summer was coming. He clicked his tongue and picked his feet up as he reached the stairs that led to ground level. He'd visited all four of the project buildings and the armory this morning and would deliver a report to the queen. Her efforts were bearing fruit, and he was eager to tell her as much.

A driver sat atop the carriage outside, and Ennis climbed into the seat beside him. He didn't know why she always sent a covered carriage. Perhaps she thought he didn't care to be seen in public anymore, but that had changed. He was doing good things. Let them stare if they liked. Let them talk. He was proud of his work and he didn't want to hide. Someday they would all know who he was, what he did for the Great Land, and they would honor his name.

The driver said nothing as he guided the two horses along the main city street toward Fairmont castle. They entered the grounds through a side gate and pulled up to a service entrance. Ennis climbed down from the carriage and shuffled into the building, taking a shortcut through the kitchen where he grabbed a bread roll and an apple. He gulped bites as he moved through a long hallway to the queen's quarters, finally arriving at the small sitting room she used for meetings.

The room had no windows but was well-lit, several large candelabras providing the necessary illumination. A small fire crackled in a fireplace on one wall, lending ample heat. The walls bore a bright mural that depicted a lavish party, painted right on the stone blocks and stretching around the room. The mural was decorated with hundreds of guests who celebrated with food and wine and on one wall, some knelt before a figure that walked in from a large, arched entrance. The figure was difficult to make out, nothing but the outline of a woman in a gown, her black hair topped with a brilliant crown. The light emanated from her shape so brightly that details were lost and many of the partygoers held their hands up to shield their eyes from her brilliance.

"Hello, Ennis."

He turned, startled. She was dressed in a short blue gown, black hair tied up in a bun. He bowed deeply. "A report, Your Majesty."

"Go ahead." Kayna moved to a nearby table to pour herself a cup of wine from a crystal decanter.

"The normal methods are moving forward as they always have. Sometimes we announce a gifted, but many die. The multiple piercings with the ceppit are productive but dangerous. Lost a racer to infection yesterday."

"We expected as much. How many total this week?"

"We've announced more than a hundred in the last few days, but only one gifted aside from the racer. A knitter."

"Bah. I need warriors." She replaced the decanter and turned to take a seat in a luxuriously cushioned settee, angled in the corner. The few shadows there were in the room flickered across her face as she took a sip.

It was true. Knitters were of little use in combat, but when trained would prove useful at keeping the rest of the army healthy. At first, however, they were scared, useless children.

"The projects have been interesting. Three have died since you began your efforts, but several show promise."

"The barbarian?"

"Yes, he's doing well. He's seen battle and has quite the will. Perhaps because he is older. There's a girl who is also doing well."

"And the young one. From Dimmitt."

"He's angry. Oh, so angry. After you stretch him, the watcher sees him leak. A lot. Far more than the others. But it fades after a few hours. Hopefully, we can make it permanent."

"I loathe the wig, but it is working. He's furious with her," Kayna said. "I can see it in his eyes. He has grown so much and fights like a rabid dog. I have to flare strength to keep him still, and he isn't even gifted."

"Yet."

"I hope you're right, Ennis."

"You're doing everything perfectly, Majesty. He cries when you aren't in the cell next to him. For hours. He says your name over and over. He'd do anything for you."

"I hope you're right. But he mustn't merely hate her and love me. I need this to work!"

"It's working, Majesty. Give it time. You'll have your cursed. Maybe more than one."

24

RESOLVE

Nara sat on the side of the high, sloping peak near the rim of the half-built fortification. She hadn't finished the water system and needed several more tunnels to ensure escape routes, but her heart just wasn't in it right now. A defensive position was nice, and this place might become useful someday, but she tired of the internal turmoil and it would be better to get this conflict over with. Offense, not defense. She would take the fight to Kayna.

Below, she could see the soldiers training with Mykel. There were more than before, at least eighty now, and she wondered if men from nearby villages had joined the effort. Eighty against what, a thousand? Five thousand? A traditional battle was simply not possible without a lot more men. She wanted ideas, and a conversation with Jahmai might provide them.

It took little time for her to descend to the training area, the exercise stopping when she got close. Some knelt when they saw her, and one of the younger lads went fully prone and started praying out loud.

"Please, get up," she said. She turned to Jahmai. "General, can we speak?" She turned and walked back into the traveler cave and sat on a stone seat. A freshly stoked fire crackled and popped, and an iron pot of something hot bubbled on a grate stretched across the flames. Jahmai took a seat beside her.

"Eighty men?" she asked.

"Eighty-three, actually. Several are out gathering food. Can't buy enough around here, so we're foraging and hunting in shifts."

"I have half of an impressive fortress started up on this mountain, but no way to feed my men. Didn't really think of that."

"We'll make do, ma'am."

"Call me Nara. Please."

"In front of the men, I'll need something else. Holiness. Mistress. Your Majesty. Something."

"Nara. I insist."

"As you wish."

She grabbed a stick from the ground near her feet and poked a log. "We need more men. How do you propose to get them?"

"I've been thinking of that. We could attack more outposts. Give terms. Like you did in Junn."

"Anything nearby?"

"Several, actually."

"Why not just go big?"

"Ankar? It's a few days away, but we could. It's twice the size of Junn. Three outposts there. And even bigger than those in Junn."

"Make it happen."

"They have gifted in the Ankar outposts, mistress. And at least three hundred men in total."

"Nara."

"Yes, of course. Nara. Ankar has been deploying gifted. We'll see at least one in each outpost. I think a steelskin-flamer pair might be in Ankar as well. Won't be easy with only eighty-three men."

"We'll find more along the way. I'm hoping for more than a hundred by the time we're in Ankar. Besides, Mykel and I have only fought on a small scale. We need to learn what it's like to face an army, even if it's a small one."

"Yes, miss," he said. "Um. Nara."

"Thank you."

"First names aren't used by soldiers, Nara, especially for their commander. Standard military etiquette. It will take some getting used to. Not the normal rules."

"We're outnumbered, tired, away from our homes, and half our force is made up of local boys with courage but no experience," she said. "Not a time to play by normal rules."

She stood and walked back to where Lieutenant Martel was directing two men to spar in heavy armor, pointing out weak areas where the metal did not protect. She stepped up to the fray and everyone stopped, turning to look at her. Eighty men marching on Ankar was foolishness, but if they wielded the hearts of heroes and carried hope, it would be better. Plus, it would give them stories to spread. Watching Mykel fight surely helped, but Nara was their leader and they needed more from her than pretty caves.

"May I join you?" she asked.

Martel stuttered enthusiastically, "Yes. Um. Majesty." He cleared his throat. "We're demonstrating the flaws in armor. Where to strike, limitations in an armored opponent's ability to move."

"Nara. Not Majesty. How can I help?"

"Well, we'll be fighting racers, and that's a big concern," Martel said. "We usually make a defensive circle and overcome them with numbers and time, but they do a lot of damage."

Mykel was standing on the other side of the throng of men but didn't move. Good. She wanted to do this alone.

"Okay, listen up," she said. "We racers are fast. We won't carry heavy items; they slow us down, so we have knives or axes, small weapons we can swing quickly, injure you, then run away before you can counter. Met a racer already myself, and she was fast. Darn fast. We don't have enough men to overwhelm them. But they have a weakness. They must move to be a threat. We'll take that away."

Several wore curious looks on their faces.

"Who knows how to make banners?" She scanned the crowd. "Flags?"

A man in the back raised his hand, and she walked toward him, the men parting to allow her passage. "What's your name, Soldier?"

"Panuk, Your Majesty. From Trapper, west of here."

Panuk was native and old, at least sixty. He was tall, with a solid stance, and his black hair was neatly combed. Proud man. Good. They needed more like him.

"Call me Nara. None of the 'Majesty' stuff. Please. Panuk, you will find fabric and make banners. Spread them among the men. Mount them on the end of spears for others to see. In the middle of battle, we will seek the gifted, but racers can do a lot of damage and I must know where they are right away. By making banners, you will help your brothers signal the discovery of a racer so I can find them quickly."

She reached up to put a hand on Panuk's shoulder. "Start working on the banners today. Red ones and black ones. Tomorrow we march south."

Nara stepped back into the middle of the circle. "If you've never seen a racer, know they are a fearful thing." She flared speed and danced around the circle, touching several men on the cheek before they could move. "We are fast and can disarm you." She flared it again and held a dagger in her hand a moment later. Several soldiers checked their sheaths. "Or we can run away." They lost sight of her until she waved from a hundred feet away, near a tree. She raised her voice as she returned to them, "But we have a weakness." Her foot caught a rock, and she fell forward, dropping the dagger. A deliberately clumsy move, but it illustrated the point. "We depend on stable ground, keeping our eyes high on our opponents. No racer watches her feet."

"You will alert me to a gifted by waving the special banners sewn by Panuk. Black for any other gifted, but red for a racer, whom I will engage." As she stepped back into the circle, she closed her eyes, summoned the earth rune and flared it. The ground rumbled and shifted, dropping in places, rising in others, the landscape under the soldiers' feet becoming pockmarked, jagged and uneven. "Two things will happen after that red banner goes up," she said. "The racer will fall, becoming vulnerable, allowing you to attack. Do so before the racer adjusts to the new terrain. The problem is that I won't know where the racer is, so I'll disrupt the ground in a wide area. If you aren't alert, you will also fall. Watch and listen. Call out 'gifted' when you see the black banner, and 'racer' when you see the red. Others will hear and will know to watch their footing."

The men clapped and cheered as she rose to her feet. Loud bellows filled the air. Some knelt and praised Dei. Nara looked over to Jahmai, a big smile on his face as he clapped along with them.

Nara continued, "You are doing something precious, my friends. And you are growing. A few days ago, we had two dozen. Today, we have many more. We will grow, and we will fight. This is a battle for the Great Land, and I intend to win. But I can only do it with your help. Work hard. Be good to one another. Your friends and neighbors depend on us to defeat the monster in Fairmont and we will not disappoint them. Now get back to work. We leave for Ankar in the morning."

Nara walked away from the men, stopping when she found a good place to look out over the valley below, and on Keetna. Perhaps that demonstration would give hope to these men. Men who might die for her. Hope can be a powerful thing.

Mykel came over to her, smiling. He clapped a few times. "Very nice. Never thought of that one."

"I'm full of surprises."

"I thought you would just wrap them up with a mound of dirt so they couldn't move."

He was still smarting over that one, clearly. "They are too fast to trap that way. Besides, I only use that method to stop big brutes who won't listen to me."

"I'm listening now," he said.

"I know you are. Thank you."

"So, it looks like you're gonna do this after all."

"I'm tired of second-guessing myself. They are depending on me. Besides, I don't see any other way."

"Me either. Ankar?"

"Maybe we get some gifted to join us. At least we'll get more soldiers. We'll need more than this ratty crew to march north."

"Need anything from me?"

"Yes. Show off as much as possible."

"What?" Mykel's face displayed his confusion.

"These men are tough-minded and eager but will be far from their homes and alone. They've seen terrible things, they've done terrible things, and may be as frustrated with Dei as we are. They are scared, even if they don't show it. When citizens join up with men who have wronged their villages, taken loved ones, there may be infighting. It could brew into chaos if we don't manage it."

"Wow, you're way ahead of me on this. Never thought of that."

"Mykel, when you lift heavy things or fight with your eyes closed, your magic is terrifying. So is mine. But we're on their side. The more we show our strength, the more confident they will be. They'll become brothers in pursuit of a common goal. It may heal the rift between them, and ease their fears. We need that to happen."

"But showing off? Making myself look better or tougher? That's just not my style."

"But you *are* better. You *are* tougher. You're the toughest warrior they've ever seen. It brings confidence. It's not our way, but that must change because bold men who are properly motivated will march forward and spread the word. Not only will they fight harder, but our force will grow. People want to be part of something victorious. Look at their reaction to what I just did. It works."

Mykel made an odd face, then sighed. "Okay."

"Okay?"

He looked out at Keetna for a moment, then turned back. "I'll do it. Want me to go arm-wrestle ten at once? Or head-butt some boulders?"

"Boulders would be perfect," she said. "Thank you."

They both laughed.

"You might want to fix the ground back there," Mykel said. "Hard to walk."

"Nah. It's their reminder we've got big, bad magic and we're gonna win."

PART THREE

War is a curious thing. Men kill for revenge. They kill for gold. They hurt one another because they have been hurt themselves. Pain begets pain, and in the midst of it, they defend their homeland. They defend their brothers. They defend their wives. They rise above themselves, displaying honor, sacrifice, and achieving a glory not possible without adversity.

Darkness can give birth to beautiful stories.

— Author Unknown

RESCUE

The sun was almost down, and Gwyn again held the advantage over the guards within the compound who couldn't see without torchlight. Over the last week, she'd made many trips over the wall, learning each building, which doors were locked, and the routes of each sentry. The northern sentries were like machines, always alert and focused, particularly when a carriage entered the compound. Sometimes, it was the Queen, but that was usually by day. Other times, it was the sick-looking man, who came often, or another who came rarely. The other man was in his fifties, she surmised, with long hair. Not just on his head, but on his face, and all over his arms. That guy was just plain hairy.

At first, Gwyn thought the sick-looking man suffered from an ailment that was being treated here, but, after a time, it became clear that he held authority and was directing the actions of soldiers. She even overheard conversations between him, the guards and some porters. About moving prisoners and such. And moving bodies. Whatever they were doing to the children, some did not survive.

The southwest sentry was her favorite, always having hot rolls and stinky cheese for his dinner. He would retrieve them from a kitchen in the large, central building and would abandon his post at least once an hour, making for easy entry and exit near his platform without the need to approach any of the other platforms.

Of all the buildings she had surveyed, the four smaller ones were of the most interest. Not only did the Queen and the sick man spend all their time here among those structures, but it was also where they took the children. A sentry manned a single door on each building that faced the inner pathway that ran down the center of the compound. Only two windows were visible on the exterior of each building, one on the north side, and one facing the outer walls. The north window sported iron bars and the other, on the opposite side of the entry door, was locked and in clear view of a nearby sentry platform. Entry to any of these smaller buildings would require overpowering a guard and revealing her presence, removing iron bars, or breaking into a window in clear view of a sentry. Timing and stealth would be her only way to get inside one of those buildings.

Five days ago, they had taken Yury into the southwest building, the one watched by the lazy, cheese-eating southwest sentry. Despite multiple attempts, she hadn't yet picked the lock on the window before he had returned from collecting his dinner, but she hoped for success tonight, a silent, quick entry. Hard to do in the middle of an armed compound, but it was the best bad idea she could come up with.

Once the sun had set, Gwyn didn't have to wait long before the southwest guard began to look restive. He stood on his platform, periodically glancing back and forth at the main building. Once, he even grabbed his ample belly and Gwyn imagined hearing his tummy rumble. It wouldn't be much longer now.

She checked her quiver again to make sure the arrows were secure and adjusted the bow on her back. Another few minutes and the southwest guard turned to descend the ladder to the ground and Gwyn sprang into action, sprinting across the open space that separated the tree-line from the compound wall. After bolting up the side using well-practiced handholds, she held herself in place near the top, looking for other sentries. The south-west guard was the only human in sight, making his way in rapid fashion to the kitchen where his dinner likely awaited. She would have some time before he came back.

Over the top and down the other side, she wasted no time moving to the target building. Catching her breath, she lingered a moment in the shadows on the south side of the building to check her surroundings. No sounds. No guards. Time to move. A hand went into a pocket, loosed a strap and lock picks came free. She eased around the corner, stopping in front of the window and putting a hook pick in the lock. She thought she had the pin combination right, but the torsion wrench hadn't yet managed to force the tumbler.

Feel. Lift. Lift. In with the torsion wrench. Turn.

Drat. It was still stiff. Frozen – or had the tumbler seized? Perhaps she'd need to heat it somehow. Everything moved better with heat. With precious few moments before the lazy guard returned, she dropped the tools into her pocket once more and darted over to grab a torch from the sconce on the nearby wall. Back at the building, she placed the torch under the lock, warming it. The fire marked the windowsill black, and she worried about it igniting the wood before the lock warmed enough to move. Just another moment. She held her breath. There, that should do it! She set down the torch, applied the hook pick and the torsion wrench and turned. Harder. Harder. Clack! The tumbler broke free, and the latch fell open.

Gwyn dropped the tools back into her pocket, grabbed the torch and replaced it on the wall sconce. She then dashed back into the shadows on the south side of the building, reassessing. Footsteps on the north side of the building moved toward the southeast platform. The guard was returning with his dinner. Hopefully, he wasn't observant enough to notice the singed windowsill and open padlock. She'd have to make entry to the building tonight, however. In full daylight, it would be easy to see that she'd tampered with the lock and she would lose her opportunity.

More footsteps. She spun to see a different guard leading several children out from the south side of the main building, moving toward the field latrine. She was exposed, saved only by shadows. Normally in a situation like this, she would hide in a high place, since few people looked up. But that was only when inside a building, not an open area. Instead, she dropped to the ground and flattened herself against the building, hoping that the guard's torch wouldn't be bright enough to reveal her location. They passed within thirty feet of her location and it was only blind luck that kept the man from looking her way.

Each child took a turn in the latrine and it seemed like an eon passed before they all finished and the guard led them back. They passed by Gwyn again, far too close for comfort, and a small girl at the back of the line turned to the left. Her eyes met Gwyn's and the girl slowed. Caught. All it would take now was for the guard behind her to notice and follow her gaze.

"Hurry up," the man said, pushing the little girl forward, causing her to stumble and fall. "I ain't got all night."

The girl picked herself up and kept walking. A moment later, they entered the large structure and the door behind them was closed and latched. Gwyn breathed a sigh of relief.

A noise behind her drew her attention to the southwest tower. The lazy southwest guard must have forgotten a dinner roll, because he was descending the ladder yet again, failing to look about as he did so.

Fortune favors the bold. With a quiet breath, she waited, once again. A moment later, the guard was out of sight and she was at the window, removing the padlock as softly as she could. The hinges at the top of the window creaked as she pushed it open. Over the sill and into the building, careful to avoid bumping her bow on anything, she soon found herself crouching on a dirt floor, a hand still holding the edge of the window above. She pushed it back to the closed position. It took a moment for her eyes to adjust to the room. She found a table with some papers, several boxes, and several side rooms. Moving ahead, no louder than a mouse on her boot liners, she passed the barred window and headed toward a stairwell that went down. As she descended, she engaged her vision to catch what appeared to be two cells on her right, each secured with metal bars and a solid steel door with a built-in lock. One prisoner slumbered in the far cell, the other remained empty. Yury? She hadn't been able to keep a constant watch on the building since they brought him here, and couldn't be sure.

To her left, there was a single room, secured by a large, wooden door. She wondered what they did in that room that required such secrecy. She tried the latch, but it was secure. Out of her pocket came the picks and she was wrenching on the torsion bar a moment later. Click.

She replaced the picks in her pocket as she pulled on the door, opening it to reveal worktables, with items on top. Moving closer, she examined the items. A bone chestplate sat on one table, fashioned with hooks and straps. On another table, she found an ivory blade, runes carved on its surface. It bore no handle, just a crude haft. Unfinished. Someone was following in the footsteps of the king. Bone weapons and armor. With runes. That would change the balance of power, for sure. Anne needed to know this.

A sound from across the basement distracted her – the prisoner turning in his cot. She left the room, latched the door, and went to the cell with the prisoner. Long hair, like Yury, but it wasn't him. His light was different, very different. It looked more like Mykel's. Brighter. He was larger than Yury, too. Much larger. Not just wider but taller. In fact, it looked as if he barely fit on the cot. She looked at the prisoner's thigh and saw a tear in the fabric of his trousers where he had been struck by the arrow. And a bloodstain, but no bandage.

So, it *was* Yury. But what had they done to him?

Anne told her to follow the boy, and she had agreed. She had her swords and a bow with four arrows. That wouldn't buy an escape, especially since she couldn't expect Yury to walk with his injury, much less fight and climb walls. But she had to try. The scorched wood around the lock would invite increased security and she would not get another chance.

She pulled out her lock picks and went to work. The latch on the metal door was stiff, but not frozen, and the tumbler moved when she used a heavy hand. The door came open with a creak, and the prisoner bolted up.

"Yury, it's me, Gwyn."

He just stared at her. A rune on each of his thighs flared and Gwyn's hand went to the pommel of her dagger. Runes! This was a bad idea. Either this wasn't Yury, or he didn't recognize her. She stepped back, intending to close the door behind her when the prisoner moved, blindingly fast, and in an instant he was behind her, an arm around her neck in a headlock, blocking her airway. She reached for her dagger and stabbed him in the arm, but as soon as she pulled back the blade, the flesh closed. She tried to speak, to tell him it would be okay, that she was here to rescue him, but she couldn't speak. He was huge, so there was no way to overpower him. And with speed like that, he must be a racer as well. Health and speed without a cepp, just like Mykel.

She felt pressure against the side of her head. He inhaled, smelling her.

"Your name is Gwyn," he grumbled, relaxing the arm around her neck slightly. His voice was deep and gruff.

"Yes, yes. It's me," she said, voice strained. "Put me down, Yury."

He paused a moment. "Yury." It was more a statement than a question. As if the word was an acknowledgment. He dropped Gwyn, and she landed awkwardly.

She turned to look at him, dagger in one hand, the other rubbing her neck. He was much taller, almost seven feet now. And wider, but disproportional. One shoulder was higher than the other, his back was slightly hunched, and his face was misshapen, slightly twisted. Like the monster he had fought in the woods, but not as bad. That's what the kidnappings were all about. Experiments. Kayna was making cursed.

"Can you fight?" she asked.

He paused, his eyes squinting in the darkness. He nodded.

She slid one of her swords out of its sheath, slowly. Yury didn't move, thankfully. Gwyn gave him the blade, handle first, then turned to ascend the steps. He was strong, but his mind seemed addled and she hoped he wouldn't attack her again. At the top of the stairs, she turned to look behind. He was following. Good. Escaping a compound filled with guards wouldn't be easy and she needed all the help she could get. But she had a sword, a bow, and a big, cursed racer wielding amnesia and an edged weapon. Should be interesting.

She turned to go to the window, then realized how narrow the opening was. Yury would never fit through. The fight must begin with the guard outside the main door. She wheeled to direct him but before she could say anything, he had opened the door and was face-to-face with the soldier. Before the man could sound any alarm, Yury put the sword through his throat.

Gwyn rushed past the dying guard, heading around the south side of the building and directly for the southwest tower.

"Alert!" the lazy guard's voice boomed from the platform above. Surely, the entire compound had heard it.

The bow went to her hand, an arrow nocked, and the lazy guard's eye socket suddenly sported the back half of a wooden arrow shaft. No more dinner rolls for that one. He fell forward, slumping for a moment, then fell off the tower and hit the ground below with a thud.

Gwyn sprinted for the wall but Yury was faster, climbing the ladder in a heartbeat. He stood sentry at the top as Gwyn moved up the wall, the shouts of armored men in the distance behind her. If anyone had a bow ready, she'd get an arrow right in the back. A few moments later, she reached the top, then was over it, breathing intensely as adrenaline coursed through her. Her feet hit the ground on the other side, and she sprinted across the open area,

Yury just a few steps ahead. As her footfalls pounded the earth in retreat, she wondered how many innocents she was leaving behind tonight. Yury seemed to barely know his own name, so he probably didn't remember his sister, either. Good thing, because there was no time for a rescue. Saving one boy would have to be enough.

She glanced behind to see several guards leaving the north gate. They held torches and were moving in pursuit but would have no chance against Gwyn's vision and Yury's speed. A short time later, they stopped running, having far outdistanced their pursuers. It was dark, and they would need a place to make camp.

"Well, big fella, I guess it's you and me, now."

Yury said nothing as he quietly towered over Gwyn, seemingly looking for direction.

"Let's build a shelter and get some sleep. Tomorrow, we find food."

"Sleep," he said.

"I hope you have some stories you can share; it's going to be boring around here. We must wait for someone, and it could be quite a while."

26

ANKAR

Nara led her men to Keetna where Able Wileman, the former banker, made purchases of food and extra wagons before they hit the road. She paid a visit to Nilly, finding her playing with a passel of little ones in the center of the town.

"Nara!" Nilly said when she saw her, running full speed and colliding with Nara and spinning in a huge embrace.

"Wow, I've been missed."

"I have something for you," Nilly said. She held up her hand, urging Nara not to move. "Wait right here."

As Nilly dashed away, Nara mussed the hair on some little ones, pinching a few cheeks and laughing. When Nilly returned, she held a piece of fabric draped over one arm, with strings and ribbons over the other.

"This is a skirt," she said, handing the fabric to Nara. "It's not tight, so you can still fight in it. And these," –she held up the strings– "are for your arms."

"What are they?"

"Some designs I made. Let me show you."

She helped Nara put on the skirt, which was soft yet very sturdy. Nilly wrapped the strings and ribbons around Nara's forearms and upper arms, taking her time to fasten them firmly. The strings and ribbons were woven together in beautiful, intricate patterns that decorated Nara's skin without being uncomfortable. "Tight but not too tight. Don't want them to slip off when you're beating up the bad guys."

"Such faith in me," Nara said.

"You're going to win, I know it." She finished the last pattern. "There. Perfect. Now you look like an angel."

"Thank you, Nilly, but you're the angel. These are beautiful." Nara touched Nilly's cheek. "Thank you so much."

They embraced again. "I have to go now," Nara said.

"Come back and visit me someday."

"I will. I promise."

A few minutes later, Nara was far down the road, out of sight of the small village and again among the men of her growing army. Ninety-five soldiers now–if they could be called that. More had arrived from the north, bearing sticks and axes. Word spread quickly in these parts, even if military prowess did not.

"What's with the new outfit?" Mykel said as he approached.

"Nilly made it. What do you think?"

"I like it, especially the arm things. Never seen anything like those. Should probably get some shoes, though. Not very dignified."

"Maybe later. Bare feet aren't that bad. Ready to head out?"

"To Ankar."

The trek south was slow but went more quickly than before, the roads seemed in better repair the closer they got to the large city. The freezing and thawing of winter months created terrible ruts and frost heaves, but Ankar had money and money filled potholes. As the days passed, they came upon many more villages, but only two were burned. The dead had already been buried, probably by neighboring villages. The Great Land was becoming accustomed to the terrible new state of things.

"The northernmost Ankar outpost is on this road, only half a day's march to go," Jahmai said from atop his horse. "If we keep going, we'll hit it before dark. It's the smallest one."

Mykel turned to Nara. "Do you want these men to fight tired?"

She looked up at Jahmai. "How many will we face?"

He shrugged. "Fifty to seventy-five men, maybe a little more," Jahmai said. "At least one gifted, maybe a pair."

"I want to win," she said. "Let's not be rash. If we take the outpost tonight, we may have two more to fight in short order, and I don't want to take on three outposts in one day. We rest soon, eat well, get a good night's sleep. Early tomorrow we go straight at them."

Another hour of walking took them within sight of a large river, huge snow-capped peaks on the other side. A wide bridge crossed the water in a narrow spot, and, in the distance, they could see the ocean.

"Those are the biggest mountains I've ever seen," Nara said to Mykel. "Other than the Twins."

"Yes. Ankar is beautiful. The river is the Sitna, which dumps into Kinnik Arm," said a voice behind Nara.

She turned to see Martel standing nearby.

"Then the water goes out into the Landian Gulf," he said.

Beyond the river and the bridge, along the far shore of Kinnik Arm, she could see buildings. Maybe only a few hours' march. Ankar. The second-largest city in the Great Land and where Anne had spent a big part of her early life.

"It's beautiful," Nara said. "We camp here tonight. Fight tomorrow."

They made fires and ate well, and they passed a fair amount of alcohol around—brandy, ale, and wine. Nara enjoyed a glass of wine. Able Wileman joined Ferron, an archer, and they both got very chatty after a few ales, then sang together in an ill-advised duet that brought many laughs and more than a few jeers. It was good to see the stuffy banker lighten up and enjoy himself. Sentries stood watch in the event a patrol might wander by, but nobody bothered them and most laid themselves down in time for a good night's rest.

———

Nara woke early and found Mykel sitting on a rock, watching the sun rise over the mountains in the east.

"Gorgeous," she said.

"I've heard stories of Ankar," Mykel said. "But they never mentioned the mountains."

"First time we visit this beautiful place, and we come to start a fight."

"Yeah, I know."

"Think we can take seventy-five men and a couple gifted with this ratty crew?"

"I think you could take seventy-five men and a couple gifted by yourself," Mykel said.

She laughed. "I'd like to recruit a few, if they'll come. I can't just bury them all under an avalanche and expect to get much loyalty afterward."

"True. So, we overwhelm them, get them to surrender, and make a 'come to the light' pitch. 'Redeem yourselves' and stuff like that."

Just then, Lieutenant Martel played a bugle to rouse the men.

"Time to go," Mykel said, getting to his feet.

They broke camp, tucking tents into packs and gathering the wagons. Then they crossed the bridge over the Sitna River, skirting the mountain range as they approached their target, passing a few merchants and travelers. A few hours later, the outpost's walls could be seen to the southeast.

"There," Jahmai said, looking east and pointing. "Enemy lookout."

"Nara followed his gaze. A rider on horseback galloped along a ridge-line trail at the base of the nearest mountain, heading for the outpost.

"Want me to stop him?" Martel asked. "I could intercept on horseback."

"No," Nara said. "Let him warn them. We will approach with confidence, speak with them, and give them a chance to surrender."

"They won't give up," Jahmai said. "Not right away."

"Just because you didn't, doesn't mean they won't."

"As you wish."

It was almost midday when they formed up on a field that straddled the road just north of the outpost. Shoe prints and scuff marks on the nearby turf indicated that soldiers had used the area to train. The outpost was just beyond reach of their bows, sporting high walls and multiple sentry towers, archers at the ready. Nara counted at least a dozen bowmen standing proudly.

"Going alone?" Mykel asked.

"You and Jahmai can come but stay back a few steps. This is my show, but I want them to see his uniform so they know they are up against some of their own."

Nara and Mykel walked up, while Jahmai followed on horseback, tabard visible over his chain mail. Less than a hundred paces from the outpost, they stopped.

A man on the top of the wall shouted, "Surrender as traitors, submit to the authority of the crown, and I will give you quick deaths."

Nara turned to Mykel. "Want to surrender?"

"Nah," he said.

"Me neither." She turned back to the outpost. "No thanks. I'll give you a counter-offer. You surrender, and we won't raze your outpost and deliver the justice your soldiers have earned. We rise against the Queen, and we will have victory today."

The man shook his head, then said something to another. Nara heard Jahmai spur his horse into action just before a volley of arrows launched into the air. She flared sight and speed as the arrows approached—slowly, now that she was in her magic. Five came straight at her. She dodged four and caught the fifth, whirling, flaring strength and sending it straight back at the leader who gave the order, sinking it deep into the wood just inches from his head. She then burst into a run at the gate, hoping that Mykel and the rest of the army would follow. As she sprinted, she flared earth and the northern wall lurched and buckled, the front gate cracking with rising stone that shifted it off its hinges. That would provide entry for her men, but she had another way in.

Arrows came at her again, but she was moving too fast and all went astray. She flared strength, leaping high in the air and landing on top of the damaged outpost wall. Two soldiers were near her landing spot, swinging swords clumsily at her racing form. Strength, speed, and protection alive in her mind, she engaged the first soldier, dodging his sword strike, then smashed his wrist with a fist, disarming him.

Before he fell, she was beyond him and on to the next, grabbing a spear and breaking it with ease, then punching the man in the gut before spinning and moving down the line. The next fell. Then the next. Five were down almost before they knew what was happening. She looked down to see Mykel just now entering the gate, followed by Jahmai and the rest of her army.

"Gifted!" screamed a man on the western wall.

Nara leaped down into the outpost's common area, feet hitting the earth near at least three dozen soldiers who awaited what they likely thought would be a siege or at least a lengthy exchange of arrows. Swords came out of their sheaths, and she felt a wave of fatigue. Dropping all of her runes, she flared sight to assess, just in time to predict arrows about to come her way from archers on the eastern wall. Flaring speed again, she dodged the arrows just as they approached. Where were the enemy gifted? Then she heard a call from behind her.

"Racer!"

She didn't recognize the voice but now chided herself for entering the outpost so quickly. Her desire to make a strong impression had left her men unprotected—an amateur move.

Several of the enemy soldiers now surged to attack her, and soon they would be upon her. She couldn't take so many at once in a melee.

She flared earth and a wall of dirt and rock rose between them, giving her ample time to dart out the gate and return to her men.

A red banner flew high, tied on the end of a spear held by a man in the front. The soldiers had retreated to form a circle, armored men on the perimeter, spears, and swords pointed out. Mykel was in pursuit of the racer but was badly outpaced. The racer was a bearded man, maybe twenty-five years old, holding a dagger in each hand. He was speeding around the perimeter of her army, stabbing her men, one at a time, so fast that they could not defend themselves.

Nara dropped speed and flared earth, hard. She willed the ground to erupt, urgency, anger, and passion in her thoughts. The earth responded with a violent quake, rocks and pits appearing beneath her army's feet and also beneath her own. It was too much, the disturbed earth stretching out over a far greater area than she intended. Many of her own men dropped, but so did the racer. She saw him fall, his face striking a rock, stunning him. Before he could rise, Martel put a spear through his heart.

She whirled to see four soldiers coming through the destroyed gate behind her. Then ten. She was flaring no runes at the moment and seemed to move through a fog, a warm blanket of fatigue washing over her. So much energy spent and far too fast. If she'd had a cepp to replenish herself, she might have been able to keep going, but she had none. She'd planned this poorly and wouldn't be able to finish this fight.

A blur moved by, and it took a moment for her to realize that it was Mykel, engaging the soldiers that streamed from the outpost before they could fall upon her. He waded through the enemy, breaking ribs and tossing them aside like sticks blown about in a storm. He then disappeared inside the outpost and her men followed, making their way as best they could on the broken earth.

Nara shook her head and took deep breaths, the fatigue fading slightly and vision clearing enough that she could move forward in pursuit of the others. As she entered the outpost again, she witnessed a grand melee before her. Mykel battled many at once and he was overwhelming them, moving with the staff as if doing some carefully choreographed dance. Dozens fell before him, and his relentless, perfectly-timed blows left the enemy no hope of victory. Several shouted their surrender and dropped their weapons, but others just gave ground, struggling in futility against Mykel and the others in what had become an unwinnable struggle.

Moments later, the end came, the enemy commander calling for his men to stop. Jahmai walked up to the man, who bled from several wounds, including one on his head. They spoke for a moment, but Nara couldn't make out what they were saying.

"How ya doing?" Mykel said. He wasn't even breathing hard.

She turned, surprised that she hadn't noticed him walk up. "How many did we lose?"

"Three so far. That's why I asked. We're about to lose another. Ferron caught an arrow on the back of his neck. He's bleeding badly."

"Where is he?" she said, looking around, still fighting the fog that was clearing from her head far too slowly.

"Back here, by the wall."

She turned and headed toward what little remained of the outpost's northern wall.

"No, Nara. Your wall. This way." He grabbed her arm and led her to one side of the wall of dirt she had summoned in the middle of the yard.

She was still disoriented. It was difficult to think, much less walk straight. Ferron sat with his head slumped forward, and one of the younger soldiers pressed a bloody bandage against the nape of his neck.

"I have it now," she said, removing the bandage slowly. The blood flowed generously as she placed her hand over the wound. Closing her eyes and flaring sight, she visualized the damage.

Muscles were severed and a vertebra damaged, as well a nearby vein. She willed the muscle, blood vessel, and skin to heal, but the vertebra was fractured; pieces had detached. Arrows from those powerful longbows did a lot of damage when they hit bone. If she healed the vertebra now, in her foggy state, it would be irregular, and she might cause damage to his nerve cord with a bad knit. She didn't trust herself with something so delicate at the moment.

"Bleeding has stopped, but his spine is damaged. I'll look at it again later. Immobilize his neck, and I'll try again in a few hours."

She rose to her feet.

"Who else?"

"Some minor injuries," Mykel said, "but not life-threatening. You need to rest more than they do."

"What happened? Why am I so tired?"

"Look around."

She shook her head and tried to focus better. The walls of the outpost had been decimated, the ground pitted in some places and mounded in others. Several irregular columns of rock had risen a dozen feet in the air. She walked outside the wreckage, surveying the field where the racer fell. More pits and mounds, high columns standing tall and several boulders the size of a wagon had half risen out of the ground. The damaged earth stretched as far as she could see, hundreds and hundreds of yards.

Dei, no.

"This is why you're tired. Too much passion, no restraint. Hold back, will ya? We can win without you breaking the Great Land in the process."

"How about 'good job' or something?"

Mykel smiled. "Impressive. They'll be talking about this in Ankar for a while. I'm glad I was here because you almost got jumped by a dozen or more."

"You were near, so I was fine. But thank you."

Jahmai approached Nara. "Ready for a report? You look a little pale."

"Go ahead," she said. "I'm fine." She reached to steady herself on Mykel's arm.

"Four of ours are down," Jahmai said. "Three dead, and we almost lost Ferron too. He's still breathing and looking better now, but you already knew that. Nice work there. I've never seen anyone knit such a grievous neck wound."

"He needs more work," Nara said.

"Still impressive. Another five of ours injured, but not badly. They'll wait. As for the enemy: twelve dead and twenty injured. Another fifteen escaped. Fifty prisoners inside, some are injured. Many will join us. The racer is dead. And you have a harvester now."

Three of her men dead. And a dozen of the enemy dead. This was her first battle report, and it was an odd feeling. They were talking about human beings like they were potatoes that fell out of a basket on the way from the market.

"Is that good?" she asked.

"Nara, you just led an assault on a well-defended fortification. You attacked veteran soldiers, single-handedly at first, while unarmed. Nobody does that. They wielded ranged weapons and held an elevated position, yet your army overcame them with a force composed mostly of civilians. Even so, you inflicted several times the casualties your army suffered and obliterated their outpost without catapult or ballista. In military terms, this was a rout. I'd call it a miracle."

"And so many want to join," she said. "What did you tell them?"

"I told them you're the most powerful blessed the world has ever seen, and you're taking Fairmont from the Queen. You resurrect the dead, punish the wicked, and reward your followers. They have two options. Get out of the way or march with the righteous and make history." He looked about at the disturbed earth. "You did the rest. My Lord, girl, this was something else."

"Resurrect the dead, Ander Jahmai? Are you kidding me?"

"You're the best knitter I've ever seen. I ran with the healing theme and got carried away."

"Stop that."

"Sorry," he said with a wide grin. He wasn't sorry at all.

"And the other outposts?" Mykel asked. "Will they move on us now?"

"When they hear what happened here? Not a chance."

"Good," Nara said. "'Cuz I need a nap."

27

A GRAND DISPLAY

As Kayna walked along the cobblestone paths, she lifted the bottom of her black robes to keep them from getting soiled. She looked about as she walked, marveling at the wide swaths of well-groomed grass and trees that separated her from the main building. The Ministry of War and Justice was more like a castle than a ministry campus, and Kayna wondered at the hubris shown by her father in making it so. The sprawling grounds comprised a half-oval central building containing the courtrooms, administrative offices, many meeting rooms, and the minister's private garden in the center. Around the periphery were several smaller buildings, interrogation rooms, execution stages, kitchens, laundries, and cells for housing prisoners that awaited trial. Throughout the campus were beautiful, winding paths, bushes, well-manicured trees, and many flowers, as if Papa planned for prisoners to marvel at his civility and refinement while they were being prodded along to their deaths. Beautiful justice.

"This way, Highness." The newly appointed Minister of Transport, Darin Ripowski, wore a lavish blue military coat as he guided her along to the main building. The coat bore multiple ribbons that he'd never earned, gold braids that crisscrossed the front, embroidered sleeves, and oversized epaulets. The tails of his coat almost touched the ground, flapping with each solid, manly stride. Why the Minister of Transport should be decorated like a general, Kayna had no idea. Darin was always quite the peacock, however, and his vanity had only grown with the recent appointment.

They entered through a side entrance, climbed several stone staircases, and traversed a high balcony, finally descending a small stairway to arrive at the courtroom where she would pronounce the sentence. The gathering was large, several hundred barristers and administrators, along with every minster on the council. The audience was appropriate for the crime but even more appropriate for the prisoner: a former man of authority, shackled and sitting cross-legged in a cage in the center of the chamber. His matted hair and unkempt beard gave witness to an uncomfortable time in the dungeon for his recent transgressions.

Instead of taking her seat, as they had advised would be normal for such matters, she remained standing. "I am not the sort of monarch you have known in the past and am beholden to no traditions," she said. "I will remain standing for today's proceedings, while you will not."

The attendees looked at one another with confused expressions on their faces before finally deciding to take their seats.

"You see before you a fine example of consequence," Kayna said, walking down to the main level of the chamber. She ran her fingers along the iron bars, looking at the prisoner who sat, his eyes wide with fear. "This man, once Chancellor, did not protect my father from our enemy. In my mercy, I did not execute him but appointed him as the Minister of War and Justice. Placed into a position of trust, retaining wealth and station, he was given a second chance, yet betrayed me again. And committed a crime."

A hushed murmur moved through the crowd.

"A crime!" she yelled. Her raised voice did not reverberate about the chamber as much as she would have liked. Still, it was loud enough. It would be nice to have a deep, booming tone for these occasions, but she had searched and could find no magic for such things. Yelling was an interesting thing, an act born of passion, capable of producing a great emotional effect when used properly. She folded her hands across her robes, trying to display a harmless image for a moment.

"I am a victim of this man. And so are you. I gave him a responsibility. A charge. To protect our nation. He had armies, he had gifted, and yet he failed. A pretender has come. She challenges me. She destroys our outposts. Robs our treasury. Captures our faithful soldiers. She even burns villages. Kidnaps children. Murders their parents!"

The murmurs grew, and one in the back said, "Hear, hear!"

"I am only one woman," Kayna said. She had prepared the speech yesterday and was quite proud of it. Pride. An interesting feeling and it only came with sincere effort and sacrifice, it seemed. One couldn't get pride in any other way.

"I am blessed by Dei," she continued, "but I cannot act alone. When I appoint someone to a task, they must complete it, with honor and diligence. They must play their part and protect this land. Neither Dei nor I will not tolerate the incompetence of faithless, honorless men, who swear oaths of loyalty one day, then allow treachery the next. We will cut them from the body of this beautiful nation as if they were a cancer. A malignancy that will be burned away if we are to achieve a productive society. A prosperous citizenry. A necessary peace."

She turned to the prisoner, who seemed to avoid her eyes, still sitting cross-legged in his cell. Kayna's stomach turned at his stench. His disgusting appearance provided a beautiful deterrent for the gathered, but they didn't have to be so close. Tomorrow's prisoner would have to be cleaner, or she'd have to rethink the choreography of these sentences.

"Archibald Holland, you are former Chancellor and former Minister of War and Justice. You are now a traitor, accused of betraying your nation, your Queen, and Dei. Do you have anything to say for yourself?" Her voice was tender, hopefully appearing compassionate to the crowd. "Anything I must consider before delivering your sentence? Excuses, regrets, or perhaps an apology? I yearn to give mercy but must hear a plea from you first. Please. Defend yourself."

He said nothing, but that wasn't his fault. To the audience, he would appear unremorseful, or so she hoped. They could not know that he was drugged, with his tongue having been removed three days before.

"He's not even sorry," a man shouted from off to Kayna's right.

"Traitor!" cried another.

"Enemy of Dei!"

"Demon. He comes straight from Kai!"

Whistles and jeers filled the room as the crowd called for judgment.

Kayna held a hand high, her head bowed in feigned sorrow. The crowd hushed.

"I have no choice," she said. "Holy Dei, have mercy on this man, a sinner. May a cleansing of your holy fire burn away his transgressions."

Then Kayna's eyes flared hot, and her hands extended toward the cage. Fire engulfed Archibald Holland, the screams began, and stench and smoke filled the chamber.

***

Kayna wandered through the ministry's private garden. She'd have to appoint a new minister and did not know whom to choose. Austere displays of power and justice were fun but assessing who would serve well in leadership roles was something else. Perhaps she should just leave it to a designee to find candidates. Let them all jockey for power and position, bribe one another, make a list of names, and she would pick the richest one. Or the most obedient. That's what good monarchs did.

She rounded a corner hedge, and a strange odor intruded on the floral scents that filled the area. Musty. It was Ennis. She whirled to find him behind her.

"Don't sneak up on me, Ennis. That's rude."

"You want to spend thousands of crowns on food?"

"Yes. And we won't buy just food. Also bedding. Shoes for kids. We'll hire builders to fix roofs or anything that is needed. This isn't just about the people; I want our soldiers to be part of something positive. To heal. We tell them to fight and they obey, but killing exacts a toll on the victorious. Men can't wade through blood and horror, then walk away unscathed. It has to weigh on them for long after."

"It does. Not that any of us are eager to admit it."

"And we never know if we will win a battle, but this is a guaranteed win. Our men will be heroes to little kids with hungry bellies. Saviors to the mothers who struggle every day to survive. Role models for men who may join us."

He scratched the side of his head. "Interesting. Not my style, but I think I like it. Might bring new recruits. But it will bring problems, too. Soldiers get into trouble when they have money and the bars are open. This might not go as easy as you hope."

"Put them in groups of two or three for accountability. Set a curfew so they aren't out beyond dark. Let them know that Mykel and I will be watching. If we hold our expectations high, they will meet them. They need this, Ander. To be the good guys for a while. One day of charity, then we march north."

"Understood."

She moved about the outpost, greeting the men. Each time she found an injured soldier, she removed his bandage and knitted the wound, however minor, remaining a while to speak with him. There were young men and old, family men, boys, and many gruff veterans, but all were grateful for her attention.

Afterward, she went looking for Mykel, wandering out the north gate, broken as it was, and into the clearing beyond. Or what used to be a clearing. It was cluttered now, with so much damage to the earth. She yearned to fix what she had broken but paused before acting. As she surveyed the area, she realized how little control she'd had. And how the fight against Kayna would be a different struggle than the Great Land had seen before. She was no lord fighting over territory or for money. This was bigger than that, and she must fight it differently. She would need to be disciplined, not haphazard with her magic. This broken earth would serve as a reminder of her need for restraint. Maybe she would come back and fix it, someday.

She circled the outpost and found Mykel training with a large group to the south among boulders, pits, and columns. They drilled with swords and spears, some even carrying shields. The ranks were swelling fast, more than doubling since the morning. She watched them form lines, then upon command from Martel, retreat into a semicircle, shield-bearers facing out. A choppy transition, with civilians trying to learn what the veterans had known for years.

She wandered to the edge of the field near some trees, still keeping in sight of the outpost but far enough away that nobody would notice her. The solitude was a rare treat, and there was much to think on. They would feed the people in Ankar, but should still have enough for the push north.

She thought about how small her army still was. Even if they doubled in size before arriving in Fairmont, this was a fool's errand, unless Nara could come up with something to even the odds against Kayna.

Yet, the battle this morning was a victory and was encouraging for the men. And she would pretend to be encouraged as well, but no matter how much confidence she feigned for the benefit of others, she didn't feel it herself. Kayna could control air currents so perfectly that she floated on them, showing a mastery of magic far exceeding Nara's. Kayna would not be foolish with her energies, and if she got tired, she could just suck the life out of someone– maybe even her own soldiers.

Mykel worried about Nara's level of control and said as much whenever he got the chance. If she didn't care so much, if she could quell her passion somehow, she'd be able to restrain herself, but when the battle began and people fell, she didn't know how to calm her spirit. How could she force herself to not care?

A fallen tree blocked her path, and she climbed over it, then kneeled and grabbed a handful of dirt and pebbles. That's all it was to most people. Dirt. Good for growing crops. Others didn't see it the way she did, yet they depended on it. Every step, they trusted it to hold them. Earth was the foundation of all life and often taken for granted.

She sat, leaning her back against the fallen tree, and put both hands into the soil. Flaring earth and sight at the same time, she reached down with her awareness. She was looking, but not for something in particular. Just looking.

Through the soil, the sight rune gave a different feeling. A different experience. She wasn't Nara anymore; she was the earth. Rock. Mountains. Sand and bedrock. She felt the footfalls of citizens in Ankar going about their daily chores as they walked upon her. Vibrations from wagons rolled along her back, and she sensed the gentle roll of waves crashing on her beach rocks near Ankar's port. Farther north, she sensed travelers camped on her hills, moose walking, and a fox digging a den under a fallen log. She sensed the movement of rocks in her belly, grinding against one another. And heat inside her mountains, alive and churning, hidden from the knowings of men.

Wow, that was incredible. She'd never flared sight and earth at the same time before. This wasn't a combat premonition, knowing enemy actions before they struck. Nor was it a vision, like the one of Dimmitt's fall. It was more like Mykel's staff rune, seeing what mattered to the staff. Using sight this way showed what mattered to the earth. And it brought peace. So big. So powerful. And it made her feel so small.

She let the runes drop and opened her eyes, the worries about Kayna and the upcoming struggle much diminished. As she stood, her balance faltered. Returning to her own perspective was a rough transition, and a bout of dizziness had her leaning against the log for a moment. Earth magic was an odd thing, and there was much to learn.

It was early the next day when they headed out to the streets of Ankar, money in hand. Nara stood on the roof of a tavern at the edge of the market, watching as a dirty-faced toddler clung to her mother's leg. The mother couldn't have been older than Nara, By her garb, it was easy to see that she was poor—her hair was matted and she wore ratty shoes and a dress that had seen better days. Two older rough-looking soldiers were offering a basket of bread to the mother, and she tentatively reached out, then took a single loaf.

"No, take it all, woman," the soldier said, pushing the basket into her chest, almost knocking her back. "And some of these," he said, dropping half a dozen copper bits in the basket.

Geez, they should be more gentle. She's afraid.

The woman put the loaf back in the basket and clasped the handle. "Thank you," she said, looking around defensively.

"You're welcome," said the other soldier, who wore a big grin on his face. "Tell everyone we are marching on Fairmont. We need able bodies, if they're willing." They walked away, fishing through pockets for coins, probably to buy more bread.

Nara watched as two other soldiers filled a handcart with fruit and vegetables, then dropped coins into the vendor's palm. They wheeled the cart down the street, calling out. "Hungry? Come get free food." A boy stood on the opposite side of the street and the soldiers stopped. "Catch," one called to the lad, then threw an apple.

The boy leaped to catch it in his left hand, then immediately put it to his mouth and took a bite. "Thanks," he said through a mouthful.

Nara smiled as the men kept rolling the cart. This was a good thing.

At first, Mykel scoffed at spending so much money on the people of Ankar. After a couple of hours watching, however, Nara saw him join in the distribution, buying dozens of children's shoes and ferrying them along the street in a wagon, inviting little ones to hop up and try them on.

Nara jumped from rooftop to rooftop as she watched the charity in action, witnessing the reactions of the parents, the children, and, more importantly, the soldiers. They loved it. They sang and whistled, and those who were suspicious at first soon relaxed and smiled. Citizens thanked the soldiers, and there were more tears and hugs exchanged than she could count.

As night approached, Jahmai summoned them all back to the outpost, pockets empty but hearts full. Several large bonfires raged in the open area, and pigs roasted on spits propped on braces between boulders and columns. Spirits were high among the army, with many laughs and songs throughout the evening.

"That was a good thing today," Mykel said as they sipped from mugs of hot apple wine. "I don't think the men are worrying about a thing right now."

"It's our job to lead," Nara said. "It's theirs to follow and fight. But leading is more than just battle. It's about leading their hearts, and I'm glad they could have this."

"Me too," Jahmai said, joining them, holding a mug. "You two are a blessing. I mean that. Whatever happens, many will remember this day. I've never seen these men so happy on the eve of a long march, and the recruits are swelling our ranks by the hour."

"How many so far?"

"You have an army of almost three hundred right now. More by morning, for sure. Able is keeping a roster and giving updates."

"How many are garrisoned near Fairmont?" Mykel asked.

"At least two thousand. Probably three, since Kayna will summon more from outlying areas when she hears what happened here."

"Three hundred against three thousand?" Nara shook her head. "We're gonna need a miracle."

"No, we won't," Jahmai said, looking at Nara. "We have you."

29

BEAST

Kayna stood in a sentry tower as training exercises took place in the open area below. Ennis never envisioned the compound to be a training ground, but General Almit didn't want either of the two projects to be far from their cells, just in case something went wrong. Staying close would allow Kayna to manage things if they got out of control. With what was at stake, she was happy to oblige.

The Dimmitt boy fought with a hammer and shield among a dozen armored opponents, his size and strength giving him an advantage over the soldiers that prodded him with wood sticks and guarded themselves with shields. Teaching the monster to fight well would be difficult, and they may not have time for him to develop much skill, but the armor was nearly complete and his ability to heal would serve well in battle. The men called him Beast, and the name had stuck. His size, ferocity, and slightly misshapen form certainly fit the moniker.

Although his growth had finally stopped, he was easily eight feet tall, thicker than an oak tree, and ate as much as ten men. He took to the health rune quickly, but even with a week of practice, he still couldn't flare the strength rune. In truth, he didn't need it— his size provided a strength that approached that of a bear even now. Still, he almost flared the rune twice today, so it wouldn't be much longer. When he found it, he would be a juggernaut on any battlefield, even without skill. But they had erred with him, going too far on the conditioning. He remembered nothing of his former life, which was good, but he'd even forgotten most words. Ennis sent an officer to hire tutors so the boy could learn to speak again, but progress was slow, especially since he murdered the first tutor they sent—a redhead—crushing her the moment she entered his cell. A foolish error.

Kayna's other project was a girl who now practiced against a large circle of dummies holding pikes and spears. She stood over six feet tall and darted about with unnatural speed, holding wooden knives she used to stab at the mannequins, shredding her silent opponents. They had found her in a village near Glennway, at fifteen years old. Her transformation hadn't cost her memory or her words, showing a resilience not seen in the males.

Health didn't work on her, though. Even after an accurate inscription, she couldn't see it, much less flare it, which was disappointing. Cursed had perplexing limitations, but Ennis moved forward with the project anyway, burning off the scar to try again. She took to the steelskin rune and recently mastered speed, a great talent in combat. Kayna wondered if they should try another rune but was cautious about getting greedy this time. With two cursed and many new gifted, her army should easily overcome Nara's little rebellion.

Kayna climbed down from the tower and approached the circle where Beast trained. As she got closer, he noticed her and turned, immediately taking a knee in the middle of the fray. She walked up to him, smiling.

"How are you doing today, Beast?"

"Goot," he said in a booming voice. Even kneeling, he was taller than Kayna, and she reached up to brush his black hair aside and put a hand on his cheek. Then she moved around to rub his back.

Beast closed his eyes. "Mama," he breathed, and his shoulders relaxed.

He called her that whenever she touched him. Mama. Odd thing. And strange how her touch calmed him so. How much he desired to please her.

"Now fight!" Kayna ordered, then rose into the air upon a gust of wind.

Beast bolted upright at her command, springing into action with eyes wide, brandishing the hammer at the soldiers who challenged him. He swung feverishly and advanced, the vigor in his assault increasing markedly with Kayna now watching from above. Even without a strength rune, the hammer struck shields and sent men flying backward.

"Harder!" Kayna said.

He charged directly into three men. One of them braced the butt of his spear on the ground, putting the tip through Beast's left shoulder. Beast bellowed and crushed the man's head with his hammer, then dropped his shield and removed the impaled spear with his left hand. The wound closed instantly, and Beast charged several more men, who ran.

"Down, Beast!" Kayna shouted, and the monster immediately took a knee, breathing heavily.

She knelt at his side, rubbed his back again, and felt him relax again under her touch.

Ennis walked up, cautiously. "Did he get strength yet?"

Kayna turned to face him. "Not today. But we're close. Tomorrow maybe. I can't imagine what he'll be like when he finds it."

"Me either," Ennis said.

"What's your report?" she asked.

"Armor is done. Fitting this afternoon, if he'll do it."

She turned to Beast, continuing to rub his back. "He'll do anything I say."

30

NIGHTLIGHT

When Nara awoke, she expected to eat and begin preparations for the march north but immediately sensed something was off. She left her tent to find soldiers packing wagons here and there, but to the north of the outpost, she heard a noise. It wasn't fighting. It was cheering.

She ran through the destroyed gate and out into the field where Lieutenant Martel, Wileman, and several dozen of her men were trying to organize a rowdy crowd of citizens, mostly young men. Were they demanding more food?

She reached to the nearest soldier, who didn't seem to be concerned. "What's happening?"

"They're here for us, Majesty."

For us?

"They want to join. They want to fight in Fairmont."

"Oh," she said. She looked at the long lines. Dozens. Maybe hundreds. "Wow."

Mykel was talking with some men off to the right, and Nara walked over to meet with them. As she approached, Mykel looked to her and spoke to the men, who took a knee and lowered their eyes.

"Stand up," she said. "Please."

They stood slowly, apprehensively, and she introduced herself, shaking hands with many of them. "I'm Nara."

The men smiled and shook her hand vigorously.

"Your plan worked," Mykel said. "They want to join. Jahmai thinks we'll have close to seven hundred before we leave today."

She nodded. Seven hundred. More than they expected, for sure. They didn't have seven hundred swords, though. Or seven hundred suits of armor. But with a couple of weeks of travel before Fairmont, they'd find time to make spears along the way. She smiled.

They might have a chance after all.

The trek north from Ankar would be a challenging one with such numbers. Jahmai explained that with such a force, Kayna would know they were coming long before they arrived, so scouts would perform reconnaissance along the advance flanks to prevent an ambush. They would avoid travel through narrow passes. And because carrying enough food for such an army would slow them down, much of it would be purchased along the way.

They piled food for the initial march into wagons. They purchased other supplies and equipment, including tents for sleeping, medical use, and a command center, and grabbed as many weapons as they could from the Ankar outposts and local weaponsmiths. Jahmai even bought two bone cepps from a nobleman whose steward sold them some armor. The cepps were empty, but Nara filled them from her own reserves right away and they now dangled from her belt. They would come in handy if she ran low on strength.

As tedious as the preparations had been, once they were moving, there was an enthusiasm in the air. Young soldiers sang and laughed as they marched, confident in victory and eager to begin the contest.

Nara spent much of the early trip walking among the soldiers, listening to their stories and asking about their families. Most of the newer volunteers were poor and spoke of how they had been mistreated by Fairmont. Some told of friends in nearby villages who had disappeared or been murdered. These people wanted to fight back, but they didn't know how. Laborers, farmers, or simple city folk, few knew anything about real combat, and that would be a big handicap when facing trained soldiers and the Queen's gifted.

They trained in the evenings, breaking into groups of twenty to practice formations. While several elite groups of soldiers trained together, including Jahmai's mounted regulars and the archer corps, many of the others included raw recruits that needed guidance. By the end of the third night, all were accustomed to the routine. Break camp, march until midday, eat lunch, march until sundown, make camp, train, then eat again. Those less suited for battle made spears from trees they'd cut down along the way. Light in the evening was provided by torches at first, enabling them to train in the dark. The routine changed on day five, however, as they stopped in the middle of a large, flat plain near a small group of woods outside the small town of Canty.

"You're not training them tonight?" Nara asked.

"Can't," Jahmai said. "It's too dark, and we're low on torches."

"We should stop earlier in the evening to train in the daylight."

"Hurts our forward progress if we do that," Mykel said, as he walked up to join the discussion. "We will run out of food before we arrive if we don't keep our pace."

"But so many are new. They need training," Nara said.

"Nara, all the training in the world won't make most of these young folks fight much better. The moment they face an armored man with a sword or spear, most of these greenhorns will break no matter what training we give them."

"Well, that's not very encouraging," she said. "Train them anyway. Tonight. Even if it doesn't help them fight, it helps them have hope. They need hope more than anything. I need hope more than anything."

"No light. How could we—"

Right then, in the middle of the camp, Nara rose on a column of earth high into the air, then flared the light rune. The entire plain lit up with her brilliance, approaching daylight in its intensity, like a new sun. The suddenness of it must have scared many because they dropped their tents or bedrolls with the sudden illumination.

"Holy Dei," some said.

"Praise Him," said others.

After a few moments, Nara shouted. "Get to work. To your drills!"

For two hours, the tired army drilled, practicing formations, charges, regrouping, and shield work. Legs ached from the long day of marching, but hopes were high, and they trained with fervor. When Jahmai finally called for them to retire, Nara stayed alight long enough for them to erect tents and build fires.

So it went for the next week. March during the day, then train at night by the light of Nara. She became their inspiration, and they became hers. Spending most of the day walking among them, she learned their names, their fears, and their hopes for the future of the Great Land. Some cried when she hugged them, others saluted. Still others knelt and prayed. Despite the frustration she felt with Dei, the men of her army seemed to have no such problem with their faith, praising Him and calling her 'angel.' Some said the evening sun who guided them was the 'Light of Dei.'

Nara tried to dissuade them at first but, eventually, gave up. Since she didn't have much of her own anymore, the piety of these simple, honorable people would be useful in carrying them forward. To win this fight, they would need every bit of hope they could get.

31

ASSAULT

Gwyn was no stranger to wilderness survival. Hunting, fishing, and making shelters were activities that occupied her life as a young watcher, but she'd never been required to perform those tasks in the company of a seven-foot-tall half-naked barbarian cursed who could barely speak. And she'd always been given a purpose, someone to follow, someone to watch. Something to do. Now, however, they just waited. For Anne. "Find the boy," the old woman said, "then I'll find you."

Their first night in the wild was uneventful, and Yury's obvious gratitude kept him close. They stole some clothing for him from a shop in a small town, and all was well as they kept moving their camp, always staying less than a day's walk from the compound. Several days later, however, he began to wander, watching the roads intently and even following groups of soldiers from time to time. His words started to come back, but he still spoke in fits and starts. Slow progress.

At least finding food was no problem, her vision and his speed making it easy to hunt. Yury had even taken to fishing. He'd stand in a stream, motionless, watching, then, like lightning, he had a dagger through the gills of their lunch, its tail flapping in futility.

One afternoon, several days after the rescue, they sat around a fire eating a fairly large sheefish, when Yury remembered something.

"I have family," he said.

There it was. This would change things. "Yes, you do."

"Sister."

"Yes."

It was bound to happen, and she worried what he'd do when he remembered. She'd allied with a giant racer who now carried a grudge and plenty of ability to act on it. But to attack a compound full of armed men would be foolishness. They'd surely have increased the guard by now, probably augmented by gifted warriors, and stealth would no longer be their ally. It'd be brute force against a vastly superior enemy with better arms and a fortification.

"We will save her," Gwyn said. "I have friends coming to help."

It was an empty promise, but it might stall him. She hoped so. Anne should find her, and if she was with Nara and Mykel, they could attack the compound straight on, even against several gifted. She pictured Nara leaping over the wall, or perhaps Mykel smashing right through. Earth would trap the legs of soldiers, and they could save every child in the compound in just a few minutes. But Gwyn and Yury alone would be a different story. They could kill a few soldiers, then would be slowed by efforts to rescue the children. There was no way of making an exit, and they would need to escape through one of the gates. That would require fighting nearly every soldier in the compound, including gifted. Suicide.

"When?" he asked.

"Um. I'm not sure. Soon."

"Two," he said. Then shook his head, struggling to articulate. "Days. I wait two."

"Okay." Frustrated, she didn't know what else to say. The boy wanted his sister, and Gwyn had failed to save her. He would go alone if he had to.

Where are you, Anne?

The two days passed, and despite her reluctance, it was time for Gwyn to make good on her promise. Both she and Yury crouched near the edge of the tree line overlooking the outpost. As expected, the compound had fortified the guard, even building more sentry towers and adding lighting. Gwyn's eyes surveyed the torches that now circled the outpost, seeing some even scattered about the open area on posts between the trees and the fortification's walls.

"We can't approach without being seen," she said.

He turned to her, smiling, then pointed at the nearest torch post. "Burn."

Burn it? She looked at the posts, torches flaring. Interesting. And it might work. Yury was fast enough, for sure. It would be hard to hit him with an arrow unless they got lucky. Even if they did, he could heal. "If you stack enough torches at the base of the wall, it will surely alight. Heck, they use oil sealer to keep that wood from rotting. Should go up pretty quick."

He nodded.

"The buildings are all made of brick, so the children should be fine, and the chaos will be to our advantage."

"Gate." He pointed at the western gate. "Out."

Their escape. They'd have to get the gate open. Children didn't climb walls very well.

"After you start the fire on the east side, we'll go around the outpost and enter over the western wall. It'll be a lot of running, for both of us, and we will battle several guards on the way to the main building to rescue the kids. I'm not sure how we'll get in, but maybe we'll get lucky."

"We go." Yury jumped to his feet, heading straight at the first torch.

"No! Not that way. Other side. East." The look on his face showed that he didn't know what east meant. "Follow me."

They headed straight south, then east, skirting the wall, then north again. There was no gate on the eastern wall, but the open area had plenty of torches.

"Whenever you're ready. Get the wall burning, then come back here and we'll circle around again."

Yury dashed away. Gwyn watched the first torch disappear— the speed of his run had blown it out. He paused at the second torch, using it to relight the first, then continued at a slower pace. He'd acquired four before a sentry saw him.

"Hey!"

Yury ran straight for the sentry, throwing one of his torches at the tower, missing. He dropped the other three at the base of the wall. Arrows flew in the half-darkness, but he dodged them easily, then raced back as they raised the alarm. He grabbed several more torches, then sprinted for another part of the wall where he dropped them at the base.

"Fire!" shouted another guard. They were slow to react. "Get the buckets!"

The front gate opened and soldiers, carrying buckets of water, tried to douse the first blaze, but Yury had started a third fire now, near the southeast corner.

Gwyn rose to her feet and started running the perimeter of the wall, expecting Yury to join her, but when she looked for him, he was nowhere to be found.

She looked at the southern wall. The sentry towers were empty, save one. She ran straight for the guard, nocking an arrow as she bolted across the open area that separated her from the compound. He saw her just as she shot, the shaft impaling his neck before he slumped, eyes wide in surprise. She threw the bow over her shoulder and launched herself for the wall, hand over hand to the top, then over the other side. As she descended, she looked around, seeing soldiers carrying buckets to the eastern sentry towers. They stormed up the ladders and threw the water over the side. One of them saw her just as her feet hit the ground. He dropped his bucket and drew a sword just in time to catch an arrow through the heart.

Gwyn ran and hid behind the field latrine. The stench was overwhelming, but she needed time to survey the scene. The rear door of the main building opened, and a guard stepped out. Aiming with her bow, she had almost loosed the arrow, when a blur took the man off his feet, dropping the soldier to the ground with a gaping wound in his neck, then disappearing into the building. Yury.

Gwyn sprinted across the yard to the building and checked the fallen guard for the keys. She found a chain with half a dozen large keys attached to his belt. After grabbing them, she dashed through the door and found two more guards inside, twitching on the floor, expiring from loss of blood, gaping wounds visible on their necks. Yury stood outside a giant cage, holding a bloody dagger. Inside, the frightened eyes of a dozen children were fixed on the barbarian.

"No," he said, looking at the children who ranged from about ten years old to maybe sixteen.

"She's not here?"

"No."

Well, they were in this far, so they might as well save the kids, if they could. Gwyn approached the cage, looking at the lock and trying to guess which key would fit. A sound from the left caught their attention, and Gwyn fumbled with the keys as she turned to see four guards coming down a stairwell from the second story. A moment later, one of Gwyn's swords disappeared from its sheath on her back and Yury was across the room, engaging them one at a time as they approached.

She fumbled again with keys. She placed another one in the lock, turned it, and the tumbler released with a click. The huge cage door swung open, and Gwyn beckoned to the children inside. Several were crying.

"Come. This is your chance. We're here to save you," she said.

Two of the older children rounded up the smaller ones and started to herd them out of the cage. Gwyn led them out the back door, following Yury. As they entered the main yard of the outpost, heat from the burning wall hit Gwyn on the left side of her face, and she tried to shield several children with her body. The entire eastern wall was ablaze, and the fire had now moved to the southern wall.

"Get to the gate," she yelled, holding her arms out to direct the children toward the west. One of the smaller ones screamed and darted back toward the door, but Gwyn caught him by the back of his shirt and pulled, then kicked the door closed. The boy turned, a terrified look on his face. Gwyn grabbed him by the arm, pulling to follow the others, who were running after Yury.

"Projects escaping!" The shout was from the north, a single soldier running straight at Yury, sword drawn.

Yury broke from the group to engage the soldier who wore a different-looking tabard than the others. Black. A gifted. Yury closed the distance between the two, sword brandished, and in a whirl of steel, his blade sliced across the soldier's neck. The man remained standing, with no apparent wound from Yury's attack. He was a steelskin. Yury paused in surprise, giving the soldier time to slash a blade across Yury's ribs.

Gwyn engaged her sight to see a cepp glowing under the soldier's armor at his waist. She thought to launch an arrow, but it would just bounce off the man's skin, so she rushed the children along toward the west gate. Yury would have to handle that one himself.

As she approached the gate, she saw a guard in the southwest tower, holding a bow, about to shoot. She beat him to it, launching two arrows at once, both landing in his torso and sending his own arrow flying far wide. Another soldier, spear in hand, was running along the western wall toward her. Her arrow found his shoulder before he could engage, and he dropped his sword long enough for her to put another shaft through his forehead. But she was running low on arrows.

Gwyn hurried the children along the wall, almost to the gate, grateful that the fire had not yet spread along the walls this far. As they approached, three guards blocked the exit and one stood in the tower, but their attention was focused on the raging fire. She directed the kids to hide on the south side of one of the small buildings, then launched her remaining arrows at the soldiers. The tower guard was dead, along with two of the others, but the third now closed in on her, forcing her to drop the bow and draw her remaining sword.

She dodged his first thrust and countered with a slash across his lower back that glanced off his armor. Foolish. She should have gone for the back of his neck. She ducked to avoid a sweep of his blade and slashed his boot, her sword biting deep. He fell, grabbing his foot in pain. She thrust forward with the tip of her sword, piercing the leather under his arm to impale his lung.

A moment later, she disengaged the three bolts that held the western gate and strained to push it open. Two of the older boys came to her aid, and the gate moved enough for them to escape.

"Go," Gwyn said as the children rushed through the opening. "Run! As fast as you can. To the nearest town. Tell everyone what is happening and hide from any soldiers."

Just then, a door on the small northwestern project building exploded open, bursting off its hinges. Gwyn squared herself to face the threat, heart pounding. She had no bow, only one sword, would have soldiers on her any moment, and now this. Stooping and angling its body sideways to get through the opening, a giant emerged and turned to face Gwyn. The creature was a foot taller than Yury and twice as wide. It didn't have a weapon or armor, but Gwyn doubted it would need one to kill her.

Holy Dei, help me.

It charged.

Gwyn sidestepped as it passed her, reaching with its massive arms. A finger brushed her, almost catching her leather tunic, and she spun in midair, sweeping her sword at the monster as she whirled, the blade biting into its forearm. It bellowed and Gwyn landed awkwardly on the ground, wrenching a shoulder with the impact before scrambling to her feet to face her opponent.

It charged again, and she ducked, then sidestepped to the right. It was fast for something so huge, but not as fast as she was, and her blade found its left thigh, slicing deep. She turned to face it again. It stumbled and braced itself against the wall, the leg wound bleeding. Then it stood upright and the wound on its leg closed. Healed.

Uh oh.

Even if she stabbed this monster in the heart, he would probably survive. It was a cursed with a health rune, like Mykel and Yury, and she would have no chance. She looked about for Yury, but he was nowhere to be found—probably still engaged with the steelskin or other soldiers.

The monster reached to the roof of the short building and grabbed the edge, ripping off a rafter, and destroying the roof in the process. A strength rune, too. This was just getting worse!

It took several steps forward, positioning itself between her and the open gate. No exit. Gwyn flared her vision to see two runes, one on each leg, flaring hot. Strength and health. And now it wielded a seven-foot club.

She turned and ran, and almost made it to the open area near the field latrine when she felt a crushing impact against her right shoulder and upper back, sending her sprawling forward to the ground. A dull pain echoed through her back and down her arm, forcing her to lose the grip on her sword. She turned to look through blurred vision and saw the giant's makeshift club lying on the ground next to her. He had thrown it, and now she was out of the fight.

Rolling onto one side, she reached for her dagger with her left hand and tried to look back at the monster but couldn't focus. The children were safe, and, hopefully, so was Yury, but she would die right here. But she wouldn't go easily, and if she could stab this monster once more before he crushed her skull, it would be the best she could hope for.

Her fingers tightened on the dagger and her heartbeat raced as the monster loomed close, standing just beyond her reach and holding another giant rafter over its head. This was her executioner, and his axe was about to fall.

Then a blur knocked the club from the beast's hands. Two wounds appeared on the side of its torso. It screamed and spun, looking for the new threat.

Yury circled back around, stabbing at the giant beast, but each time the wounds closed. The giant retrieved its club and engaged, but Yury was too fast and delivered strike after strike, wounds appearing all over the monster's chest, then fading as the beast flared health.

Over to the right, Yury stopped, far from the giant's reach. His torso was drenched in blood, and he was heaving hard, obviously exhausted. His light was low, and he was running out of strength. She looked at the giant, whose light burned brightly. Yury was outmatched.

"Run!" Gwyn said.

But Yury charged, and the giant's club took him square in the chest, knocking him at least twenty feet. He screamed in pain and rolled, stunned, probably with broken ribs. Hopefully, he could heal and still escape with the strength he had left.

"Yury, go! It's too strong!"

Gwyn struggled weakly to her feet and brandished the dagger at the beast, hoping to delay him long enough for Yury to escape. Her head swam with the pain in her shoulder and back, and she strained to focus on the monster before her. It turned its attention to her once again, then charged.

Then she felt the grip of strong hands tightening around her, followed by a rush of wind through her hair. In the confusion, the dagger in her hand slipped free. She struggled to escape the tight grip on her, but pain racked her body. Through dreary eyes, she caught images of the retreating walls of the outpost. She was being carried, but it wasn't the monster who held her.

Yury.

She closed her eyes and let him whisk her away.

32

THE PASS

Nara stood on the high hill at the vanguard of her army, overlooking the final pass that would take them into the slopes that descended into Fairmont. Jahmai wanted them to skirt this chokepoint, veering far to the east, worried that Kayna's forces would ambush and destroy them as they move through the pass, but Nara wanted the army to rest and refused to take the detour.

To the northwest, the twin peaks of Mount Fi towered over the other mountains, adding to the dread of the impending conflict. The battle would be joined tomorrow, most likely. If they could get through the pass and form up, that was. But the troops would be tired, and a debate had raged much of last night. Rest today and go through the pass tomorrow, or charge forward today and end up fighting tired in the morning?

Nara had finally ordered them to rest while she watched for enemy troop movement. They would go through the pass early in the morning, before sunrise, long before Kayna's general could form up his lines.

Mykel joined her on the high hill. "Reminds me of Dimmitt."

Nara cocked an eyebrow. "How so?"

"Not really, I suppose. Big city, giant mountains. Nothing like Dimmitt at all. I guess it's just the feeling. You and I standing together and looking down, right before the announcement. Wondering what tomorrow holds."

"Oh. I see what you mean. Last time we were in this position, things didn't go as planned."

"Tomorrow will be different."

"I hope you're right."

He smiled with confidence. "I am."

She looked back, scanning the peaks above the pass for enemies who might rain arrows down on her troops.

"No enemy," Mykel said. "I've been racing around the hills and there are only a few scouts. She's not worried about me at all."

"Apparently not."

"She thinks she can take you. And she thinks her army can take ours. She's probably right about the army part."

"Yeah, I know. It will all be up to me."

Mykel shrugged. "I'll help. She doesn't have an answer for what I'm bringing to the fight. Not at all."

Evening came, and the troops rested but Nara stayed awake on a high cliff, watching on the slopes below for signs of enemy activity.

Far in the distance, she saw torches moving on the plains just outside Fairmont, but they weren't close enough to bring alarm.

The fight would occur on the lower slopes of the Twins. Strange how that had worked out. Bylo believed the Twins' importance to the church was based on an error in translation, yet this battle would rage under their watch.

She thought about the scripture that Bylo thought so important:

'And the phyili was put asunder; separated, but not destroyed. Each defied the other, bringing conflict, pain, and death to many. In the end, only one remained.'

She hoped that the part about pain and death to many was

wrong. War was far from ideal, but she didn't know of another way to end this, and it was too late for a change of plans now.

Dawn was still hours away and with no sign of the enemy approaching, Nara moved down from her vantage point and toward her troops. Some rose and prepared for the final push, Jahmai among them.

"When do you want it?" she asked.

"Any time. Try not to shine much farther ahead than our troops. They know we're here but won't expect us until dawn and I'd like to give as little notice as possible. Time to get through the pass and form up before they can block us."

"Agreed."

She climbed high on the cliffs once again, finding her way in the dark with her vision, rising through the hills and low mountains to find a small outcropping that faced the path below. Flaring the light rune, she shined on her army, bringing dawn far earlier than normal.

A short time later, the soldiers marched and drove their wagons ahead, guided by the temporary sun that was their inspiration. Horses, archers, infantry, all moved as fast as they could through the pass toward Fairmont. Mykel and the other scouts manned the peaks, watching for enemy activity and giving reports to both Nara and Jahmai. Kayna's general remained low on the plains, just outside Fairmont. At least three thousand troops camped with him, but they hadn't yet formed battle lines.

Three thousand enemy troops. Wow. She was far outmatched, but her army had hope, and they were the forces of good, locked in a battle with dark forces. If Dei existed, and the scriptures were true, then he had defeated Kai in an epic struggle long ago. He refused to let evil have the final say, and although He seemed to care little about individual people, or the pain that some people spread about, He might care about the big stuff. Nara hoped so. If there had ever been a demon of Kai on this earth, Kayna was it.

They must win this fight. There was no other choice.

33

BATTLE LINES

Dawn was breaking, and as Anne approached the outskirts of Fairmont, she considered what must happen next. Gwyn would be waiting somewhere to the east, but as Anne looked ahead to the slopes of the Twins, she could see the torches of Fairmont's army as they marched, forming up a camp on the plains between the city and the mountains. Nara's army would be in those mountains and coming to clash with the enemy soon.

Anne wouldn't make it in time. Too old. Too slow. Her back was weak, her calves ached, and far too few had given her rides, making this one of the longest walks she'd endured in many years. If she could find Gwyn soon, perhaps the message would arrive in time. Everything depended on it.

The sound of a racing wagon behind her forced Anne to step off the road, and she raised her walking stick in protest at the driver as he passed, going far too quickly in the near-darkness. The back of the wagon was filled with sacks, probably grain for Fairmont's armies.

She summoned the resolve to step up her pace despite the discomfort, and, several hours later, found her way into a forest near the northern slopes of the Twins. After another hour of wandering the woods, she took a rest, sitting on an old, dead stump.

"I wondered when you'd get here."

Anne turned to see Gwyn, whose right arm rested in a sling. A large Roska stood behind her.

"Hello," Anne said to Yury, nodding her head in greeting.

"Hi."

"You're quite tall," Anne said. "Didn't expect that, I guess."

"Did we surprise you?" Gwyn asked.

She nodded. "Don't sneak up on old women," Anne said. "It's rude."

"I've never surprised you before. Are you okay?"

Anne tried to stand but failed, slumping back down. "He doesn't show me much anymore, but never mind that. I have something for you to do. Can you travel?"

"Yes."

She pulled the cup from her pack and handed it to Gwyn. "Get this to Nara," she said, then pointed in the direction of the pass near the Twins. "She should be in those hills. Coming through the pass this morning, if she hasn't already."

"What does it do?"

"It's her most important lesson. The one she missed when she ran off to save the world, the silly girl."

Gwyn cleared her throat and adjusted her sling. "Um, there's something else. Kayna has a cursed."

"Does she? That won't go well. Doesn't surprise me, though." She looked at Yury again. "Looks like you have one, too."

"Kayna's cursed is an angry one. And huge. I hope Mykel can take him," Gwyn said. "Even without a weapon, he was too much for us."

"Just get Nara the cup. She'll figure out what it means. And be careful with that shoulder."

Gwyn leaned in to give Anne a gentle embrace. "Sure you're not coming?"

"I'll head that direction when I've taken a rest. Now go." Anne turned to Yury. "Take care of this one, big boy. She's important."

———

Gwyn and Yury set out at a furious pace, heading for the pass. It had been several days since freeing the children at the compound, and in her injured state, she had not been able to make sure the children found safety. When they went looking, she and Yury found tracks leading to nearby villages, so she hoped they were safe from Fairmont for now.

The pain from Gwyn's injuries had persisted, and her back and shoulder protested each step. Something was torn, perhaps even broken. Another few days of rest and she might draw a bowstring, but she would not wield a sword for a while.

As the sun climbed the horizon, they skirted the woods at the base of the Twins, far from the assembling army near Fairmont. Their path carried them high through the hills and into the peaks, where they saw a second light, growing in intensity as they came closer. It was multicolored, and almost as bright as the sun but coming from the wrong direction.

Nara.

Once they got close enough, they could see that the army that accompanied Nara was small, nothing like the numbers Fairmont now assembled on the slopes nearby, and far too few wore armor. There were perhaps three dozen horses, so there would be minimal cavalry, and even fewer carried bows. Most of the army appeared to be civilians with wooden spears, if they could be called that, not even bearing steel spearheads. Pointed sticks. It wouldn't be enough. Not against Kayna. Not against her army. And not against her cursed monster.

Gwyn climbed the peaks toward Nara, guided by the blinding light that was her friend. Soon, she was by her side, her arm in front of her face to shield her eyes from the intensity.

"I've never seen someone disguise themselves as a sun before," Gwyn said. "Might want to let the real thing take over from here."

Nara turned, extinguishing her light, eyes widening. "Gwyn!"

They embraced.

"Easy on the shoulder," Gwyn said. "Still smarts."

"What happened?"

"Lost a fight with a giant. I'm lucky to be breathing."

"This him?" Nara asked, pointing to Gwyn's large companion.

"No. Different giant. Much bigger. This is Yury."

Yury stepped forward, offering a hand, and Nara shook it, his hand engulfing hers.

"Boy, you are big," Nara said. "Welcome to our little rebellion—we can use all the help we can get." She turned back to Gwyn. "Where's Anne?"

"Coming. I think. Slowly. I have something for you." Gwyn reached into belt pack and pulled out the cup, then handed it to Nara.

"What's this?"

"A message from Anne. She said you'd figure it out."

"I'll look at it later," Nara said, stuffing it into her own pack. "I have so much to tell you, but first, let me tend to that shoulder."

Kayna sat on a simple throne atop a stage near the back of her assembling forces. General Almit was still giving a briefing on the pending conflict, armored in full plate with the royal tabard on his chest.

"Why didn't you rush them this morning?" Kayna asked.

"Last report was they were two days out," he said. "They came fast and started early through the pass today. Surprised us. Not sure how they moved so well in the dark—something is motivating these troops. We could have attacked with some forces, but the full army was slow to assemble. So many were still on details to villages. Your orders, Majesty."

"How many do they have?"

"Less than a thousand. Most are irregulars. Civilians with makeshift weapons. Spears. Axes. Less than three hundred actual soldiers. Maybe seventy archers, but they will have a lot of range at first. Their backs are to the Twins, and the forest covers their flank. Great position for them, until they break and run. There will be no escape except for the pass. I already have a hundred archers that will move on the pass to pick them apart when they try to escape.

"Gifted?"

"Our watchers pick out four gifted, maybe five. Aside from the cursed."

"And her."

"Yes, aside from her. We have the cursed, six bears, three racers, and a handful of flamers. Some steelskins here and there, but some may be new. I'm not expecting much from those."

"That's all?"

"Many are absent without leave, Majesty. Unhappy with the state of things, I guess. Traitorous of them to abandon us like this. We've made efforts to track them down, but gifted are bolder and harder to control than normal soldiers."

That was unfortunate. Not that it would make the difference. Still, she held the advantage and would get her chance to put this nonsense to rest. Despite the elevation advantage, Kayna had almost four thousand troops, more than half of the Great Land's entire army in one place. It was a shame she couldn't have assembled more, but the barbarian raids in the north and the village raids kept them too busy. Nevertheless, Almit would charge with heavy cavalry, hundreds of archers, more than a dozen gifted and two cursed. She might not need to fight at all.

"Tell Ennis to get Beast ready. Armor, hammer, and shield. He's eager to please and has been fabulous this past week. Hold him back for the initial clash, though. I don't want to risk him when they are strong. After that, send him in. Break their spirits."

"Yes, Majesty." He did an about-face, then took a step to leave.

"And, Jordan?"

He turned back, taking a position at attention. "If things go badly, I'll step in. Just make sure I have what I need."

"We've stayed many executions, Majesty. You'll have plenty."

Kayna smiled. "Excellent work, General. Thank you."

34

——————

ADVANCE

Nara stood next to Jahmai at the front of the assembled army, high on the slope, surveying the enemy below. Kayna's numbers had grown since the scouts saw them last night, and they had plenty of archers. The front line was, at least, eight ranks of infantry, perhaps fifty men wide. They bore spears and shields that would best withstand a charge by putting the butts of the spear shafts in the ground as Nara's cavalry tried to break their lines.

"We shouldn't attack first," Jahmai said. "Wait and let the enemy move uphill, with our archers picking them apart on the initial contact."

It was a safe tactic that didn't account for Nara's abilities. Nor did it start the conflict off with passion.

"Smart, but playing it safe won't get us a victory today," Nara said. "No, we need a spark to light a fire in the hearts of our Troops. Get some courage flowing. We will not sit back and be victims; we will attack first."

Nara turned and looked at her army. As she surveyed the soldiers, citizens, young men and women, she wondered which would die today. Tired, but bearing smiles on their faces, they stood at attention. Proud to be here.

Derik was near the front line, his leg now strong, shield held tight. Lieutenant Martel sat mounted at the front of the cavalry off to Nara's right, his back straight, arm held in a salute. Mykel stood next to Gwyn and Yury at the far left. Gwyn held her bow, and her shoulder was now strong. Yury had a small sword and leather cuirass, light and good for fast movement. He would be useful today. Mykel had no armor, as always, bare feet eager to move as his toes squeezed the turf. He held the staff tight, base planted in the ground, his eyes forward, and his presence comforted Nara.

Hardy people, these warriors of hers. Outnumbered and enduring many days of marching, they now faced superior numbers, better weaponry, and many gifted. Gwyn said that Kayna had a cursed, but, hopefully, it would be no match for Mykel. As Nara surveyed her waiting troops, she wondered what to say before the battle began. How would she share her pride without also sharing her fear for what the day might hold? She wanted to talk of Dei, how He blesses them, and how He would keep them safe, but she knew it wasn't true. Dei didn't seem to concern himself with the individual sufferings of His people. If He did, the land would be a very different place indeed. No, He seemed to care only about the big picture, and she would not mislead them with false hopes.

"At ease," she said, and the entire army moved to a wider stance, placing their hands at the small of their backs in a relaxed position.

She flared the sound rune to amplify her voice. Her words rumbled with an unnaturally deep tone. "There will be no parley today. I will not meet with the enemy general or the monster who calls herself Queen. I will strike no deals. No land exchanged for peace. This is neither a dispute between lords nor a show for political gain. This is bigger than that, and I intend to kill her."

It was odd to hear those words come out of her mouth. She had failed to kill Kayna when she had the chance and hoped she would have the resolve to follow through this time. Her army did not sense her hesitation, however, instead cheering at her words. After a moment, she held up a hand to quiet them.

"Never have I heard of an army marching on Fairmont. The histories say nothing of rebellion against dark lords or ladies. We do something new today. We stand up for what is good and what is right."

She walked parallel to the front line of her troops, squads of mixed infantry, soldiers, and citizens who had trained together for far too little time. "I'm proud of you. You are not here for money. Probably not for glory either. You're here because people have suffered, and you're willing to stand with me against a villain and put an end to the injustice."

Nara paused, then stopped in front of a young man holding a spear. "This is Theron," she said, trying to make her voice as loud as she could. "He lives in a village near Kinnick and joined us on the march north. A detail killed his father and kidnapped his brother while he was fishing for their dinner." She walked along the line. "Theron loves horses. Wants to work in a stable someday. He has spent much of the march helping our cavalry care for their mounts, brushing their coats, checking their shoes. But today he holds a spear. Today he fights."

She stopped in front of a young woman holding an axe. She was tall, broad-shouldered, and athletic. "This is Penny. She is nineteen, the daughter of a weaver, and lives near Ankar. Penny has a beautiful voice and loves to sing. A detail took her friend Paola." Nara pointed to an older man in his fifties with a silver beard, holding a small sword and wearing a leather cap that covered his ears. "Over here is Kitt. He used to cook for the northern outpost of Ankar. He won't feed soldiers today; he'll fight by their side."

Nara flared earth and rose slowly on a pillar of rocks and soil. "You are more than a citizen army. You are the spirit of this nation. Each of you represents what is good about the Great Land. You are the people who work hard every day, feeding your families and friends, and you expect a just monarch to protect you and nurture you. You deserve peace, but you've received persecution. I am neither a goddess, as some of you have called me, nor an angel;

I'm just someone with an important job, to lead you forward into a void that must be filled. Someone must stand up for our children. For our elderly. For our mothers and fathers. That someone is Penny. It is Derik. It is Kitt. It is you. And it is me. We have a date with destiny today, and I don't know how it will be written in the end, but know this." She flared light and shone on them for a brief moment, then let it fade. "The power of heaven lies deep in our hearts and only fear holds us back from letting it loose to do great things. Follow me with courage and love, fight for your fellow man, with your fellow man, shoulder to shoulder in this righteous effort. Fear has no place on these slopes today. Banish it from your thoughts, move boldly forward, take heart, and we will win the day. There is nothing that can stand against us."

The army cheered, clapping and banging swords on shields, the hoots and calls lasting until Nara waved her arms for them to stop. She hoped those words were enough. They would know soon. She looked at Jahmai, who nodded, then she turned back to her army. "Attention!"

Hundreds of bodies snapped to attention, cavalry raising their spears in salute.

"Cavalry with me," Nara said loudly, then turned to face the army below, willing the earth to lower her back to the ground. She stepped forward, then looked at Martel at the front of the group. In time with him, she began to run forward, flaring speed to match the pace of the galloping horses. She looked to the right and saw Mykel advancing as well, the infantry forming up behind him in a spear-point formation and breaking into a run.

It took only moments for Nara's initial thrust to cross several hundred yards of sloping terrain, and the first volley of arrows from Nara's archers rose high overhead, coming down on the rear ranks of Kayna's troops. Several shafts found their way through shields and struck home, men falling in response. A heartbeat later, while still in a full sprint, Nara flared earth, and the ground erupted along Kayna's front line, the first two ranks of soldiers losing their footing. Many fell, and those that remained upright soon scattered, unable to meet the cavalry charge with their spears. Nara's cavalry plowed through Kayna's front lines, devastating the first few ranks of the enemy.

A few moments later, Mykel and Yury hit the other side of the infantry almost as hard as the cavalry's heavy horses, scattering men on the unstable ground.

The battle had begun.

Nara flared speed and strength, darting among the enemy, smashing wrists and breaking ribs, thinking of Sammy as she did so. And Nilly. Of the little girl she had found near Took. Anger drove her forward. When she was deep in the belly of the infantry line, she dropped to a knee and flared motion, sending the enemy flying in every direction away from her.

Moments later, Kayna's second line of infantry stepped forward to join the fray. Nara ran, leaping over enemies to reach her own lines once again, hoping that the initial thrust would both motivate her troops and demoralize Kayna's.

A black banner rose off to her right, and she scanned for Mykel. He didn't see it, fighting well forward of the rest of her troops, his back to the banner. Nara sprinted for the area and saw three enemy gifted in black tabards plowing through the lines. Gwyn was near, launching arrows at the gifted, but the shafts bounced harmlessly off the leader. The two that flanked him carried giant mauls that they wielded in sweeping arcs, crushing Nara's troops and sending them flying.

A steelskin and two bears.

Nara flared earth. A stone pit appeared under their feet, and all three were swallowed up in an instant. The sudden impact with the rock floor of the pit wouldn't have hurt the steelskin but might have injured the bears. Just then, one of the bears leaped out of the pit, but he no longer held his maul. Two arrows from Gwyn took him in the chest, and he slumped, dead. Nara's troops cheered and pushed on.

From behind her, she heard "racer!" Turning, she saw a red banner in the center of the fray. She flared earth again, trying to keep her wits about her and quell the passion. The ground around the banner shook, becoming pitted and uneven. There were screams and shouts, then the banner came down. Racer dead, and because of Nara. How many more deaths would she cause today?

The rush of fear and energy from the start of the battle subsided as Nara looked about to gather her bearings, and she began to notice the screams of the wounded. Several medics were dragging victims back behind the lines for care, but there was no time for her to assist; she had to fight.

She rose on a short pillar of earth to better view the battlefield. To the right, Yury battled another racer, a tall woman who was giving him quite the contest. Mykel was still at the front, crushing skulls and launching the enemy in every direction. She sensed him through the earth, confident and powerful. He'd received a few blows but suffered no great injuries. The battle was going well.

A wave of fatigue swept over Nara, to no surprise. So much activity in a short time. Her hand reached to her belt, fingers finding one of the cool bone cepps that dangled there. She closed her eyes and absorbed the energy, replenishing her strength. She leaped down from her pillar and darted to the right toward cries of alarm from her infantry, only to see two flamers, side by side, cutting a swath through her troops, burning them alive. Each held a cepp in their hand, magic that fueled their attack.

She called the magic of their cepps and it came, filling her reserves even more and robbing them of their power. Moments later, spears cut the two flamers down.

A great roar from the rear of Kayna's army caught her attention. She looked toward the middle of the enemy throng and spotted a giant soldier in white armor, shield, and helm charging directly up the middle of the formation. Nara used her vision and was nearly blinded by the light from his armor. Imbued bone armor! He held a giant war hammer, and when he hit the front line, he swept the weapon back and forth, decimating Nara's infantry, knocking soldiers back dozens of feet with each blow. Ten fell in a heartbeat. Another ten. Many broke ranks and fled toward the flanks. He was huge!

Then he turned and looked at Nara, his eyes burning like hot coals. He bellowed and sprinted straight for her, even knocking some of his own troops out of the way as he ran.

Kayna's cursed.

Nara flared earth, and a wall of rock erupted from the ground in the monster's path, but he flared strength and charged through it like it wasn't even there. She summoned another wall, thicker, and it held his initial charge. But instead of going around, he just struck the wall with the hammer, the stone shattering under his awesome strength.

He ran for her again and she noticed that both the armor plates and the shield had runes on them. It was the variant of the protection rune that also decorated Mykel's staff. Nara reached out to the armor, calling its magic to her as she did to the king's armor so long before, but it did not respond, the protection runes blocking her. She tried again, commanding the magic to be hers, but it refused.

Nara flared speed and protection as the monster came close. Some of her infantry tried to intercept, but the beast sent them flying with a strike from his hammer and a bash from his shield. The rest broke and ran.

Three steps away from her, the beast screamed, and she dodged his initial blow easily, dancing to the left. He looked even bigger up close, towering over her. Easily eight feet tall, the monster dwarfed everything on the battlefield, its footsteps thundering as it moved. Arrows bounced off the enchanted armor, helm and shield, as did spears, swords, and axes.

She dodged another strike, and the beast screamed in frustration. As it pursued her, it engaged her infantry, crushing those who attempted to intercede. Nara retrieved a fallen sword and darted in, dodging the monster's attempt to shield-bash her and stabbing between two armored plates, finding its ribs. The bellow of pain it gave nearly knocked her to the ground as she passed by, looking back to see it whirl, undeterred. It charged her again, and she saw it flare health. Health! A cursed with strength and health and bone armor she could not drain.

She flared speed again, hard, with all the strength she had, and launched forward at the beast, dodging another blow from his hammer and searching for a weakness in the beast's armor. As she passed, she flared strength and sliced at a hook that held two of the back plates together. The plates came apart slightly, exposing the underlay of padding.

Just then, a body flew into the monster at full charge, knocking it to the ground. Nara dropped the speed rune and watched as Mykel engaged the creature, the staff now whirling and striking it but the blows having little effect against the armor. The beast howled in rage and charged Mykel, sweeping wide with both shield and hammer, missing repeatedly as it passed. Though his blows seemed to have little effect on the beast, Mykel had the sight rune and could dodge his enemy's attacks.

They battled, trading blows as the monster swung in a wide, sweeping arc with its long arm, finally catching Mykel in the shoulder with the hammer at end of a lucky swing. Mykel tumbled a dozen yards before flaring health. He re-engaged, landing blows on the beast's back where Nara had damaged his armor. But with both Mykel and Nara distracted by the monster, they were no longer pressing the attack against Kayna's troops, and the enemy was now gaining ground.

Nara looked at the battle lines. Enemy cavalry were picking apart her left flank, easily outnumbering Jahmai and his heavy horses.

The beast bellowed again, slamming its shield to the ground. Mykel lost his footing momentarily, then took a shot from the giant hammer directly in his chest. The blow was incredible, sending Mykel flying straight back into a group of enemy soldiers, bowling them over. The beast turned again to Nara, anger in its eyes. She could feel the hatred rolling off the monster, directed squarely at her. It charged, snarling. Why did it loathe her so much?

She flared speed again, hard, knowing that to conserve her energy at this moment would mean failure; the creature was moving too fast. If Mykel could get his arm around the beast's neck, maybe he could strangle it into unconsciousness. She would need to get that helmet off, first. Straight forward she ran, then leaped high, sweeping her sword at the monster's neck where a strap secured the bone helmet to the breastplate. A somersault in the air carried her gracefully onto the earth behind him, then she turned again. It bellowed and spun, frustrated that it couldn't get its hands on her. Nara flared earth with her failing strength, and the ground beneath the monster came up to encase it in a thick cylinder of rock, paralyzing it in place, encasing both its shield and hammer. The rock wouldn't hold it long, but it might be enough for a moment or two.

Mykel sensed her intention and leaped in, landing on the shoulders of the monster to grab the helmet. Good. He pulled it free, falling onto the ground near Nara, and they both looked up at the monster's face.

Recognition struck her in the breast like a physical blow. The monster's features were misshapen, but the face was unmistakable. As if to confirm her suspicions, the beast looked around, scared for a moment, flaring strength to break one hand free. Then it scratched its chin. Exactly like a certain boy she knew. A beautiful friend she thought to be dead.

Dei, no.

The straight black hair, the big brown eyes, the high cheekbones. It was Sammy.

Nara looked at Mykel, who rose to his feet slowly, eyes focused hard on his brother. Then Mykel screamed and dropped the helmet he was holding.

The eight-foot-tall snarling, raging monster was an eleven-year-old boy. Sammy flared strength, screaming, and broke the stone that bound his other arm, then freed his legs. He charged at Nara again. Mykel was still frozen in place, shocked. Everything seemed to be in slow motion, confusion, fatigue and grief overwhelming

Nara. She couldn't move, so overwhelming was the shock of this. She flared protection just as Sammy grabbed her, his mammoth hand around both her ankles. He lifted her and smashed her to the ground, her head impacting the hard earth. She flared protection and strength, trying to wrest herself from his crushing grasp but was unable. He was just too strong.

"Sammy," she said. "It's me–"

He smashed her against the ground yet again, stunning her. Unable to move, she flared sight to get a picture of her surroundings and saw Mykel on Sammy's shoulders. Mykel's arm slipped around Sammy's tree-trunk sized neck and squeezed. Sammy smashed Nara on the ground again, crushing her against the earth. Her head swam, her strength drained by the protection rune that was keeping her alive, and her thoughts faltered. But Mykel's chokehold was having an effect, and Sammy's grip loosened. She reached for the remaining cepp on her waist and absorbed the energy, flaring health as she did so, clarity returning.

The beast that was Sammy slumped forward on its knees, Mykel's arms still around its neck. "Stop, Sammy. Stop. It's Nara. And me!" Mykel cried in frustration as he strangled his brother. Sammy finally let go of Nara.

The battle raged around them, Kayna's superior troops, in greater numbers, gaining ground fast as Nara rose to her feet. They were losing. Kayna had broken their hearts, and Nara hadn't seen it coming.

She flared sight and imagined the attack on Dimmitt, concentrating on Sammy as she did so. The vision came quickly, aided by Sammy's proximity. Nara saw children and adults gathered around the stage near the church. A man atop the platform pointed at a boy who fidgeted with a snare. The boy placed the snare in his pocket as he climbed the steps, but Nara couldn't see his face. A harvester reached for the boy, holding a ceppit in the other hand. The harvester said something, then the boy began to suffer. She concentrated harder, focusing on the boy. For just a moment, she saw the face. It was Simon, Sammy's friend. It wasn't Sammy at all. Lina was wrong.

Nara's heart sank. This monster was indeed Sammy. Kayna had captured him, altered him, turned him against his own family. The cruelty of it stabbed deep, sapping her of resolve, and revealing her own folly. She had been fooled, and her ill-advised anger had tainted every choice she had made since Dimmitt.

She stood and looked at the carnage that grew about her, soldiers running, screaming, and dying on spears and swords as the enemy advanced. It was all her fault. She'd had a sense of the mistake, back in Keetna, when building the cavern. She knew this path was wrong but hadn't trusted herself. Instead, she'd plowed ahead, thinking violence was the only way to resolve this conflict. Another mistake on a huge pile of wrongs committed by her hand. But there was no turning back now.

Kayna's archers rained arrows down on the rear lines. Jahmai called for a retreat, but there was no place to go except the pass. Nara turned to see Mykel tearing the plates of armor from his now-unconscious brother, snapping clasps, hooks, and tearing straps. He then hefted Sammy's giant, unconscious body onto his back with one hand, holding the staff in his other, and strode toward the pass.

Nara turned to look at the advancing men. Far in the back, she saw a rolling platform being pulled by horses. On the platform was Kayna, seated on a throne. Behind the platform was a string of men, half-dressed and shackled to one another, arm to arm.

Nara was both exhausted and demoralized, but Kayna would soon rise, and there would be no way to match her strength.

35

NAMES

Nara ran up the slope, following her retreating forces toward the pass as arrows from Kayna's advancing archers continued to come down. She flared protection and turned—the enemy infantry was in full advance. She flared motion to knock aside a dozen arrows, but she couldn't stop them all. A nearby soldier fell with an enemy arrow shaft through his calf.

Nara flared motion and pushed at more than a dozen of the enemy that were almost upon them, forcing them back into the next line and giving her time to reach the fallen soldier. It was Kitt, the cook, and he was a bloody mess. She flared strength and picked him up, carrying him over her shoulders and running up the slope to join the others. More arrows came down, one narrowly missing them, but she was able to get Kitt into the hands of several others before turning to reassess the retreat.

Jahmai rode up to Nara's side, giving the report.

"They still have almost three thousand fighting men," he said. He looked haggard, and his cheek bled from a shallow cut, blood streaming down to his chin. "We've lost hundreds, probably half of ours, but we have captured their big cursed and killed maybe eight other gifted."

Nara nodded, keeping an eye on the advancing troops, ready to delay them enough to ensure a successful retreat. "If we can escape through the pass, I'll collapse it to bar the way."

"Good idea," Jahmai said. "Try to stall them long enough for us to get all the way to the—" An arrow pierced his throat.

"Ander!" Nara caught him as he fell from the horse, then looked behind them for the source of the arrow. More rained down now, cutting her fleeing troops apart. Then she saw them. Enemy archers were at the pass, high on the rocks above, dozens of them, blocking the escape. They were trapped.

She pulled the arrow from Jahmai's neck, then put her hand over both sides the wound, flaring sight and knitting. The blood escaping the wound slowed, then stopped as the vessels and skin healed. She helped him back atop his horse, but the loss of blood had weakened him.

"Get to the pass," she said, clapping his horse on the rump. "Get them all to the pass," she yelled as the horse trotted away.

The arrows rained down by the hundreds, and Kayna's troops slowed their advance, letting the archers do the work. Nara flared motion and pushed the archers, one at a time, off the cliffs, but her attention was split as she also tried to knock away arrows flying down on what remained of her army. She stumbled on a corpse as she strove to reach a fallen spearman. The corpse was Derik, his eyes open and staring at nothing, sticky blood pooled on his chest from a sword strike.

Grief struck her hard as she looked upon the young man who'd followed her despite great pain. Who followed her because he believed she would save them all. And because he wanted to atone for his wrongs. She had let him down. She had let them all down.

Nara bit her lip as anger boiled up inside. Not just at Kayna but at herself for leading these people into a bloodbath. There wasn't much strength left in her, but she would use her remaining power the best she could.

She turned to the cliffs and flared speed, then raced through her army and through the arrows that rained down. She reached the entrance to the pass before the first of her retreating forces, just as an arrow impacted her shoulder and she stumbled, rolling in a heap of dust and pain. She rose to her feet, chiding herself for leaving protection down in the midst of an arrow storm. She needed her energy, however, and endured the pain, running until she was at the entrance to the pass.

Looking up, she flared earth and the high rocks shook. Eyes closed for better concentration, she flared earth even harder, commanding the earth to fall.

High on the east side of the pass, the rocks moved, shifted, then slid, becoming an avalanche. She could hear the screams of the remaining archers on their perches as the flood of soil and earth enveloped them, swept them off the cliffs, and ended their deadly assault. The rocks came down, thundering directly into the path of her retreating army. She flared sight and earth, sensing the footfalls of the few who'd escaped the avalanche as they climbed up and away. Retreating. Good. She didn't have much strength left, and she needed it for one more thing.

She ran toward the fallen rocks that blocked the pass, the last of the rockfall settling as she arrived. Commanding the earth with her remaining strength, she willed the debris, stones and soil to flatten, to make a path again, clearing the way for her army's escape.

"Come!" she shouted to the closest of her army. Tired, scared citizen-soldiers funneled into the pass, limping and stumbling. Mykel still carried Sammy on his back, and as she ran back toward the battlefield, Nara saw Gwyn and Yury helping injured soldiers into wagons for the retreat.

As Nara returned to the rearguard, Kayna's forces surged forward again, in full advance, now that she had beaten their archers. It was over. There was no way Nara's army could escape through the pass in time. As if to add to the despair of the moment, more than a hundred cavalry broke free of Kayna's army, in full gallop toward the pass and only moments away.

Her cepps were empty, and the weakness in her legs made it clear she had little strength left. She looked about, desperately searching for energy she could make hers. There was nothing. She was alone, again, an army about to crush her, and there was nothing she could do about it.

Anne moved along on her cane, stumbling out of the woods on sore feet as she looked toward the slopes above. The battle raged ahead, and she heard the thundering hooves of horses and riders.

Nara hadn't used the cup. It was all she needed to find victory, but Gwyn had failed to deliver it. Or worse, Nara had dismissed it, caught up in the drama of the confrontation. Without it, Nara could never win this fight, and the end was now near. Perhaps some lives could be saved. Perhaps Nara's. Or maybe Anne could just buy them a little time.

She stopped in place, dropped her backpack, and fished through it. Upon finding the handle of the small ceppit, she pulled it from the pack until it rested on her palms. Smaller than most, but every bit as effective, this was the only chance to save Nara.

She gripped it in her right hand, took a deep breath, and thrust it into her left shoulder, burying it. She screamed with the sudden pain, enduring it as best she could, shuddering with the shock of it but waiting for the magic to do its work, looking for some new power or awareness to rise.

Nothing came. The patch held.

She pulled the ceppit out and stabbed her left thigh through the meat, even as blood from her shoulder made a growing stain on her old tunic. Again, she steeled her resolve to endure the pain, closing her eyes, waiting, looking, hoping to see something more. A moment passed, but no new magic showed its face.

The pain in her thigh grew, and she withdrew the ceppit and opened her eyes. Blood from her shoulder and thigh now pooled on the ground. She plunged the ceppit into her other thigh and fell to her knees with agony but held it in place.

She waited. It shouldn't take this many, should it? She'd never done this before, and it was risky. So much blood lost now, and she was getting dizzy. Closing her eyes again, she concentrated, the screams of advancing troops threatening to distract her. Focusing on her inner self, she saw something on the periphery of her vision.

"Come out, little rune," she said. "Announce yourself. Who are you?"

It came closer, still blurry, indistinct, but slightly sharper. She removed the ceppit from her thigh and tossed it aside, then placed her hands on the ground, focusing with all her attention.

The design came into view. It was the earth rune.

Perfect.

She flared the rune with all her remaining strength and yelled at the top of her lungs, "Uf-fhal!"

And the earth rose.

Nara marveled as the ground beneath Kayna's army shook, then exploded in a shower of rocks and dirt, pits and columns appearing, boulders emerging. The entire cavalry charge would have decimated Nara's fleeing forces but, instead, now collapsed abruptly as horses crashed into one another, fell into pits, or stumbled with the shaking.

Who had done that? She looked around the battlefield, perplexed, not finding the source of that magic. Then she saw it—an old woman on the far side of the slope, collapsed.

Anne. How had she done that?

Nara flared speed and ran, using the earthquake's distraction to cross the distance. As she arrived, she found Anne slumped over, her good eye closed, barely breathing. Blood around her soaked into the earth. So much blood.

Nara fought back a brief dizzy spell, then flared sight and knitting, closing wounds on Anne's shoulder and thighs. It wouldn't replace the lost blood but might keep her from getting worse. Perhaps she'd have a chance, now.

"Oh, dear Anne," she said. "What do I do? I need you. Don't die. Please. Tell me what to do. Should we retreat to Keetna, save who I can? Or keep fighting? Tell me, please. I don't know what to do!"

Anne was mouthing a word, but no sound came out, her shallow breath rasping. Her hand squeezed Nara's insistently, and she tried to say the word again. A single syllable. Nara couldn't tell what it was.

Anne squeezed Nara's hand again, gritting her teeth, then tried to speak, but Nara still couldn't understand. Her lips were trying to form words, but no sound was coming out. Nara focused harder, and then she saw it.

Cup. She was trying to say cup. How foolish, she had forgotten about the cup Gwyn gave her. Nara pulled the cup out of her pack. Wear marks on it made the cup look ancient, and a strange rune was newly scratched upon its face, one she'd never seen before.

She placed it on the ground in front of her, then looked up to see Kayna's forces reassembling. What remained of her cavalry was gathering and would charge again soon.

She looked at Anne, who rested her head on Nara's lap. Anne reached up to touch Nara on the chest. She pushed. Twice. Her mouth moved.

Barely audible, she whispered, "Go," then closed her eyes and fell unconscious on Nara's lap, certainly on the edge of death. But there was nothing more Nara could do.

Oh, Anne, not like this!

She tenderly lifted Anne's tiny form away from the bloody soil, then laid her gently on clean grass several feet away. The vibration of galloping horses got Nara's attention and she looked up to see that Kayna's cavalry had begun another charge.

The cup bore a rune—perhaps that would be useful. Nara raced back to the cup and sat on the ground, looking at the rune. Hands on the ground below to brace herself against another dizzy spell, she closed her eyes and pictured the rune in her mind. It came quickly. She flared it.

An odd feeling came over Nara as images flooded her vision. A boy, sitting on a slope, looking over a long valley and a river. He was eating a sandwich. There was a girl nearby — no, she was closer than that. The image became clearer. The girl was sitting right next to the boy on a blanket, having a picnic lunch together. Young lovers? It made little sense. How could a picnic help fight a battle?

Nara opened her eyes, eager to stall the charge somehow. She stood to her feet and took several steps forward. She couldn't get there in time. She stooped to retrieve an arrow that was sticking out of the ground, preparing to throw it at the lead horse. Perhaps it would stumble and disrupt the charge.

The rune was important, however. Important enough for Anne to insist with what might have been her dying breath. It nagged at her. She was missing something. Summoning the image of the cup's rune again, she flared it. The odd feeling returned, and images streamed through her mind, but they were different this time. A shop in Fairmont, a man sitting on a stool, working. He was a fletcher, shaping the shaft of an arrow with a whittling knife. The image changed, now that same man was polishing an arrow-head. She looked at the arrow in her hand.

Could it be?

She whirled, looking at the ground where she sat on the earth a moment earlier, her hands on the soil. Sloped ground, with a view of a valley below. A valley with a river. It was the perfect place for young lovers to have a picnic.

The rune read memories. Memories of places. Of things!

Her eyes darted toward the cavalry charge, hoping that it wouldn't devastate her fleeing troops and that she'd have time to act, despite her lack of strength. She stooped to grab the cup, held it firmly in her hand, then flared the new rune again.

Images of a cavern came to her. Huge, bigger than the one near Eastway. Flowing water, fire weeds, birds, grass. And a classroom. Children at seats. A teacher with wavy auburn hair, drinking water from a cup as she moved about the room.

Come on, Anne, what are you trying to tell me? Teachers and caverns? How can this help?

She flared the rune harder, focusing on the cup in the teacher's hand. It wasn't just any cup, it was this cup, the very one Nara held now; the shapes were identical. The woman moved about the room, leading the class in a recitation. No, not a recitation. The teacher was saying single words as she pointed, the children repeating them. Nara focused on where the teacher was directing their attention, following her finger through the blurry image. High on the walls of the classroom were images. Symbols. She focused harder. They were runes!

Nara listened to the words as the teacher pointed. The runes were hard to make out, many designs she didn't recognize. Then she saw the fire rune and heard the teacher.

"Aysh," the woman said.

The children echoed. "Aysh."

The teacher pointed toward the sound rune, "Ni-shma."

"Ni-shma."

She pointed at the earth rune. "Uf-fhal."

"Uf-fhal," said the class.

The runes have names!

Nara threw the cup down, flaring speed and running for the cavalry just as they approached the rearguard of her retreating army. As she ran, she screamed, "Uf-fhal" and flared earth as hard as she could. The ground shook with each of her footfalls as if she were a giant smashing the earth with a hammer. It was asking for orders, shouting obedience in time with her steps. Far greater power than she had ever felt before from the earth, and it asked for none of her energy, using only its own. Incredible! She commanded it, the ground rose, and she was upon a roiling pillar of rocks and dirt, racing toward the enemy riders. She called to the soil of the slope, and it collapsed under the cavalry, burying them, aborting the attack just before impact with her fleeing army.

Nara turned, looking down at Kayna's still-approaching troops. One against almost three thousand. Weakness in her legs reminded her that most of her strength was gone, but now she wielded a new weapon, her favorite, and mastery of it requiring none of her own strength now that she knew its name.

She reached down and ordered the earth to yield some of its own power, to fill her spirit with the strength she knew it had, but it refused. It would go where she willed and change its shape as she commanded, but its spirit was its own and would not be shared.

It might be enough. Her friends needed to escape, and there was a Queen that needed to die.

She told the earth to carry her forward, and it obeyed.

36

CATACLYSMOS

Mykel dropped his staff and set Sammy down in the middle of the pass as several hundred men, soldiers, and horses galloped past him in full retreat. Nara had cleared the way for their escape, but as he looked around, she was nowhere to be found. Was she leading the retreat or staying behind to stall the enemy?

Sammy breathed but still slept, a large red mark from Mykel's strangulation still around his neck. As he examined his brother, it was clear that Kayna's magic had twisted the boy. Not just making him grow, but altering his shape. His eyebrows weren't even, and his jaw was now pronounced. Oddly, Mykel now realized how much Sammy looked like Pop. But Pop was never this big.

Sammy was supposed to be dead. They had been wrong, somehow, and finding him this way was a curse in itself. He lived, however, and Mykel was grateful. Thank Dei for that. But Sammy was changed in such a horrible way, no longer the delightful boy who ran about the woods and blushed when he was teased. He was a rampaging monster and had violently attacked Nara. He could have killed her, even though they had been friends. Kayna had changed more than his body, somehow teaching him a hatred for Nara. His mind had been twisted and when he awoke, that anger might resurface. Mykel couldn't leave Sammy without first knowing where Nara was.

"Where is she?" he asked of soldiers that ran by. "Nara. Where is she?"

They continued their retreat.

He flagged down a mounted spearman. "Where is Nara?"

The man pointed back to the battlefield.

She was still fighting. Alone. Without her Guardian by her side.

He grabbed the staff and took a last look at his broken, twisted brother, angry at himself for not having been in Dimmitt to defend him. He then turned and broke into a full sprint for the battlefield.

Kayna rose to watch the rout, Nara's forces in full retreat through the pass. As Kayna's cavalry made a charge to end the enemy, however, the ground erupted, and most of her cavalry were completely swallowed up by the earth. Gone. It was just that fast.

She squinted to see a lone figure on the slope. It was Nara, red hair blowing in the breeze as she rode a pillar of rocks straight at the royal army. Curse Dei!

Nara's charge was fast and straight, directly toward Kayna and her troops. Brave girl, but she couldn't take that many.

Moments later, the ground beneath Kayna's infantry sprouted sinkholes that sucked soldiers down by the dozens. Columns appeared under the archers' feet, launching them into the air. The entire slope quaked in chaos, shifting, rising and falling at the whim of her sister. Rocks came up to the surface, then fell, churning the earth, sucking in her army and crushing, then burying hundreds of royal troops.

Some of Kayna's elites charged forward, but many of her soldiers broke ranks, having no way to move or attack when the ground they depended on had now become their enemy. Cowards! But Nara was no normal enemy. She commanded the earth beneath their feet today, and it was obeying her.

Kayna refused to lose her army over this. Or her crown. Curling a lip in frustration, she rose with the air, calling to a sergeant nearby, and pointed behind the platform at the string of prisoners. "Keep them close to me," she said. "Looks like I may need them."

Nara's first wave of attacks fell upon the front lines, sinkholes and churning earth killing many and confusing others. There was no time for lamenting the lost lives—she was up against an entire army herself, with little energy left in her spirit. If she could delay them long enough for her own army to escape, this would be a worthy effort.

Anne had faith in her and believed that Nara was the only one who could defeat Kayna. Now Anne was dying herself, on the other side of this battlefield. Sammy was misshapen and had been turned against her and Mykel. Children from across the Great Land had been captured and tortured. If she failed, the darkness would persist.

Nara was the only hope for an end to the horrors. She wouldn't give up yet. Not when there was any chance of ending this fight with a win. She wielded the name of the earth, and although weak, she wasn't out of strength just yet.

Directing the pillar that carried her to the right, she blocked the passage of any remaining horsemen from slipping around toward the pass. Then she realized—she didn't need to block them herself; she could let the earth do it. She willed it to be, and a giant pit, hundreds of feet across and a dozen feet deep, appeared on the slope between Kayna's army and the pass. Let them detour around that!

Again, she focused her attention on Kayna's army, which was in disarray and confusion. Many more were fleeing. They may have held the battlefield for a while, but they didn't seem eager to stay. Nara stopped advancing, hoping they would all retreat, only to be disappointed when she saw Kayna engage. Up from her platform the Queen rose, followed by a man on horseback leading a string of dirty, emaciated prisoners. Fuel for their mistress. Nara should have figured as much.

Nara had no such energy to draw from, but she had complete command of the earth, which now required almost no strength from her. "Uf-fhal!" she said again, flaring earth and reasserting her mastery over her best weapon. She hoped it would be enough.

Kayna came close, floating about twenty feet above the pitted slope, matching Nara's height on her shifting pillar of earth. Nara was now eye-to-eye with the source of the Great Land's troubles.

"I should have killed you when I had the chance," Kayna yelled.

"And I you."

Then half of the prisoners collapsed, writhing and shrinking, their life force sucked into Kayna from almost a hundred feet away without her even glancing at them. Nara used sight to discover that Kayna's body was decorated with cepps. Rings on her fingers, bracers on her arms, and greaves under her dress shining so brightly they all had to be made of coral. Like the king's armor.

Nara attacked first, sending a pillar of rock straight up at her sister, but Kayna easily dodged. Kayna was not vulnerable to the unstable earth that had scattered her army. She floated above it all, and Nara now realized how different this fight would be. Nara's success had depended on her enemy standing upon the earth, but earth couldn't touch Kayna. And Nara didn't have the strength to attack any other way.

Wait. Yes, she did.

Behind Kayna, a thirty-foot wall of earth rose, then Nara flared the fire rune, screamed "Aysh" and let a torrent fly.

The power of fire, when its name was called, dwarfed any destruction Nara had ever seen before—a raging inferno erupting from her fingers toward her hated sister. It launched Kayna backward to impact the wall with a thundering sound that sent her into the dirt barrier, the crushing impact making a thunderous noise.

But Kayna had protection flared and recovered a moment later, a gust of wind sustaining her flight as she moved away from the earthen wall. She must have shielded herself from the fire with a gust of air, because her dress was only partially burned, now tattered and smoking. Her skin was scorched in places, raw and red, including her left shoulder, where the damage extended deep into the bone. Some of her hair was gone, burned away, but the health rune flashed, and Kayna's body became whole once again, her face now twisted in a snarling rage. A gust of air launched the Queen forward.

Nara raised a rock wall to stop Kayna's charge and give her time to send another burst of fire, but Kayna flared chaos and the wall fell apart. An instant later, Kayna was upon Nara, a hand around her arm, squeezing like a vise and spinning.

Supreme strength, far greater than Sammy's, swung Nara toward the ground, but Nara flared protection just before impact. The collision took the breath out of her, and she was dizzy, unable to focus. She looked up just in time to see fire coming down from the heavens.

Again, she flared protection and also summoned earth to block the attack, but the earth was too slow, flames hitting her before the barrier could intercede. Her clothes singed and skin burned, even with the protection rune active. Kayna had so much strength, powered by coral cepps and devoured souls, her might was greater by far, and using protection had depleted Nara's meager reserves even further.

Pain from the burns racked her body. She flared health and moved away on a pillar of earth. Movement caught her eye. Mykel was racing through the pit that blocked the pass. He leaped out of the depression and onto the slope, running directly for Kayna.

Kayna turned to follow Nara's gaze.

"So, your lover comes to save the day, does he?"

Nara shot flames at Kayna, but just as she did so, Kayna flared motion without even looking in Nara's direction, launching Nara into the air hundreds of feet away. The wind whistled through her ears as she fell, but before colliding, she transformed the earth below into soft dirt to ease the blow. It was still hard enough to twist her right forearm unnaturally on impact. Nara cried out as the pain burned hot.

She grabbed her broken arm with the other hand and pulled it straight with a scream, then flared health to knit the bone. Just a bit, not much—she dared not use all of her energy. Her legs grew weaker, and her vision blurred again. Looking up, she saw Kayna's form high in the sky, silhouetted against the rising sun. Watching.

Struggling against the fatigue, Nara rose to her feet. Her legs would not run for her, so she commanded the earth again to propel her, high toward Kayna once again. But before she could finish her approach, a giant rock flew through the air and struck Kayna, knocking her sideways.

Mykel was throwing huge rocks at the Queen, screaming as he did so. Boulders far larger than a man's head catapulted toward Kayna, most of them missing his target. Such strength he spent in his effort, but it was the only way he could attack her. Just then, beyond Mykel, Nara saw a large figure running at a full sprint for Mykel.

Sammy.

Struggling to focus her vision, Nara put up an earthen wall to block him, but Sammy charged right through it, tackling Mykel and knocking the staff far from his reach. Arms locked about Mykel in fury as Sammy beat on his brother with thunderous blows and Nara could see Mykel's protection rune failing.

Motion out of the corner of her eye alerted Nara and she turned to see Kayna flying on the wind toward her, chaos flared. Nara threw up an earthen wall, but it disintegrated. She flared protection, but it shredded.

This was it. This was the end.

Even the name of earth would not defeat Kayna. The name of fire had done no better.

But she hadn't tried sound.

Sound, you are the key, I know you are, she thought. *What was your name?*

Then she had it. Ni-shma.

She flared the sound rune and called, "Ni-shma!"

The power of sound's name being uttered propelled Kayna backward, forcing her to steady herself in the air.

Again, Nara flared the rune, screaming ever louder, "Ni-shma!" The ground shook with the power of Nara's twice-amplified voice, columns of rock in the landscape below shattering with the power she uttered. An avalanche crashed down in the pass, thundering and building as if bowing in obedience to the power of her voice. So much power in the names!

Power that might change everything.

Her thoughts turned to earth. So many times, she had flared the earth rune, and it was a friend, a willing partner. She'd shaped it, coaxed it, let it ease the pain of her headaches or asked it to carry her strength to Mykel as he fought. But when she asked for it to yield her its energy, it refused. Time and again, it said no. Things were different, now. She had the name of earth, and she had the name of sound, and she could use one to command the other. With power in her voice, Nara now flared the earth rune with all her might and screamed with her very soul, "UF-FHAL!"

She heard a giant crack, and the spirit of the earth broke open.

The power that came up from the earth was nothing like she expected, overwhelming Nara with euphoria like no other. It was alive with power but also with memories that stretched eons. Time seemed to stand still as images flooded her mind. Scenes from mountains, valleys, and hills across a vast expanse of ages where people walked, where trees dug their roots, and animals burrowed their homes. She felt the presence of other nations across the globe, castles carved from the rock of the earth, homes built from the clay of her riverbeds. The entire world was Nara's now, a slave to do her bidding, and she held unlimited power, power held secret since the beginning of creation. She could change the course of rivers, raise islands, crush entire armies, or swallow cities. But, at the moment, she had only one goal.

Nara tapped her new source of power, flaring protection and health. Her body repaired itself, just as Kayna threw chaos. It was a mosquito attacking a castle wall. A toothpick against an iron shield. Kayna threw fire, a raging inferno in power and in anger, but Nara didn't even feel it.

Kayna continued, unrelenting in her attack on Nara, but to no effect. She sent fire and gusts of air. She screamed and screamed, but Nara was untouched. Nara flared the motion rune from several directions, paralyzing Kayna in midair as if she were a puppet.

"It's over," Nara said, voice thundering. The confidence in her heart was absolute, the power she bore unlimited. Her voice was a raging river, her words a thunderous mountain. She reached deep into the ground beneath her, summoning the spirit of the rock and the dirt, not asking but demanding the magic that would end this fight. Her spirit surged with ancient power.

A gargantuan fissure opened in the ground, shaking the battlefield below. Avalanches streamed down the slopes of the Twins, and Nara sensed a tremor shaking the Great Land, the Yukan, and beyond. She was one with the earth, sensing its movements, and that which rested upon it. Buildings in Fairmont, Ankar, and Junn shook under the strength of the growing quake, falling into dust with the power of a subjugated earth. The world was unmaking itself.

She sensed the spiked peak of the Twins shift, then fracture as it tumbled down its own slopes. The planet was crying in pain.

Because of her.

Like harvesting a human being, Nara was stealing life she had no claim to. Castle walls crumbled, and children were running from their collapsing homes.

Because of her.

Many would die in this cataclysm. Through the magic of the earth, she felt their suffering. Their panic. Mothers screamed in anguish across the land, their voices silenced as they expired.

Castles shattered, libraries and churches burned, and innocent people went quiet. Nara was murdering the world.

It doesn't belong to you.

The voice was deep but didn't ring in her ears. It was in her mind. She looked around. Mykel and Sammy were still fighting below on the chaotic landscape, Kayna was paralyzed with a face full of fear, but Nara couldn't find where the voice came from.

Let it go.

The voice brought clarity, shaking the euphoria that had over-whelmed her. For a moment, she came to her senses and realized what she was doing. She was destroying everything she had tried to protect, embracing violence that gave birth to pain. Instead of seeking Dei and His favor, she had succumbed to pain and anger, embracing not life, but death, overstepping her bounds. She had crossed a line into the realm of the divine, where she had no rightful place. She had the power to end Kayna, right here, but the cost would be too high.

Let it go.

That was *His* voice. It had to be. So long she had yearned to hear it, and now He came at this moment? To tell her to give up?

Trust me.

A tug-of-war ensued in Nara's mind. Let go of the power, the sweet, sweet power, and embrace death, or use it to save the Great Land. But she wasn't saving the Great Land. She was annihilating it.

At that moment, she realized her greatest fear, that she was a dark thing, not born of Dei but choosing the way of Kai. A demon of destruction and death, a bringer of calamity and anguish, much worse than her sister.

"What am I doing?" she said with a whisper that was heard for miles.

The horror of her now complete realization cleared her of the intoxicating effect of the magic. Dei's words had helped restore her senses, but she didn't know how long she would retain the clarity.

"I can't do this," she said. "This isn't me."

Let it go.

Nara let the power go. Back into the earth the magic flowed in an instant, straight down into the soil, the bedrock, to its home, where it belonged. The earth stopped shaking, and Nara fell to the ground as the pillar under her collapsed into dust.

Now free of her bonds, Kayna flared air, coming straight at Nara like a bolt from a crossbow. She flared chaos and Nara's skin sprouted sores, limbs contorting as the life siphoned out of her body. Horrible pain.

Flare protection. Now. Deep within yourself.

The voice again! Nara obeyed, flaring protection with her last ounce of strength, but it was too late for her body. She flared it much deeper, around her spirit. Cloaked in the rune, she closed her eyes a moment before they turned to dust. The agony faded, growing distant now, as if it was happening to someone else. She felt her legs disintegrate. It was a curious feeling, safely housed in the protection rune as her body gave up its life.

Then the pain stopped, and her spirit was free.

37

HISTORY

The pain was gone. Nara floated in a detached state of being, fear and panic a distant memory. She looked about to see one of the Twins as it crumbled in slow motion. Kayna, clothes burnt and visage manic, floated over a slope while she harvested the life of a human being. The person was blackened, shriveled, with her limbs, her skull, then her whole body turning to dust. It was Nara's own body. She was dead now, but somehow not afraid. Why not?

She looked around again to see Mykel sprinting across the broken field. He had subdued his brother yet again but now raced to save his love. He was too late.

A tug from inside her brought a curious feeling, then the landscape faded away like a waning light. A different light dawned in Nara's vision, and she felt a rushing sensation as she hurtled down a tunnel. Her progress slowed as the new light grew, welcoming her with a strange warmth, comforting and peaceful.

A heartbeat later, she found herself standing on a beautiful field, high snow-capped mountains visible in the distance. Flowers decorated the field for farther than she could see, in colors she didn't have names for. So beautiful! The lights of other people walked through the field, but they were far away, and she couldn't see any details.

Nara stood there for a long time but didn't know what she waited for. The warmth on her skin was comforting, and she felt she could stand there for hours. A gentle breeze danced through the flowers and grasses as the other lights in the field moved about. Was this heaven?

One of the lights came nearer, and as it did so, the image flickered, the brilliance of it fading until it was a single form. A woman. She was not tall, and neither old nor young. She moved with a glow through the flowers and grasses of the field, gracefully and confidently. As she approached, Nara could see that her hair was a deep auburn, long and wavy, and her face bore large brown eyes and a wide smile.

"Took you long enough," she said, then gave a hearty chuckle.

It was Anne. She was alive, and so much younger! She carried no cane and wore no patch over her eye.

Nara ran the last few steps and embraced her mentor with all her might.

"Well, now. Look who misses me so much!"

"I thought you were dead!" Nara said, and pulled back but kept a solid grip on Anne's hand. "On the slope near the Twins, you were bleeding, and I knitted you, but you were pale, and I thought you were dying. It was terrible."

"You weren't wrong."

A wave of knowledge came over Nara, washing away the elation that had clouded her senses. "Oh."

"Yes, I'm dead," Anne said. "Finally. It took me long enough."

"And me too, then. Dead." The realization was clear, but she felt no panic. No fear. "Kayna won. Mykel will die too. We lost. I had the strength to beat her, but I gave up. I failed."

"Hold up, not so fast," Anne said. "You don't have the whole picture just yet."

"Tell me."

"Let's go for a walk."

They stepped through the field, Nara looking about but still holding Anne's hand, the warmth of it providing stability in the peaceful, wondrous confusion of this new place.

"This is heaven, then?" Nara asked.

Anne smiled. "Words. They don't do the real thing justice."

"That's not an answer."

"Heaven is a word that men use to describe what they want to happen after things happen that they don't want to happen."

Nara laughed. "I can't believe I understood that."

"This is what comes now for you. It's hard to say more than that."

"But I'm not on earth anymore?"

"No, you're not."

"Is Dei here?"

"The Creator is here, but that's true of any place. He is everywhere."

"I don't understand. And you died just before I did, so how can you know these things?"

"Time doesn't work in this place as you imagine it should."

"Oh."

They came near a creek, its water trickling through the rocks and swirling in little pools where the flow turned. Nara let go of Anne's hand, kneeling to retrieve a rock in the creek. Its feel was smooth and rough at the same time. Through her fingers, she sensed its strength and its calm. It wasn't like any other rock she'd ever held. Everything was brighter here, purer. And far more complex.

"Teach me everything," Nara said.

"There is too much to share. And you don't have time."

Nara stood and turned to face Anne. "What do you mean? Don't I have all the time in the world?"

"Because you have more work to do, my dear. Much more."

"I'm dead. I saw my body shrivel up. Kayna killed me."

"Oh, look who knows so much!" Anne said, then chuckled. "Dead for a few seconds, and now she knows everything."

Nara scrunched her face in confusion. "What work do I have to do?"

"You must rebuild it. All of it."

"All of what?"

"The Great Land. You showed more restraint than I expected but still caused quite the damage. Cities damaged, many dead. Libraries buried or burned. Knowledge lost. You even brought down a mountain. Never heard of that one before."

Memories came back to Nara, how she stole the essence of the earth, intent on using it for destruction. She had become far worse than Kayna at that moment. "I am terrible. I did all that."

"Yes, you did. Now you owe a debt."

"Okay, but—" She stopped.

"But what?"

"I have a question."

"Go on."

"Why?"

"Why what?"

"I'm not sure. All of it. Why the constant struggle, by every-one? The fear and the pain. All of our lives. Build things only to see them destroyed. Love people only to lose them. Why?"

"That's the best question of all, isn't it?"

Nara waited for her answer.

"First, I'll start with fear and pain. It may not be obvious, but fear is actually pain. They aren't different things. Fear is pain you choose to suffer in advance. Pain you inflict upon yourself, even if the actual pain never arrives. Silly thing, fear is."

"I never thought of it like that."

"So really the question is, 'why so much pain.' I'll try to answer." Anne paused as if preparing her thoughts. "Nara, have you ever heard a great story?"

"Well, of course I have. You've told me some."

"What do you notice about stories, specifically, how do they go?"

Nara pondered that for a moment. "Well, there is a beginning, where you learn who the people are. Then they get into some trouble and find their way out. If it's a good story, they do. If it's a bad story, they die and the bad guy wins. That sort of thing."

"Very good. Nice summary. Now let me tell you a different sort of story. You have a beginning, you meet some people, but they don't get into trouble. They are happy. They are challenged by nothing, never strive for anything, never cry, never fight, and never lose anyone they love. They just live. Happily. Peacefully. The End." Anne clapped her hands as if she had just given an excellent performance. "What do you think of my story?"

"That was terrible."

"Exactly. There must be challenges."

"So, Dei allows pain because it makes a good story?"

"In a way, yes. And history is *His*-story. His. Not ours. But the story grows us as well. And teaches us. We learn that with power comes responsibility, for one. Power affects many people, and this is a great lesson. Your choices as a young girl in a village mattered little to the Great Land, but think of what you became. How your choices affected it in the end."

"The more you control, the more you can help. Or hurt."

"Very good. Think also of the stories that tell us of great heroes who struggle against great foes. The tales are better because of the scale that comes with them. Slaying a dragon is far more inspiring than a grand quest to make a stew, wouldn't you say?"

"Depends on the stew, I think," Nara said, smiling.

"Ha! Yes, it does." She smiled in return. "But stories also teach us that without loss, there can be no gain. If it's easy to do, it possesses no value. On the contrary, valuable things are such because they are rare. Food is more delicious when we are hungry. Companionship is more important to those who are lonely. Love is precious because there is so much hate."

"Oh."

"Love is a special one. Real love is sacrifice. Paying a price on behalf of another without receiving a reward. The Creator is like this. Pure love. The source of all strength and goodness, but in your path, He allows hurdles. Obstacles to overcome as you struggle and grow. Your struggles are beautiful to Him. Everyone's are. They are part of His story."

"But he could just take them away. In an instant, he could remove all pain. I don't understand why He won't do that. To let people struggle and die seems so pointless."

"Look around you," Anne said, pointing out at the fields.

Nara saw the many lights again, although the forms were indistinct. The lights skipped through the flowers, and when one came close to another, they almost joined, spinning, dancing with one another. "They are people. Like me?"

"People, yes, but certainly not like you. This isn't the only place like it, and they don't have your path. Few do. But do you see any of these in distress right now?"

"No. They are peaceful."

"They suffered. Just like you. Like everyone. They struggled, and they felt pain. Some died while still children. Others wasted away with pain for years. But look at them now."

They looked so peaceful.

"A young child whose mother forces her to eat her vegetables might cry and scream," Anne said. "Lots of drama and lots of pain. Children have a way of feeling everything quite powerfully."

"And?"

"The child grows and becomes wise about such things. She learns the importance of doing things she doesn't like. She stops screaming about vegetables. She learns to exercise, run, even when it hurts, in order to become strong. How did this happen? How does a young thing go from screaming about her dinner to working long days in a field to feed her family? How does a warrior grow up to face enemies and fight for his homeland?"

"Pain makes them grow, but I still don't get it. Pain that kills you can't make you grow."

Anne pointed again to the lights in the field. "Do they look dead to you?"

Oh. Of course. Like most people, she'd led her life with the assumption everything ended at death. Even when Father Taylor talked about heaven, it was just too far away, and didn't seem real. But death was real, she'd seen it many times, and the horror of it stuck in her mind long after attending a funeral or seeing someone fall on a battlefield. But now she was here with Anne in some sort of after-place. This wasn't death at all. Not like she knew it to be, anyway. In fact, that word didn't seem to work very well. Not anymore. Nara felt vibrant, alive, with senses more alert than she'd ever known and peace more profound than she could have imagined.

"So, if you can see the big picture, death is just vegetables? Exercise? It sounds ridiculous, but I get what you are saying, I think."

"Exactly!" Anne clapped. "Now take it a step further. Those that can't see it. Like when you fought against Kayna. You killed to stop the killing. By your own hand, you delivered pain. You weren't a parent telling your child to eat vegetables; you were a foolish, scared child fighting with other foolish children, trying to prevent pain by causing more. When you buried a soldier in his grave with your magic, it wasn't just his pain you caused. You caused his wife's pain because she would be a widow. His children's pain as they became orphans. His mother would suffer. His friends. One life lost, yet so many suffer. You multiplied your folly, causing echoes through the land."

"I'm just like her. Every bit of me."

"Yes, you are. We all are. Every bit of us. We cause pain, we suffer obstacles, we fret, we frown, and we scream at the heavens to save us, angry that the Creator doesn't seem to care."

Exasperated, Nara let out a long sigh. "I tried so hard, but I wasn't good. Not at all. All that work and I was a horrible person."

Anne put a hand on her shoulder. "Everyone is good, Nara. And everyone is horrible too. We bear the seeds of both extremes within us. Here's some advice: borrow His perspective in this. Don't think yourself so wonderful if you deliver a kindness on someone, for the Creator gave you the means to do so, did He not?

But also don't think yourself to be so horrible when you deliver pain. He gave you that power too. He just hoped you wouldn't use it."

Nara was searching for what to ask next but felt a tug inside, like when she was rushed away from the battlefield toward the light. "That feeling again. I'm about to go, aren't I?"

"Yes."

"To where? Back to the Great Land?"

"Yes."

A sense of urgency rose in Nara as if she was about to lose an important opportunity. "Hurry, Anne. What else can you tell me? I want to remember so I can teach everyone. So I can help rebuild and fix things."

"It won't happen like that. You won't remember much. Just feelings. But know that He loves you, my sweet girl. He loves us all so much He can't contain himself. He is the sun, shining on you every day, as befits His nature. He gives you strength, even when you don't know where it's coming from. He yearns to ease your suffering but loves you so much that He wants to see you grow, and He won't rob you of that chance. He is eternal, and He waits for you. Go. Love. Fix what you have broken. And have patience, my dear. You'll need it."

Suddenly, the field disappeared. Nara was rushing down a river of speed and sensation, light disappearing then another light growing, her head spinning, her world shaking.

Then the pain. It came in fierce bursts, racking her form from head to toe. Attacks. From Kayna. She couldn't see her, but she felt her sister's presence. They battled again, but not like before. No, that battle had been lost. She was fighting Kayna in her mind, now. How could that be?

She sensed Kayna's presence, her anger and frustration, as she hurled pain at Nara, but this was a different sort of battle. It was a contest of wills, not of skill. A contest of passion, not of magic. They were together, in the same shape, one form but two personalities, clashing in the chaos, locked in a struggle for dominance. But the rules were different here, and Kayna did not have Nara's strength of will. Nor her passion.

As if it were a rune, Nara flared passion with all her might, overwhelming her sister with pure intention, angry and hot, crushing the dark twin with emotion, ardor, and intensity. Facing a vastly superior enemy, Kayna folded quickly, becoming like a fish hiding under a quiet lake. Not gone, but instead silent. Submissive. That fast, Nara had won. The contest was over.

Nara opened her eyes, but the images were cloudy. Clarity trickled into her muddy thoughts, but her vision remained slightly blurred. She was on her back, her body was in pain, and there was a figure standing over her.

Mykel. His arms were reaching out, but something was wrong. It was his face. So angry. And his hands. They were around her neck, squeezing like a vise. She couldn't breathe, and her throat was in agony, her head pounding with pain and pressure.

She tried to push him off her, and as she reached toward him, she saw coral bracelets on her forearms. Rings on her fingers. Her spirit had moved. The final battle of wills had taken place in Kayna's body.

And now, thinking she was the evil Queen, Mykel was killing her.

38

PEACE

"You killed her!" Mykel screamed into Nara's face, his breath hot and wet. "Spawn of Kai!"

The world around her faded, and all Nara could see was Mykel's face, close, angry, twisted in pain and suffering. She tried to flare strength to push him off but couldn't find the rune. She tried to flare health to keep from dying but couldn't find it either. Protection? It was there, but it was fading. She flared it, but her hold on it faltered. Her runes were leaving her.

It's me, she wanted to say to him. But his strength was too much. In an instant, she would be dead.

"Stop, Mykel. It's not her!" It was Gwyn's voice. "Stop!" Gwyn screamed.

Through her blurry vision, Nara saw Gwyn punching Mykel in his face, then in his ribs, but his powerful hands still strangled Nara.

Then a sword impaled Mykel in the right side of his chest. His stranglehold around Nara's throat immediately relaxed.

"Let go of her!" It was Gwyn again, standing behind Mykel. She had just stabbed him. "That's not Kayna!" Gwyn screamed.

Mykel let go and stood, while Nara tried to steady her dizzy head. Her throat hurt and her breathing came weakly. She remained on the ground, watching to see when he would attack her next. Mykel was standing face-to-face with Gwyn, a sword still sticking out of his chest.

"What are you doing?" Mykel asked, angrily.

"I know that looks like Kayna, but I was watching. She was draining Nara, then Nara's light moved. It didn't drain out like it should have, Mykel. It moved! Into Kayna. Then the lights merged. And changed. It's one light, solid now, and it doesn't look like either of them."

They both looked down at Nara, who struggled for air, but she still couldn't speak. Not yet. She might have one word, if she tried really hard. But even more horrible was the fact that Mykel still had a sword sticking out of his chest. Nara pointed to it, Gwyn removed the blade, and the wound closed quickly.

"Her eyes are different. White," Mykel said as he knelt by Nara's side, an angry expression on his face. "Who are you?"

Tell him. You have the strength.

The voice was familiar. Deep, powerful words that rang in her soul. She now knew where they came from and somehow wasn't surprised. Summoning all her strength, Nara squeaked out a single word: "Bitty."

A flash of recognition and shock came upon Mykel's face. Then worry, and Mykel grabbed her. "I'm so sorry," he said, embracing her tightly. "But how?" Tears and sweat wet her cheek as he pressed against her, his long hair falling around her face and breast. "How could this be? Oh, Nara, what have I done? I don't understand. I don't care. You're alive!"

He lifted her from the ground, and she put a hand to her throat. So little air entered her lungs, her so breathing raspy and weak.

"Heal yourself, Bitty. Do it now. You can't breathe."

She tried to flare health, but it was gone. She shook her head.

"Get a knitter. Her throat is damaged," Mykel yelled to Gwyn, his eyes still focused on Nara.

There was a risk of her airway closing with swelling if she didn't get a knitter soon. Hopefully, Gwyn could find one among Kayna's fleeing soldiers. The lack of air made her dizzy, but through the fog, she heard the sound of heavy footsteps. A large form coming close. Sammy.

Mykel sighed. "I thought I had you down again. You just keep coming, don't you, big boy?"

Sammy looked from Mykel to Nara and back again, confused, then scratched his chin. Worrying that there would be another fight between the brothers, Nara held her hand up, motioning Sammy to stop. She pointed to him, then pointed down at the ground.

Sammy took a knee.

Still struggling to breathe but resolved to find peace here, Nara pushed against Mykel's arm, signaling for him to set her down. When her feet touched the ground, her legs were weak and shaking, but with Mykel's assistance, she was able to stand. She took several breaths, then motioned for Mykel to help walk forward, approaching Sammy to place her hand on his shoulder. She knew that he was her Beast, and he liked to have his back rubbed. She reached up and massaged his shoulder blade, feeling him relax under her touch.

Her breaths were coming easier now, but there was still a risk of her airway closing if she didn't get a knitter soon.

"Nara?" Mykel said. "Look." He pointed at her hair.

She reached back and grabbed it, pulling it forward so she could see.

Her hair was slowly changing from black to silver.

"You're not going anywhere," Mykel told Nara, as he gently barring her from standing on the battlefield slope, high above Fairmont. "Not for a while. Sit here some more."

"They need help down there," Nara said, eager to be part of the effort to heal the city. Several hours had passed since the earthquake and the victory over Kayna, but she was still so weak. Yet the damage to the city was her fault, and she wanted to be part of the solution.

"You're no good at all to them right now."

"Collapsed buildings. People trapped. I could direct the efforts."

"Jahmai is doing just fine without you. You can still barely breathe. Rest for a while longer. Please."

He was right. Thankfully, Gwyn had found a knitter whose healing helped to improve Nara's condition, but her throat still ached, and a deep fatigue had overwhelmed her so profoundly that it was hard to even move. She had no strength. None at all.

Gwyn, Yury, and Lieutenant Martel were reassembling the armies to help the fallen in Fairmont. Citizens needed rescue from collapsed buildings, shelters needed to be organized, and injuries needed tending. She had asked Sammy to join them and he had quickly obeyed. If only Mykel would do the same.

"Please go help," she said to him. "I can barely move, but you are still strong. They need help down there. Please."

"In a while," Mykel said, fingers fiddling with the ivory staff that lay on the ground next to him. "Right now, I'm staying with you. I'm your protection. At least until you get your runes back."

"They're not coming back," she said. "When you were strangling me, I had hold of protection, but it faded too. I only have two, now."

"Two runes. Sounds familiar."

"Yes, it does," she said. "That's not all that sounds familiar. Gwyn, Yury, and Sammy. That's three."

Mykel gave her an odd look.

"The Humble Guardian of old. Anne's Guardian. The histories said that he had three mighty men that gathered with him for every battle."

"I forgot about that. But Gwyn is a woman."

"Even better," Nara said.

Mykel smiled. "I agree." His gaze lingered on her. "But I'll have to get used to your new hair. I liked it better when it was red."

"A lot has changed, not just my hair. She's here with me," Nara said. She needed him to understand this. Everything was different, now. "No, that's not right. She is me. I remember everything she lived through. Growing up with Papa. Life in Fairmont. Draining the life out of all those people. But I remember Dimmitt too. I remember it all. I'm Nara, and I'm Kayna."

"But you talk like Nara. You look like her too. Except for the hair. And the eyes."

"We're twins, Mykel, of course I look like her. But my eyes don't work well. Everything is blurry now."

She closed her eyes and the sight rune popped into her vision instantly, although it looked slightly different than the versions she'd seen. More ornate. Richer. More powerful. When she flared it, she could see like never before. She could see things around her, she could see things that happened recently—the battle on the slope, her army escaping through the pass, and even the earthquake in Fairmont that brought some of the buildings down. A rich, powerful sight rune. On the periphery of her vision dwelled another rune, far more subtle. It was constantly flaring, yet very quiet, and hard to see. It wasn't difficult to guess what it did.

"I don't care if you're different. I'm just glad you're alive. I'm so sorry. About your throat and all."

"You didn't know. It's okay."

They were quiet for a time. So much had happened, and there was so much yet to do. The earthquake had done deadly work; Fairmont was a disaster and needed help. Other cities and villages would also be suffering. She had been Queen, but that would end, now. Many would blame her for all of this, and she deserved it. But she must help them rebuild, and she would need Mykel to keep her safe from those who would turn their anger toward her. He really was her Guardian, now.

"Anne is dead," she said.

The words were hard to say because they didn't come with the feelings she had expected them to bring. Mourning. Pain. Sadness. None of that. Maybe it was because Anne wasn't dead at all. Her body had failed, but Nara was confident that Anne was now more alive than she had ever been, and she couldn't bring herself to grieve. Still, she missed her and would miss her in the years to come, for sure.

"I know," Mykel said. "Gwyn found her corpse. I wasn't going to tell you yet, but–"

"I met her. I must have died too."

He raised his eyebrows.

"It's hard to explain, and I don't remember it very well. But I talked with her."

"What did she say?"

"Something about being patient. And having work to do, but there was more. And I've been thinking. This has all happened before, Mykel. She didn't tell me that, but I know it to be true. The destruction of the Breshi. It happened like this. And Anne was part of it."

Nara struggled to remember the conversation, which must have occurred when Kayna harvested her, or killed her, or whatever it was that happened.

"I felt peace where we were. And Dei loved us. But I'm not sure if that's His name. Anne never called Him that."

"Did you meet Him?"

"No. I would remember that I think. But I learned some things. I just can't remember what they were."

"I'm just glad you're alive," he said. "And we won, Nara. It was crazy, but we won. Kayna's army has scattered."

"Many have died. It was a high price to pay."

"At least Sammy is alive. He's different, but he's alive. He doesn't remember me, but I don't care."

"Of course you care. But with time, he may remember. When I changed him, it destroyed most of his memories. And I manipulated him. It was easy because he never had a mama, and he wanted one so badly. Did he ever tell you that?"

The look on Mykel's face was one of shock, then it changed, his brows furrowing and lips pursing. This was hard for him. He didn't understand that Kayna wasn't dead. She was every bit as alive as Nara, although Kayna's lack of passion had made her easily overcome. How could she explain this to him?

Maybe she just did.

"I told you, I'm not the Nara you remember," she said. "It will take you a while to realize this, I'm sure. But I am the horrible person who ordered the kidnapping of Sammy. The death of all those people in Dimmit, too. And I am the person who grew up with you. I loved you my whole life. I love you now. We battled against the darkness together, and we have work to do. My foolishness caused a lot of pain. We need to help them all. Please accept this. Not now, but someday. Accept this. Accept all of me."

The look on his face changed to one of doubt and confusion.

"And forgive me."

He looked away, then stood up but didn't leave. "I don't know."

Give him time. He'll come around.

It was Him again. Now she knew why Anne was always talking to the trees and the sky. Perhaps she was never alone all those years after all.

"I'll need your help."

She looked up at Mykel, but he didn't meet her gaze. She struggled to rise from her sitting position and reached to put a hand on his shoulder. "Take all the time you need."

"I have a question," he said, turning to face her.

She must look terrible, with cloudy eyes, pale hair, and wearing a torn, scorched dress.

"Ask."

"In all of this, with how we were wrong about Sammy, how we were angry about what Kayna did to the villages."

"Not what Kayna did. What I did."

"Listen. Are you still mad at Dei?"

She paused to think about that for a moment. Her heart had changed. She wasn't sure if it was because of the battle, the regret she felt about her own actions, or how Kayna was now a part of her; a quiet, but important part of her. She felt different, now. Her passion was tempered, the anger at her circumstances now faded, having transformed into an urgency at what must be done in the weeks and months ahead. But there was appreciation as well. And peace. Peace because she knew that there was a plan and that she wasn't the one in charge. The weight of the world was no longer on her shoulders.

"Maybe a little, but not like before. He has a story to tell, Mykel. It's a painful one, but somehow it works out and I understand that, now. I'm more disappointed than angry. Disappointed in myself. I want to do better, I try to do better, but I fail, and that frustrates me. But I know that this is His story, and we're just players in it. Actors on a grand stage that will someday fade away. We don't have to like our roles, but we should love Him because He's worthy of it. And because He loved us first. He is good. And He plans good things in the end. It's all going to be okay; I know that now. He has crafted a beautiful story, with a beautiful ending for each of us."

Mykel nodded, pausing for a moment as if taking her words to heart.

"Maybe I should go help." He kneeled to pick the ivory staff off the ground, then held it by his side as he looked out over the city below. His tall, proud form gave her confidence that he would have an important role in reshaping the Great Land in the years to come. She was grateful to have him.

"There is more," she said, then looked up at the sky and gave an appreciative smile. "Something else has changed. For so long I prayed and heard nothing. I begged, and He was silent. In the middle of great pain, I prayed. And in quiet moments, I prayed. But He never responded with anything more than a feeling. Or a gentle breeze. It was a big part of what angered me because I felt so alone. It's different now because I know He hears me. He hears us all. He's our Father, our Creator, and He loves us dearly."

She reached out to Mykel, grabbing his left hand with both of hers. He turned his head and she looked into his eyes and gave him a big smile. "And I can finally hear His voice."

ABOUT THE AUTHOR

David A. Willson lives in the great land of Alaska with his family. His passions are faith, movies, books, traveling with his beautiful lady, and hanging out with his kids.

www.davidawillson.com

facebook.com/lookingfordei

twitter.com/dav_willson